READING
SERAPHINA

STANLEY SILVER

This book is dedicated to the memory of my late father, Des, and to my niece Zadie, the beautiful new angel in our lives. I also give thanks to all who have encouraged and inspired me during this journey of writing my debut novel.

Finally, to the adventurers of Planet Earth, this book is for you. Keep dreaming, keep striving, keep learning, and never give up on the incredible, luminous and vibrant creatures that you are. I love you.

ONE

Stars littered the sky. The moon's light gazed down on to the sea and seemed to move to the shore on the tips of gentle waves. There, water and sand opened up to paved streets and ornate buildings. Stillness engulfed the entire city. Majestic buildings surrounded the harbour, like guards protecting the city from the sea. A palace, a lighthouse, a library.

From the vast harbour, a labyrinth of laneways crawled into the city. One of these alleys disappeared behind the library, concealed in the shadows.

A dull banging interrupted the silence. A large stone brick moved from a wall. With each tap, it jutted out a little more until finally, the stone fell and out tumbled a young woman. At the last moment, she threw her arms out to break her fall, barely making a sound.

'Maximus,' she whispered. 'You pushed me!'

The cheeky dog stood where the brick had been, wagging his tail. As he hopped down, Seraphina smiled.

She strained as she lifted the stone brick back into its place, a drop of perspiration sliding down her face, and the effort chasing away the chill she had felt.

She came to the edge of the alley. The hairs on the back of her neck stood tall as she peeked out and scanned the street. Nothing. She stepped out into the empty street and began to relax.

Seraphina looked down at Maximus and grinned, before sprinting into the night. The wind blew through her long hair as Maximus dashed alongside her. She spotted a crate and a cart to her left. Her body moved as quickly as her eyes, stepping off the crate, then the cart, and soaring into the air. Her head tucked under her body, and there was a glimpse of the city behind her. She hit the rooftop running, and Maximus heard her tinkling laugh as he followed at street level.

With a feeling of exhilaration and adrenaline pumping through her body, Seraphina darted across the rooftops. She leapt and somersaulted with ease to cross between the buildings. The sea became closer with each jump. She saw a gap ahead that looked a little unfamiliar and slowed down. Taking a few steps back, she squinted.

Wait, she thought. *I've done this before.*

Seraphina smiled and sprinted towards the edge.

Maximus watched from below as she tore through the air. He lowered on to his front feet and paused, watching her clothes flap in the breeze, her long hair streaming behind her. She disappeared over the gap and he heard her feet hit the rooftop. Then, fast steps fading into the distance. He sprang up after her in pursuit.

Seraphina's heart thumped in her chest. Her breathing became heavy as she accelerated towards the end of the buildings. Instead of stopping, she somersaulted over the edge and disappeared into the night.

Losing sight of her, Maximus dashed to the edge of the building and tore around the corner. It was only then he saw Seraphina hopping off a cart and heading towards her usual spot on the wall.

Her breathing relaxed, and she looked out over the city, one way, then another. The contrast was vivid. Behind her was where the Egyptians lived. In front of her stood the Hebrew village with its small shacks. Even the humblest Egyptian home dwarfed those of the Hebrews. She looked down. The street on which she stood was the dividing line.

Seraphina smiled and gave a big sigh. She loved these twilight adventures. It was her only freedom from the confines of the library. Here she could be free. Free to run. Free to dream. When her mind wasn't busy studying, it conjured up visions of a future that lit a fire in her heart.

The Hebrew village always gave her an eerie feeling. Yet she was drawn to this place. Maybe it was her inquisitive nature.

She had never known her parents, and one of her fantasies was that they lived in the village. Seraphina was a Hebrew name, after all. Her name was all she remembered from the time before she had come to live in the library. She shook her head and looked out over the sea.

Just then, she sensed she was not alone.

She froze.

Her neck and shoulder muscles tensed up, and she kept her gaze on the water.

Blinking, she thought to herself, *this is silly, there's no one there.*

Her body relaxed. She turned away from the water and scanned her surroundings.

Seraphina flinched. She had not seen the woman in a while. Every so often, Seraphina would see her at night like this. She just stood there, calmly looking at Seraphina with a slight smile on her face.

A long simple dress hung from her tall frame, with a white rope tied around her waist. It was the style commonly worn by Hebrew women. She had a strong, sturdy build that contrasted with her soft features. Her face was a kind one, with a smile that broadened as she continued to watch Seraphina. Seraphina rose to stand, and the woman did not move. Something told Seraphina she should find out who this woman was.

No one else was around, and Seraphina began walking towards her. She glanced down for a moment, just to make sure Maximus was coming.

When she looked up, the woman was gone. Seraphina dashed to the corner where the woman had been standing. She looked around. There were two streets. Seraphina checked both. Where was she? Whoever it was, she was gone for now. Seraphina started back towards the waterfront, and for a moment she thought she saw someone. Standing behind the wall, she waited a few moments.

It was nothing. She looked down at Maximus and nodded towards home. The two scurried off into the night.

TWO

Julius Caesar sat in his offices. Surrounded by chattering advisors, his mind was elsewhere. He looked at his surroundings.

The Egyptians certainly knew how to build a grand palace. It aligned with his own appreciation of luxury, and he used extravagance and opulence as symbols of his ambition and achievement.

If there were ever a man with ambition, it was Julius Caesar.

Egypt was a jewel, and to him, it represented endless possibilities with its rich and ancient culture, wealth in the form of precious metals, and decadent food.

It was also a valued centre of knowledge, but most of all, it was a gateway to the rest of Africa. It appealed to Caesar on many levels.

He had recently been appointed dictator of Rome and although he still had some battles to deal with there, he had started to look to the future. Dominion over Africa was a goal of his that other men would not even consider.

That is exactly what made him Julius Caesar. As far as he was concerned, it was the natural next step. Many described him as ruthless, but he smiled at such words and took them as a compliment.

It was usually his enemies or critics who would say such things, but most of them had now either been executed or thrown in the dungeon.

The young queen of Egypt, the beautiful Cleopatra, had allied herself with Caesar. He had taken advantage of a sibling feud, and now had a direct hold on power in Alexandria.

However, he did not trust the Egyptians. He needed someone reliable, but also strategic. He would give Cleopatra the impression that she was in charge, but in reality, his army would control the city. His top general in Alexandria had recently retired, and he now had a crucial decision to make.

Trust did not come naturally to Caesar, but he was a practical man. He simply could not handle the region himself. It was too important now for him to be in Rome to face his opponents there.

He had to find the right man for the job, though.

Alexandria had formally come under Roman control many years ago. Nevertheless, Caesar believed in imposing his authority, just having it wasn't enough. It helped to remind the locals who was in charge, remind them of the power of Rome's army, and it also ensured the soldiers didn't become complacent.

Despite his misgivings, he had found the man for the job. He had a similar ruthlessness to his own and Caesar saw much of himself in the man. There was also a healthy disdain for the Hebrews and Egyptians, which for Caesar made him the only man for the job.

His name was Rufio, a talented and ambitious Brigadier. He had been stationed in Alexandria for over a decade, so he knew the city well. He had risen through the ranks on merit alone which impressed Caesar, tired as he was of men who rose on the heels of nepotism.

He had noticed Rufio several years ago. It wasn't any observation of the man, but rather what his superiors had said about him. There was fear in their tone, when they spoke of a brutal and ambitious man, and Caesar liked this.

A man who was feared by his superiors.

That was his kind of soldier.

Just over a year ago, his last promotion had been approved by the Senate, and Caesar had started paying a lot more attention, and now, here they were.

The soldier had arrived, but Caesar kept him waiting. He chatted idly with his advisors and observed the man while Rufio waited patiently. He seemed nervous, but excited. Rufio had already quelled several minor disturbances in the city with ease. He knew this man would not hesitate, and anyone who opposed him would suffer the consequences. Caesar was barely listening to the chatter of his advisers now.

Caesar knew he had found his man.

'Brigadier Rufio Lucius Gabinius, step forward.' Caesar's boom surprised Rufio.

'Yes, sir,' said Rufio, stepping closer to the great man.

'Do you know why you are here?'

'Yes, sir. You are considering appointing me to the position of General, which would give me command of all the garrisons in Egypt, and authority as governor over all the people within its borders.'

Caesar smiled. The man's brutality and ambition were already beyond doubt. He was an effective soldier, and Caesar now saw the strategic thinker in him. He had obviously used his connections to find out. Then again, maybe he gave him too much credit. After all, the outgoing general had just retired.

In any case, Caesar's admiration was growing by the second. The brashness of his response alone was reason to be impressed, and he told Rufio as much. The two of them discussed Rufio's duties although Caesar was careful to keep the conversation hypothetical.

Rufio played along. It was obvious he would be appointed. He just had to act humble and confirm to Caesar what he already knew.

'My most pressing priority is that total control is maintained over the region of Egypt, in a way that enables us to expand the number of garrisons we have stationed here. We also want to ensure that any troubles with the locals will not be an issue.'

Rufio did not hesitate. 'Sir, you have summoned the right man. My service record details my experience in this region. Throughout my career, I have been stationed almost exclusively here in the city of Alexandria, and I have diffused every rebellion that the Egyptians or the Hebrews have orchestrated. I personally have made examples of those rebels, and there has been no civil unrest in this city for over five years.'

Then Rufio surprised Caesar. 'I and the soldiers under my command will serve you faithfully, and the future will see an expansion of Roman territory here in Africa.'

Caesar was speechless. It was as if the man was reading his mind. There was no sense in delaying any longer.

'Very well, Rufio. You are now the general, commanding all Roman armies in this territory of Egypt, and governor over all its people. Your orders in future will only come from me. Otherwise, you may do as you see fit to maintain order in Egypt and command our armies here.'

Rufio asked how he was to handle Cleopatra.

'Keep her happy,' said Caesar, 'but you are the one in charge. Always remember that. You are dismissed.'

Rufio saluted and thanked Caesar. A huge dream of his had just come true. He turned and as he left the chamber a sinister grin crossed his face.

He walked out, thinking of all the possibilities his new position would give him.

THREE

Love. It was a concept that had always fascinated Seraphina. In the library, she had read through centuries of philosophy on love, absorbing the teachings of Socrates, Aristotle, Plato, and many others. It made her think of love in her life. She knew she loved Afiz, in the way a child loves a parent. But Afiz was not her father. She had learned about many other types of love, but none seemed to be so profound as the love between human beings and their offspring.

She flicked through a scroll on a new topic – empathy. It was a fascinating subject, but texts on empathy were rare. She looked up for a second and remembered the other night. What she had been thinking, before the mystery woman had shown up. Seraphina dropped the scroll and picked up another one.

There it was! She read the beginning to herself.

Trataka meditation is a method of meditation that involves gazing at a single point for a prolonged period of time. It is said to increase one's ability to concentrate, increase the power of the mind to recall past memories, and bring the mind into an enhanced state of focus, attention, and awareness…

Afiz knocked on the door and came in. 'Seraphina,' he said,

'you're not even ready.' He crossed his arms and looked at her, feigning frustration.

'Ready for what?'

'I told you we were going to the market today. What's going on?'

He watched as she scrambled to her feet. As she hurried around the room, she pointed at some scrolls. She was studying, and had lost track of time, she said. Afiz told her to hurry up. He tried to maintain his annoyance, but she was too funny, always off in her dreamland.

She got ready, and he could tell she was flustered. 'I'll be waiting downstairs,' he said, 'and don't keep me waiting long or I will leave without you.' He tried to sound as stern as he could.

As he stepped towards the door, Maximus followed eagerly. Afiz paused and stared down at the dog whose little eyes were full of hope. Afiz looked up at Seraphina, who had the same look in her eyes. 'Bring him, but keep him in your bag, and don't forget your robe,' said Afiz.

Closing the door behind him, he cracked a smile and lumbered down the stairs, chuckling to himself.

What was going on in that girl's mind today, he wondered.

As he made his way through the library, his mind drifted to Seraphina's past. He had always thought Seraphina might be Hebrew. She looked Hebrew, and she even spoke Hebrew.

There was a tinge of Egyptian there too. Even as a child, Seraphina spoke a little Coptic. Seraphina's origins were a curiosity to Afiz, but he never dwelled on it for long.

The sunlight shone into the main atrium of the library. Afiz exchanged the usual morning greetings with the people there as he passed through. Some were scholars, some coworkers.

A robed figure waited patiently at the entrance. He knew Seraphina had a secret way in and out of the library. While he wondered exactly where it was, Afiz was content for it to remain a mystery.

The loose robe draped over the tall, lean frame and a big bag hung on the left shoulder. His assistant was ready to start the day's work. He smiled at Seraphina's mischief, and out they went into the bustling streets.

Alexandria's marketplace was vast, sprawling, and disorganised.

Afiz had learned over the years that what he was looking for could turn up anywhere.

Seraphina breathed it all in and smiled. Her gentle footsteps followed Afiz, and her eyes hungrily devoured her surroundings. She loved Alexandria.

The busy streets full of vendors.

The wild traffic of horses, chariots, and people.

The conversations in the streets.

The beautiful buildings.

Something bumped into her side. Maximus was fidgeting. Her gaze returned to the street, and Afiz was a few hundred metres away. He was talking to a man Seraphina didn't recognise. She gulped and hurried to catch up to him. Afiz continued chatting, his eyes shifting in Seraphina's direction for a moment.

The man smiled in Seraphina's direction, and led them into his house. He said he wanted to show Afiz some new items.

The old man was more observant than they realised. He noticed a slight movement in Seraphina's bag. As they walked in, he paused for a moment and nonchalantly left a scrap of bread and some water on the floor. He placed them right next to the bag, which Seraphina had put down, then smiled again and went out to the back of the house.

Afiz and Seraphina exchanged glances, then followed him outside.

A gust of wind blew her hood back. Seraphina froze for a second in the sunlight, and her arms rose to grab the hood. She checked herself, then lowered her arms.

The old man's eyebrows arched, and his face softened. 'Hello, child. Why do you hide such beauty?' the old man asked.

Seraphina remained silent.

Then, he spoke to Afiz as he grabbed Seraphina's chin and inspected her. 'Is she Egyptian? She looks Hebrew.'

Afiz was astounded but managed to respond. 'Egyptian. She is fairer because she works indoors a lot.'

Seraphina remained calm, although she grimaced at the man's grip. Little did she know that her mother had Egyptian blood in her. It showed on Seraphina, and it helped to lessen the old man's suspicions.

It didn't really matter, because he would never speak a word of this to anyone. He was very fond of Afiz and enjoyed his visits. Besides, the old man lived alone and spoke to hardly anyone except his customers. 'Hmmm,' said the old man as he let her go.

She stood motionless, then shifted her weight to her other foot. Her eyes darted towards Afiz for a second, then back to the vendor.

'My skin has always been a little lighter,' said Seraphina. 'I spent almost all of my life inside either working or looking after my mother.' She spoke in perfect Coptic. Afiz grinned slightly. 'Perhaps I wear this robe too much,' she said with a grin.

'Well, there's no need to be shy around here,' said the vendor. He nodded towards the inside of the house, and Seraphina turned to look. The bread and water had been reduced to crumbs and droplets. She laughed. No longer needing to keep up the ruse, Seraphina snapped her fingers. Maximus came bounding out of the bag. She watched as he dashed to the vendor's feet, wagging his tail. The vendor picked him up and petted him.

Seraphina looked up for a moment, the sun bathing her face in light. Exhaling, she watched the vendor play with Maximus. She giggled at his antics. It was funny to watch him being so silly with a stranger.

The vendor put Maximus down and went off with Afiz into his workshop.

Seraphina crouched down to Maximus, her long black hair almost touching the ground. As she cuddled him, the two watched as Afiz and the vendor did their business.

She could only be interested in writing implements for so long and she became bored. Her eyes turned to the courtyard, and she stood up. The smooth stone felt good under her feet. The vendor had some interesting plants in his garden, and she made a mental note to learn the species later. As she sat back down and waited for Afiz to finish, she decided that life under a hood was not for her. Not anymore. She closed her eyes, breathed in, and tilted her head towards the sky. A red hue tinged the darkness under her eyelids, and she smiled at the sensation of warmth.

Afiz had quite the haul. Scrolls, ink, reed pens. They thanked the vendor, and he asked them to come back soon.

Without her hood on, Seraphina was conspicuous. Most women worked indoors, so it was an odd sight to see her on the streets.

Afiz was a little worried. Maybe they thought she was Hebrew. He looked back at her and realised something. They were looking at her in admiration. Afiz had not thought about it until just then, but his dear Seraphina had grown into a beautiful young woman.

The sun will make her that little bit darker, he thought.

More Egyptian.

He looked around. They had walked too far. So often he scolded Seraphina for drifting off with her thoughts. This time he was the culprit.

It must be rubbing off on me, he thought.

He looked back at Seraphina who was, not surprisingly, in her own world. She gazed at the buildings and up at the sky. She seemed to enjoy life without a hood over her head. He smiled and thought he'd have some fun with her. 'Excuse me, do you know where we are going?' he asked her. She kept walking. 'Hello? HELLO!'

She stopped and looked around. 'Where are we?'

Afiz shook his head and smiled. 'Never mind.'

He turned on to an unfamiliar street. Seraphina followed. The buildings along the street got smaller as they walked.

There is something familiar here, thought Seraphina.

They were at the edge of the Hebrew village. She saw the water to her left and knew exactly where they were without letting on.

Afiz stopped at the intersection to get his bearings.

As Seraphina waited, she noticed an older couple. They were standing at the corner of the next block. Their eyes were fixed on her.

How weird, she thought.

She looked away for a moment, then looked back. They were still there. She turned around to see what was behind her, thinking maybe they were looking at something else. No. Nothing there but a brick wall. She looked back, and they were looking straight at her. The woman! That was the same woman from the other night!

Seraphina stayed calm and did not react. They were definitely Hebrews, and she wondered who they were. Theirs was not an uncomfortable or unpleasant stare, more a familiar one.

Afiz was lost, muttering to himself about which direction to take. Suddenly, the Hebrew woman moved forward. The man grabbed her hand, and she stopped.

The pair looked at each other, then looked back at Seraphina. A second later, turning around, they walked back into the village. The entire encounter had lasted ten to fifteen seconds at most.

How weird, thought Seraphina for a second time.

She looked at Afiz, who was completely oblivious.

Her curiosity got the better of her, and she went to follow them.

'Where are you going?' asked Afiz. 'It's this way.'

Seraphina turned back, acting as if she'd made a clumsy mistake and followed Afiz back towards the library.

Once inside, the two of them sorted the supplies they had bought. Seraphina watched Afiz as they worked. His eyes were down, his face hard with concentration. When they finished, Seraphina headed towards her room.

The sound of his voice stopped her. 'Tomorrow, we'll go and buy you some new clothes.'

FOUR

Rufio was aware of the politics behind his appointment. He knew that Caesar needed a certain type of soldier, and he knew he fit the bill perfectly.

Cleopatra and her younger brother were caught up in a feud which had become bitter, and the young queen had aligned herself with Caesar. It was a wise move, and Caesar had now taken control of the city.

Her younger brother, Ptolemy, had fled with those loyal to him.

Caesar and Rufio shared the desire to eliminate Ptolemy. For now, it was not urgent; Caesar was in control, and could easily influence the queen, and the army had the city under control providing a positive check on Cleopatra's power.

Caesar was dealing with his own problems back in Rome. Several powerful senators had lined up against him, and the situation threatened to descend into all out civil war. Usually, Caesar would appoint a senator as protector of a place like Egypt but that wouldn't work in the present situation, hence the need for Rufio.

The senators could not be relied on for now. One of them might leverage Egypt's riches, as a bargaining chip in the negotiations back in Rome.

Caesar knew that appointing Rufio ensured his hold on the region. Few men would grasp all of this and although Rufio was indeed a shrewd strategist, he was also practical about his ambition.

For now, he commanded Roman Egypt.

Cleopatra was merely a child and all he had to do was placate her.

Rufio was enthralled by the idea of having free reign over the locals, particularly the Hebrews. In one sense, he loved the Hebrews. After all, he had built his career on subjugating them. The Egyptians looked down on the Hebrews too, which made them willing accomplices in the oppression of the Hebrews however present-day politics kept the Egyptians in check from becoming too overbearing.

Roman influence had been strong in the city for over a hundred years and by now the locals knew the benefits of keeping the peace.

To Rufio, Egyptian or Hebrew, they were not people. They were commodities.

As he contemplated his advancement in his military life, he found himself drawing a comparison to the rest of his life.

He did have one weakness when it came to the Hebrews. Their women. He found their beauty enchanting but his, sometimes impulsive, nature had caused several incidents over the years. There had never been any serious consequences, however, but he had been lucky.

Rufio had never married.

He never saw the point.

He would either have a wife in Rome who he would never see or a wife in Egypt who would resent living so far from home. It was unheard of for a Roman to marry a foreigner and here lay the irony in Rufio's views.

If it was permitted, he gladly would have found an Egyptian or even a Hebrew woman to marry. It would never happen though, and the idea remained an unspoken desire.

He turned his mind to other things. How could he best use his new position?

Before he had a chance to even start making a grand plan, his son walked into the living room. The sight of him filled him with pride but then with concern.

He called out to Quintus, asking him to come into his office. Quintus greeted his father and sat down at his father's table. Rufio saw in his son a terrible weakness. He was a slave to his emotions. Rufio resented this at times, but he also knew when something was wrong.

'Is something bothering you, my boy?'

Quintus was the only person Rufio truly cared for. Many years ago, when he was in Rome for some official duties, Rufio had an encounter with a Vestal priestess.

A brief love affair ensued. He had planned for the girl to come and join him in Alexandria, but fate intervened, and by the time he had returned to Rome, she had become sick and died. Rufio was devastated, but in time, the pain if not the memories passed. He had not known the woman that well but had hoped it could become something lasting. After the priestesses gave him the bad news, they had something else to show him. They had hidden a child, a small baby boy.

The Vestals were virgins. Affairs were forbidden but they had fallen in love. However, once Rufio learned of the girl's death, he never again admitted that to himself.

The priestesses knew they had to hide the baby, otherwise, he would face certain death. The Romans were auspicious people, but the priestesses just could not let this baby suffer such a fate. They saved Rufio's child, and in doing so, risked their lives. Rufio admired the women and would be forever grateful to them.

What would he do with this child?

Once he held him, he knew there was only one choice. He would take him to Alexandria, and Rufio would raise him.

Quintus shook his head in reply to his father's question and looked out the window. Rufio indulged him for a moment.

Quintus was a young man now. He had a loving nature and was very reliable. He had spoken to his son about enlisting in the army, but those conversations hadn't gone well. His son had very odd ideas for a boy of his age and background. He embraced all people as equals. He did not believe in resolving conflict with violence. He genuinely cared about the welfare of all people, even those he didn't know. These ideals were diametrically opposed to his father's.

So, they argued. A lot.

Still, Rufio loved him with all his heart and moderated his more extreme views at times to avoid the argument he knew would follow.

'Look at me when I ask you a question,' said Rufio.

Quintus looked up and Rufio asked him to tell him what was the matter. Quintus told him what he had seen that morning.

'I saw two of your soldiers drag and beat a Hebrew man in the street this morning.'

Rufio smiled. 'Well, there must have been a good reason. Soldiers don't just go around beating everyone they see.'

Quintus looked at his father without saying a word.

'Was there a reason?' asked Rufio.

Quintus explained that an Egyptian man had accused the Hebrew of stealing.

'Well, the penalty for theft is a serious one,' said Rufio.

'I understand that, but your soldiers did not even take a moment to ask the Hebrew man what his side of the story was, nor did they question the Egyptian man who made the accusation, they just proceeded to beat this man. He could barely walk once they were finished.'

Quintus was visibly upset. Rufio started to explain his view on what the Hebrews were like. He always tried to make his son understand.

'Father!' interrupted Quintus, his voice now raised, 'You cannot paint an entire people with a single brushstroke. At the very least, your soldiers could have placed the man under arrest and conducted some sort of enquiry into the matter. The great Roman Republic has laws and courts, and for a good reason.'

Rufio resented the sarcasm. Getting caught up in an argument with Quintus would do no good. After all, he cared about his son, and the opinion he had of his father. He wanted to talk to Quintus about enlisting, but now was not the time for that conversation.

He considered the best approach. Many of his colleagues thought of Rufio as strategic. He knew that all he did was manipulate. He never saw a difference between the two words. So, he manipulated, strategised, or whatever people wanted to call it.

He got the outcomes he desired, and that's all he cared about. His son was no exception.

Right then, he decided, Quintus needed to be placated.

'Son, I see the wisdom in what you are saying. Now that I've been promoted, I will be meeting with the centurions. This will happen in a few days. I will talk to them about how the soldiers are to conduct themselves.'

This pleased Quintus. He smiled and nodded, thanking his father. He had a concerned look on his face still. 'What promotion?' he asked.

'Oh, I didn't tell you?' said Rufio, knowing full well that he had not. 'Caesar himself has appointed me as his general to govern all of Roman Egypt.' Rufio could not suppress a smile as he told his son the news.

'Congratulations, father,' said Quintus. He approached him and kissed his hand. 'That is a huge achievement.'

In truth, Quintus was deeply concerned. His father now had a huge amount of power. Like Rufio, he was a strategic thinker. He did his best not to show he was worried, but he knew his father's views all too well.

To anyone who was not Roman, this promotion was bad news. Especially the Hebrews, who his father constantly maligned. He dreaded what might come of it.

Looking at his father, he tried not to think about it. Quintus excused himself. He wanted to go for a walk while there was still some sunshine left in the day.

Rufio watched his son as he left. He was curious about what was on his mind. He had deliberately waited to tell him of his promotion.

Quintus' reaction was interesting.

At least the boy is learning to hide his feelings, thought Rufio.

Quintus had given no obvious indication of how he felt. Or at least he had tried. He gave himself away when he kissed his father's hand. It was unlike him to be so proper. He wondered what Quintus' true feelings were on the subject.

He would have to wait and see.

Almost as quickly as Quintus had left, Rufio's thoughts reverted. There was a lot to do in the coming days, weeks, and months. He foresaw a rapid expansion of the Republic into Africa. It would be him who would lead that expansion. There were untold riches to be reaped, in the lands to the south and west. He relished the thought of plundering those lands without mercy. He thought of what he had promised Quintus.

Would he speak to the centurions?

Chuckling to himself, he shook his head, poured himself a chalice of wine and continued to fantasise.

FIVE

There was a knock on the door. Seraphina sighed and opened it.

'Afiz, do we have to do this tonight?'

It was late.

Tonight, was the monthly chore of cleaning the library. It was a routine Seraphina despised. She would much rather read scrolls and debate with Afiz, than tidy up, put away scrolls, and fill up the ink.

The silver lining was, that when they were finished, the library was an amazing sight. Everything would be perfectly organised, down to the last detail.

Afiz smiled and gave his usual lecture. 'Seraphina, we are caretakers for perhaps the greatest library and centre of knowledge in the entire world. We both have the privilege of reading the words of the brightest minds our planet has ever produced, and to do so in a building that is akin to a palace. I hope it has also crossed your mind that you and I are in the rare position of having this beautiful building to ourselves on a regular basis. That is an honour, and a privilege that I dare say no one else in the world has like we do. So why, why do you complain on this one night each month when we take the time to give some care to this building and the wealth of knowledge it houses?'

Seraphina was impressed by the speech. She always was, but she was not going to give up that easily. 'Yes, but it's so boring.'

Afiz agreed. He laughed and waved at her to follow him. It was time to get started.

Maximus watched Seraphina. He knew he would have to stay in the room. Otherwise, he would get bored and tear around the library. Then there'd be even more tidying up to do.

Seraphina slammed the door shut. Stomping down the stairs, she tried to make as much noise as she could. At least she was making her displeasure known. As if Afiz couldn't already tell.

'Alright,' said Afiz, 'we will start by making sure all the scrolls are in their correct place in every part of the library. We will clean the shelves as we go, then the tables and finally, we will replenish each pen, stylus, and jar of ink as necessary before we sweep the entire floor of the library clean.'

Seraphina was more than familiar with the routine. She and Afiz had done this every month since she was six years old. They got to work. Seraphina started in the engineering and science section. As she organised the scrolls, she was tempted to stop and read one. Gradually though, she got on with it. After a brain numbing half hour of sorting her mind began to wander. She thought about her new memories from a few nights ago.

Then there was the mysterious Hebrew woman. Who was she? She wanted to know. The dreams, the feeling of terror in her memories; all of it needed an explanation. The litany of questions continued to plague her.

'Afiz,' she said, 'do you ever wonder where I came from?'

He had been concentrating on his work, and his first reaction was to tell Seraphina to get back to hers. Then he looked up, and saw the earnest look on her face.

'Why do you ask, Seraphina?'

She told him she had been thinking about it a lot recently. She told him about the dreams and the memories she was not sure were real or not.

She mentioned the questions that had been running through her mind and checked his face for a reaction. Seraphina was worried that he'd want to get back to work. Seeing his smile, she felt comfortable telling him what was on her mind.

'I wonder what happened on that night, before you found me outside in the back alley. I remember being very afraid. I think I had been running. I also remember crying and feeling very sad. I ended up here at the back door. That is when you took me in.'

Seraphina looked down as she spoke. She concentrated on her words, this had been going on for weeks, and she wanted to get all her thoughts out.

'For years now, I have walked the city with you. I've always noticed something familiar about the Hebrews. I see some who look like me and some look at me in a certain way, almost as if they recognise me. The other day, when we were lost, I saw something.'

'What was it?' Afiz kept his eyes on his work.

'At the edge of the city, a Hebrew man and woman were watching me. I don't know why but they definitely seemed to know me.'

'I don't remember anything like that.'

'You were figuring out where we were.'

Seraphina's first question had caught him off guard. It was clear she had a lot on her mind. His dear girl was vulnerable and confused, and he wanted to comfort her.

'I have often wondered what happened that night. What brought you here to the library. In fact, I have thought about it nearly every day for the last eleven years. I have always thought you could be a Hebrew, and I know you think the same which is why I've never really brought it up. I see how the Hebrews are treated and it worries me. You are very dear to me. I would hate to see you mistreated.'

Seraphina leaned on the table, her back hunched. It was a difficult conversation. It felt as though her world was ending, at least in part. She, Afiz, and Maximus had a wonderful life, and she didn't want anything to change that. Yet, there was a feeling of inevitability. As though things were changing, and Seraphina felt sad and powerless at the thought.

Afiz could see she was struggling. He tried to offer words of comfort.

'If anyone asks, we will say you are Egyptian. You speak the language perfectly, after all, but the key is to never mention to anyone else that you think you're a Hebrew. I understand you want to learn about your past, and I will help you as much as I can, but we must be cautious. As much as I want you to have the answers you seek, I also want you to be safe and If anyone ever found out a Hebrew girl was living in the library, it could be disastrous. So, can we agree that we will try to work things out together, cautiously?'

Afiz saw Seraphina nod, and breathed a sigh of relief. If anything ever happened, he knew there would be consequences for both of them. The Alexandrians saw the Great Library as a precious gem, a source of pride to them and if they discovered Seraphina, it would cause problems. If Afiz was lucky, he would only lose his job, but more likely, it would be much worse.

He hesitated to think of what might happen to Seraphina. Afiz cringed at the thought. It would be even worse if the Romans found out.

He would prefer to avoid such a scenario altogether.

Seraphina still looked sad.

He got up and came to her side of the table and placed a hand on her shoulder. 'So, tell me what this woman looked like.' He listened to Seraphina's description. He saw her eyebrows drop, and she stopped talking. Then her eyes dropped to the ground. She looked as though her mind was elsewhere. Afiz assured her they would come up with a plan. They would find this woman and see what the connection was.

He watched her for a moment. Her eyes came back to him and he saw a smile. A small one, but it was there.

He gave her a brief hug, which was very out of character.

They got back to work, in silence.

SIX

The following day Afiz was thinking.

How are we going to find this woman?

He had promised Seraphina. So many questions were obviously running through her mind.

Her parents, thought Afiz. *That's what this is about.*

Personally, he'd always thought something terrible must have happened that night. Seraphina had been a mess, but she was healthy and well fed. Someone was taking care of her, and yet she had no memory. It was puzzling to him.

Maybe her mind blocked it out, he thought. *It was natural. She is becoming a young woman, of course she's going to wonder about these things. There are so many unknowns in her past. Still, something must have triggered all this. What was it? It didn't matter. She wanted to know. One way or another, she would find out. She deserved to know.*

He wanted to help her. He just couldn't think of how.

He had lost track of time.

He needed to run some errands and visit the harbour master. A well-renowned philosopher had been invited to the library. He lived in a place called Valentia, many, many miles from Alexandria and Afiz needed to find out exactly when his ship would arrive. Maybe the news of a visiting scholar would cheer up Seraphina.

She had been so sad the past few days.

As he walked up to her room, he racked his brains. There had to be a way of finding this mysterious Hebrew woman.

He walked into her room, full of energy. 'Good morning, Seraphina,' he said. The young girl looked up for a moment, and seeing Afiz's cheerful face, looked back down. She was sitting on the edge of her bed, slouched over.

Afiz's smile faded away. A heavy energy hung in the room.

'Come on, Seraphina, it isn't like you to slouch,' he said, sitting down next to her. He gave her a little nudge. She straightened up and sighed.

It was very melodramatic, thought Afiz but he kept his thoughts to himself.

Seraphina was just sad at the moment. At least he hoped that was the problem.

'I have a surprise for you,' he said.

'Really? What is it?'

He told her about the philosopher. A very, very famous philosopher, who was on his way to Alexandria. He started to explain where Valentia was.

'I know where Valentia is,' said Seraphina.

He continued undeterred. Explaining about his busy day to come. While he spoke, he noticed she was perking up.

She looked at him, and a tiny smile formed on her lips.

'Really?' she asked.

Afiz smiled. 'Yes, and one of the things we have to do is go to the harbour master's office. We must find out exactly when he is arriving. I promised Imhotep, and we have other things to do.'

Seraphina tilted her head from side to side. A rare moment of indecision.

'So, are you coming?' asked Afiz.

'It would be nice to go outside today,' said Seraphina, almost to herself.

'What about you, Maximus? Do you want to go out on this beautiful sunny day?' asked Afiz of the little pup.

Maximus got in on the act. He ran to the corner of the room. Dragging his bag to Seraphina's feet, he tugged at her trousers. Then a little whimper.

Seraphina looked down at the adorable puppy. His energy was irresistible.

She knew that the walk and the fresh air would do her good, so she got up, and Afiz left the room so she could get ready. As Seraphina came out of the room, Afiz watched in admiration.

'What?' she asked.

'Nothing,' said Afiz. 'Well, you look very smart in your new outfit.'

Seraphina smiled. She looked down, and thought she looked the part. It was a long dress, in typical Egyptian style with a matching headband. It was one of several new outfits Afiz had managed to find for her.

'It really suits you,' said Afiz. Seraphina thanked him for the compliment. Afiz started down the stairs, and she followed. Afiz turned and gave her a quizzical look. He couldn't remember the last time she actually walked down the stairs with him. She always used her secret passageway. Seraphina looked at him and shrugged her shoulders.

The office of Alexandria's harbour master was near the edge of the city, on the waterfront for obvious reasons. Seraphina smiled as they made their way through the city.

It's right near my favourite spot, she thought.

The streets were so different in the daytime. Busy, teeming with life. Even walking along them, instead of sprinting and somersaulting, was an adjustment.

Part of her wanted to all the same, and she looked down at Maximus. He seemed to have the same idea.

Not right now, she thought.

When they arrived, Seraphina was relieved to get inside. The marble building was cool and made a pleasant change from the stifling heat outside. Even Afiz had rushed inside to escape the heat.

Maximus was very well behaved, and once they were inside, he was so silent no one would know he was there.

The harbour master came out to greet them. He was a serious type. Afiz started to chat with him but Seraphina quickly got bored with the conversation and her mind drifted off. She looked down at herself. The midsection of her dress was all colour, and the intricate patterns culminated in a thick gold strip at the top.

She felt the headband. It was wrapped around the top of her forehead. It felt a little awkward.

Probably because it's new, she thought.

She watched the people out in the street.

She was taller than most of the women she saw, in fact she was about the same height as Afiz. Seraphina had always thought of Afiz as a giant.

Now I'm as tall as him. She joked to herself. *Am I an adult now? What's next for me?*

She smiled at her silliness.

Afiz had finished with the harbour master. Seraphina had completely tuned out. Afiz had turned to leave, and Seraphina hadn't moved. She roused herself to leave with Afiz, but as Afiz said goodbye near the entrance, Seraphina could not believe her eyes.

There she was. The Hebrew woman.

She hadn't noticed Seraphina. She was doing nothing remarkable, just chatting to a friend and carrying a few vegetables. Once they were outside, she stopped to get Afiz's attention.

'Don't look, but she is right behind you,' murmured Seraphina.

'The Hebrew woman?'

'Yes. Just turn around very slowly.'

Afiz did as he was told. No one noticed him, and Seraphina realised she was being a bit overdramatic. The woman was at least thirty metres away and the streets were very busy. So, they watched and waited. The woman finished her conversation and started to walk away.

'Come on,' said Afiz, 'let's follow her.'

Seraphina hesitated for a second then she started following the woman. Afiz joined her. 'Slow down, we don't want to attract any attention. Let's just see where she is going.' They slowed to a stroll. They were now in the Hebrew village.

The locals noticed them in passing. The young woman was elegant. One of them was looking more closely.

Her features looked a little Hebrew, she thought.

Afiz and Seraphina kept moving, avoiding any direct eye contact. They stayed on the woman's trail, keeping their distance. She hadn't noticed them and seemed to be in a rush.

After a few twists and turns, she disappeared into a small house in the centre of the village. Seraphina made a mental note of where they were. Afiz kept walking so as not to arouse suspicion. If they stopped to look at the house, they might be noticed, and he preferred to be careful.

The two of them looped around and walked back out of the village. It amused Seraphina that Afiz was excited by their find. She liked this adventurous side of Afiz, which she had never really seen before. Seraphina was also very grateful. Afiz hadn't hesitated, and now they knew where this mystery woman lived. Whatever was going on, she now knew she could count on Afiz's support.

Her mind turned to the Hebrew woman. She had to meet her although Seraphina wondered what would come of such an encounter. That question consumed her, distracting her for the rest of the afternoon. As Afiz ran his errands, Seraphina had a strong feeling in her gut. Her world was about to be turned upside down.

SEVEN

Cleopatra sat on the lavish chaise lounge, gazing up at the beautiful ceiling, the picture of leisure.

She glanced across the room. There sat the great Julius Caesar. She thought of all that had happened. Not long ago, she had been forced to share this palace with Ptolemy, her despicable younger brother.

She was glad to be rid of him. After all, her father had trained her to be queen, yet his will decreed that she was to share the throne. It made no sense to her.

She thought of her father, and still missed him. She had loved him dearly, and he had been a devoted father, despite his many duties. He had always made time for her.

On top of that, he had been a wise king. Many had criticised him for capitulating to the Romans. Cleopatra knew better.

Her father's approach was wise. The Roman Republic was expanding, and this shift in power was inevitable. Her father had foreseen that, overseen the transition, and peace had endured.

Still, it upset her that she had to be queen alongside her brother. She was older, and more mature. Her father had said as much. She certainly had a more methodical way of approaching matters.

Her brother was a different story. Much younger, he was narcissistic and self-centred. An absolute brat of a child. Caesar's arrival in Alexandria had been fate. She had known about the visit, and smelled opportunity and after smuggling herself in to meet with him, she persuaded him that their interests were aligned.

Caesar knew she despised her brother. Yet he was enamoured with her. Her courage, her passion, her initiative, and above all her mesmerising beauty. Caesar knew the situation was not so simple. It didn't matter though. Caesar saw the opportunities before him. It would be beneficial to have Cleopatra as an ally. Egypt would become part of the republic, and the locals would see their queen in charge of things.

If Caesar kept Ptolemy at bay, Cleopatra would be indebted to him. She would do anything to have the throne to herself.

So, he made a promise, on the night they met, that she would rule Egypt alone. It was unlike him to make such a promise. Caesar had been seduced, but even so, he would be the one who benefited the most.

He began staying at the palace as their bond deepened, but one day their relationship took a political turn. Ptolemy had come to the palace for a meeting with Caesar who he found with Cleopatra.

The young king flew into a rage, claiming that he had been betrayed.

A mob gathered at the palace. His generals attempted to incite them against Cleopatra and Caesar. Ever the orator, Caesar eventually won over the crowd by reminding the people of the late king's wishes. Cleopatra and Ptolemy were to rule Egypt together. The people had great respect for the late king, and order prevailed.

It had been Ptolemy's decision to flee the city afterwards.

A lot had happened. She had mixed feelings for Caesar. She loved him for removing her brother from power. He had even captured Ptolemy, after he'd fled the city.

She hated him for releasing the young king, just to placate his followers. While Cleopatra and Caesar were both ruthless, his ruthlessness was tempered with age and opportunism, but Cleopatra's was fuelled by rage and ego.

She had raised the issue of her reign and whether she could remain in power. Caesar assured her he had matters in hand. He asked her not to worry, and to trust him and for now, she was content to do so.

There were rumours though. Her brother was amassing forces and preparing for civil war. She still worried, but not too much. After all, here they were in the lap of luxury. They had all the power and were in the throes of a deep romance.

'How long will you stay this time?' Cleopatra interrupted the silence.

'Perhaps a few more days. As you know, I have pressing matters in Rome to deal with, but the situation here is equally important,' said Caesar.

'I would love to see Rome one day.'

'Once things are calm, you can visit. The city and the surrounding countryside are beautiful, and you can stay in one of my homes when you come.'

This excited Cleopatra. She had already set her sights far beyond Egypt, but not wanting to give away too much, she changed the topic.

'That sounds lovely, when the time is right. So, tell me, this Rufio, he is now your top general here in Egypt?'

'That is correct, my love,' said Caesar.

'What kind of man is he?'

Caesar told her about Rufio. He explained how trustworthy he was, and this reassured her.

'You can rely on him for anything you need. His command throughout Egypt is beyond question. He will ensure you are safe when I am not here.'

'Surely my own guards can take care of that?' asked Cleopatra.

'I prefer to rely on Rufio than your guards. Rufio has been through more training, and the Roman legions in Alexandria are some of the best trained and battle-tested in the entire army. Your brother is my only concern. Even here in Egypt, I must keep an eye out. Some senators back in Rome may use their influence here.'

Smiling at Cleopatra, Caesar told her how important Egypt was to him. For her, he would do anything to make sure Egypt remained safe and secure.

Cleopatra returned the smile. A lot of politics and power games were at play.

Putting all that aside, she knew he truly loved her.

EIGHT

Alexandria was in a festive mood. The Beautiful Festival of the Valley was being celebrated to the south, in the great city of Thebes and while the Alexandrians did not formally celebrate the festival, they thought it a great excuse to remember their ancestors.

They had a wonderful time doing so, filling themselves lavishly with food and drink for the better part of a week.

In principle, Rufio did not approve. However, the celebrations kept the locals happy. They seized on the opportunity to enjoy some of their more traditional customs. A bit of indulgence never hurt. Besides, happy people were less likely to rebel. His soldiers appreciated the festival too. The city had an upbeat atmosphere at this time of year.

Rufio thought it would be a nice day for a stroll through the city and had asked Quintus the day before if he wanted to join him. He thought Quintus would enjoy it, given his fondness for all things foreign.

'We can watch the Egyptians celebrate their customs,' he said.

Quintus had agreed, which pleased his father greatly. He always looked forward to spending some time with his son, as it wasn't something they got to do often.

It was a short chariot ride to the city and before long, they could hear the celebrations.

The city was alive. Rufio noticed only a few Hebrews on the streets. *They're spending the day with their families,* he thought.

There were food stalls in the streets, and wine being sold in the marketplace. Everyone was getting in on the action. A band of trumpets, lyres, flutes, and drums was in full swing.

Quintus marvelled at the atmosphere. Even Rufio was enjoying himself. His father danced a little to the music as they passed the band which made him laugh. Seeing his father smile and be silly was a rarity.

Quintus watched the Egyptians with great interest. He loved their dancing and music. Their traditional clothes were dynamic and interesting.

Rufio watched his son. It was nice to see him enjoying the day. He didn't like the way he looked at the Egyptians. It was a look of admiration. Of course, Rufio couldn't understand that, but today, Rufio wouldn't worry about such things. They were having fun. Aside from that, there were other things he wanted to discuss.

'So, Quintus, how are things going in your final year of school?' asked Rufio.

'Very well, father. It looks as though I will graduate in the top three positions in my class, and I have a good chance of finishing first,' said Quintus.

This made Rufio proud. He smiled and put his hands on Quintus' shoulders. Looking into his eyes, he said, 'That is an excellent result, my dear son.'

Like any son, Quintus wanted to make his father proud, so he appreciated his father's kind words. They continued walking around and everywhere they went, they were surrounded by one big party.

Quintus was happy.

It was a beautiful day.

There was joyful energy in the streets.

He was spending time with his father, and actually enjoying himself. His father had even told him he was proud of him! It was a great day indeed.

It would be great to do this more often, thought Quintus.

Rufio sensed his son was relaxed and happy.

Now was as good a time as any, he thought.

'Finishing school in such an excellent position will give you a lot of opportunities,' said Rufio. As he said this, he watched some nearby dancers to appear nonchalant. 'Have you thought about what your options are and where you might go after school is finished?'

Quintus had thought about little else. He loved that his father was taking an interest and told his father there were several colleges he was interested in. Some were in Rome, with the others scattered throughout the republic. Quintus was hoping his father could help him and said as much. They kept walking through the city, and Rufio asked him what he had in mind.

'You could use some of your connections,' said Quintus. 'I would love some more information on these colleges. Maybe I could even go to Rome to visit one or two of them.'

Rufio found the idea interesting. He told Quintus he would gladly help once school was finished.

Quintus continued, 'I have some other ideas too and there are excellent colleges in Antioch and Byzantium as well.'

Rufio wasn't really listening, but played along for his son's benefit. A group of men nearby laughed loudly. Rufio cocked his head at them. They were intoxicated, but they noticed his stare and moved on.

Turning back to Quintus, he frowned and said, 'The best colleges are in Rome.'

'I agree, father. The best options do seem to be in Rome, but I want to look at all my options.'

Rufio nodded sagely and after a few seconds said, 'So, these other ideas you mentioned?'

Quintus hesitated. 'Ah, yes. Well, I would love to explore the possibility of working directly with a renowned scientist, or a philosopher, or perhaps even an engineer. There are several excellent ones I know of. Again, I was hoping you might help me.'

This interested Rufio.

'Quintus, do you think it will work? I mean, the people you speak of would be experts and renowned scholars. How are you going to match wits with them?'

'Well, Father, I was thinking I could approach them with the idea of them being my mentor.'

Rufio nodded his head. It wasn't a bad idea, but this wasn't what he wanted to talk about. He made a show of looking like he was in deep thought as they continued to walk through the festivities. Quintus saw the harbour in front of them and then there it was, to his right. The Great Library of Alexandria. Quintus stopped and looked up at the majestic building.

'I love this library,' said Quintus. He admired the architecture. 'Not just the beauty of the building, but everything inside. The scrolls, the scholars. They study in there every day.'

Rufio was frustrated. 'Yes, I know what they do in a library,' he said, trying to make a joke. It missed its mark. 'It is a wonderful place, one of the gems of the city.'

Rufio remembered when he first had come to the city. The library was one of the first things he had seen. That was a long time ago now and his enthusiasm had waned quickly. He tried to steer the conversation once again.

'I remember the first time I saw this place.' Rufio looked up and down the building, feigning interest. He waited for Quintus to ask him a question.

'When was that, Father?'

'Many years ago, when I first came here from Rome. I was not much older than you are now. I was on a ship full of freshly trained legionaries. Someone had made the decision to dispatch us here once our training was complete, and we had relatively little warning that we would be leaving our homes and families behind.'

Rufio saw that Quintus was waiting on his every word. Something about this interested him. He looked back at his son.

There is so much compassion in those eyes, he thought.

He must have inherited it from his mother.

'That must have been difficult for you,' said Quintus. He had rarely heard his father speak about the past. If only he realised what a manipulation it was.

'Yes, it was. I felt sad leaving my parents.' That sentiment was a genuine one, but he did not reflect for long. Shifting gears, he said, 'But I trained to be a legionary because I wanted to serve in Rome's army. I do not regret my decision. Even though I have had to make sacrifices, serving in the army has done a lot for me. I have had the privilege of commanding scores of excellent men. I have worked hard to rise through the ranks and now this entire region of Egypt is my responsibility.'

Quintus nodded as his father spoke, and acknowledged him. 'Yes, Father. I can see how well you have done. You have had an amazing career. I see how well respected you are by your fellow soldiers, as well as the senators and other officials I have met.'

Rufio saw an opening. It was time for the question he had wanted to ask all day long.

'Have you ever considered the possibility of service? Even if only for a while?' Rufio straightened his posture and stood tall in front of his son.

He had been hunched over until just then. It was to seem vulnerable to his son while he discussed his past. Rufio was shameless and manipulation came so naturally to him. He saw this conversation as a necessary step. He had to set his son on the right path. He saw the value of an academic education. He even saw the power and prestige that would come with such a career path. However, there was nothing more powerful or prestigious than the Roman army, at least, not in his mind. These were things that Rufio had exalted more than anything else in life. The path his son took in life was a reflection on him. It therefore spoke to his own prestige that his son should follow him.

'Father,' mumbled Quintus, 'you know that is something I am not interested in.'

'I understand that, my dear son. You often speak of being open-minded and how important that is, so, when you say you are considering all of your options, I only ask that you honour your own words.'

Quintus dragged his feet. Coming to a halt, he put his hands on his hips and faced his father. He nodded without looking at him.

'Military life is not for me, Father,' he whispered.

Rufio smiled and took his son by the shoulders.

Quintus flinched, and his eyes widened. 'I know that the army exists to make war. It has expanded the borders of the Roman Republic. This has been achieved through massive bloodshed. The Romans have the notion that their way is superior. Superior to all other cultures, and ways of doing things.'

The boy did not mince his words, thought Rufio. The Romans? He spoke as if he was detached from the group.

You are a Roman, he thought.

He remained calm and continued to debate with his son.

'Interesting. Is that all you see when you think of the Roman army?'

'To be honest, Father, yes.'

'Well, we have been walking around the city for a number of hours today. Have you seen any of the mistreatment against Egyptians and Hebrews that you often complain about to me?'

'There are hardly any Hebrews on the streets today.'

'There are plenty of Egyptians though. You did not answer my question.'

'The answer to your question is no. At least for today, that is.' Quintus' voice was rising, his words sounding harder.

Rufio was undeterred, and felt he had the momentum. 'Might that not suggest something to you?'

'Like what?'

'That our soldiers are well trained, and that they follow orders. After our conversation the other day, I gave a directive. Already, that directive is being followed throughout the entire city.'

Quintus' anger subsided for a moment. He had a small smile on his face. 'You already spoke to the centurions?'

Rufio lied. 'Of course. It was important to you, and I saw the sense in what you were saying.'

Quintus looked at his father. Then he looked away for a moment as he considered his father's words.

Rufio sought to press home his advantage. 'That doesn't impress you at all? That an important order could be implemented with such speed and ease?'

'Or it might suggest that your soldiers have decided to take a day off from their usual arbitrary brutality on a day of festivity.'

Rufio knew he was getting the better of his son. It was unlike him to snap back with a fierce remark like that.

'Whatever your opinion may be of the Roman army, son, I think that remark is out of line. You speak of treating people with fairness. You speak of keeping an open mind. As your father, I suggest you apply those things to yourself. To your own evaluations and judgements.' Rufio held up a hand to stop his son interrupting. 'I understand your position. I can even see how you have formed some of your opinions. Balance is important. The army keeps the peace throughout the entire Republic. Every day, they ensure the people feel safe; that they can live their lives free of war and violence. This security provides a huge benefit to society. People can pursue their endeavours, their passions. Whether it be science, or the arts, or something more unique.' Rufio placed his hand gently on to his son's shoulder. 'The army provides updates to the Senate which helps our government to improve our society, not just for military matters. We're talking about everyday life here. The army provides a valuable public service and I only ask that you consider these things in forming a more balanced viewpoint.' Quintus was now engaged. He listened as his father continued. 'There is the training provided to the men in combat, tactics, and teamwork. These are valuable skills that remain with the men for life. Regardless of how long a man serves, these are invaluable.'

'I understand all of that, father,' said Quintus. 'Yet I stand by what I said. I am not convinced. I believe that the army does more good than harm to society as a whole, but my interests and my future lie elsewhere.'

His father gave him an arrogant smirk. Quintus listened as Rufio brought the conversation back to the library. He was relieved. Maybe his father had heard him.

They discussed the architecture of the building. Then they admired some of the other buildings nearby. The museum was fascinating to

Quintus.

It served as a college itself, and a rather grand one. Quintus had considered it but one of his motivations for leaving Alexandria was to be free of his father. Although he loved him, he was far too controlling.

'You know, Quintus, I am very lenient with you. Most fathers are not so open to debate. I allow you to make your own decisions on most things. I support you in every way possible. You've had a very comfortable life so far. I do not ask for much of you, and I think it is fair for me to expect certain things. One of those is that you consider the advice I offer.'

Rufio paused to allow Quintus to respond. He looked at his son for a few moments. Nothing.

'I am disappointed, Quintus. You are so open-minded when it comes to others. To the Egyptians and the Hebrews, and yet you are not receptive to me, your own father; your own flesh and blood. The Egyptians and Hebrews are strangers to you, but I see you respect them more than you do me.'

Quintus bent his head. He nodded to himself for a moment. Even so, despite his father's urgings, he had to follow his heart. His father was wrong. He knew what he had seen: soldiers abusing their power, bullying those less fortunate, the terrible attitude that soldiers always seemed to have. That's what his views were based on. He looked at his father, and saw the same in him, maybe even worse. He was the very embodiment of Roman superiority. Quintus didn't want that for himself and would avoid it at all costs. He decided, for now, to placate his father.

He sighed. 'You make a good point, Father. I will think about it.'

Rufio smiled at his son. He was so easy to read.

'Do not patronise me, son. I know your mind is already made up but so is mine. When your schooling is complete, you will go to Rome. Not to colleges or philosophers and not to scientists or engineers.' Quintus started to interrupt, but Rufio put up his hand again to silence him. 'You will spend six months learning to be a soldier. Just outside the city, there is a camp; one of our finest training camps. After that six months is complete, we will talk.'

Quintus was devastated. 'I beg you to reconsider, Father,' he said, hugging him in despair. He felt his father shrug him off violently and fell to the ground. Quintus looked up at his father from the ground.

Rufio looked down on his pathetic son. 'You are weak. If you refuse to keep an open mind, you will learn the hard way. Maybe after the six months, I could consider other avenues, but you must at least give it a try.' Rufio's frustration intensified, watching Quintus shake his head as he spoke. He barked at him to get up.

Quintus rose. 'Father, please do not do this.' Rufio was unmoved.

All he respects is aggression, thought Quintus.

Finally, he gave vent to his anger.

'I worked hard all these years. I did that, so I could choose what I want to do with my life. I did that work, not you. Just because you are my father, you think you can do this? You have no right to define my destiny. I don't care what other fathers do. You've always told me to be my own man; to make my own choices, but what a hypocrite you are! When you don't get your own way, look at what you do.'

Rufio remained firm. The boy was crying. He would not be deterred by such pathetic pleas. Even from his son. He simply smiled down at Quintus.

'I am getting my own way, Quintus. Accept this. Don't fight me. You are an intelligent boy, and very capable, but you are still a boy, and I am your father. If I see you going astray, it is my duty to set you straight. You don't always know what is right for you, and I have the benefit of experience. You will excel in the army, and before long, your views will change. This will all be a distant memory. The reason the Republic expands is not bloodshed. It is because of our way of life. It offers something that no other civilisation can or ever will.'

'What might that be?' Quintus' voice was laden with sarcasm, and Rufio did not appreciate it. Rufio leaned down so he was eye to eye with his son. His movements were deliberate and aggressive. He then raised his voice, something he almost never did. It scared Quintus.

'What it offers is an opportunity. An opportunity for excellence in life. It offers people the chance to escape an uncivilised world. It offers people the security to build a life for themselves. To build a life knowing that it won't be taken away just because a horde of barbarians came across their village. That, my son, is the future, and whether you like it or not, you will be a part of it.'

The argument was over.

Rufio turned and walked away from his son.

Quintus watched as he walked off, and as his father disappeared into the distance, he felt his dreams fade away.

NINE

Seraphina waited impatiently outside the vendor's house.

Afiz was taking his time. She was so bored that she'd started to count the bricks.

Only Afiz would find work on a day like this, she thought.

She looked around. Everyone else was enjoying themselves, and *they* were working. Two men were having an argument near the library.

Well, not everyone else, she thought.

She sulked while she waited.

All Alexandria is celebrating, and here I am waiting for Afiz to finish a conversation about pens. Or ink. Or other such nonsense.

At least she was outdoors though. She looked back at the two men. On closer observation, it looked like a man and his son. Their conversation certainly was animated.

Seraphina grew curious. What were they fighting about? They shouted at each other. Then, the older man stormed off. She had been thinking about which scroll to read when she got home but now, she was fixated on this young man. He was beautiful. His face was fair, with high cheekbones that descended into a strong jawline. His eyes were an intense blue, and his natural expression was a soft smile.

Seraphina smiled as she observed him. His thick, dark hair complemented his facial features and although he stood tall and strong, there was a gentleness about him.

At this moment however, he looked sad.

She watched him for a while, then looked inside the house. Afiz was still deep in conversation.

Why not, she thought.

She walked up to him, thinking how she'd never paid this much attention to a stranger.

'Hello,' she said.

'Hello,' said Quintus.

Seraphina looked away. She shifted her weight from one foot to another. Suddenly, she was shy. Why did I approach this young man?

'What is your name?' asked Quintus.

Seraphina looked back at him, wondering again about what had compelled her to speak to a complete stranger. His eyes danced as he observed her. She couldn't help but smile.

'Seraphina.' It came out as a croak; her throat had gone completely dry.

'Sorry, what was that?' asked Quintus.

She held her hand to her mouth and coughed to clear her throat. 'Seraphina,' she said with a smile.

'Beautiful name. I am Quintus.'

Seraphina nodded with a smile. She felt her breathing return to normal and started to relax.

Quintus glanced around, trying to think of something to talk about. He mentioned his love of the library.

Seraphina's eyes lit up as he spoke about the library. She stayed silent for the most part, nodding and agreeing with his comments until she saw Afiz come out of the vendor's house. He was standing on the doorstep, looking for her.

'I have to go now.' She dashed off in Afiz's direction.

All Quintus could do was watch as she scurried away.

TEN

Tonight, was the night.

Seraphina did not know why she was so nervous, but she couldn't wait any longer.

It was time to visit the Hebrew woman.

She had no idea what she would say or do.

Maybe storm her house and interrogate her, she joked to herself.

Seraphina hoped something would come of it. Was it a wild goose chase? It did not matter. She was going.

Maximus would have to stay home though. She was worried he might be too noisy, especially while she was creeping around the Hebrew village. It was one thing to run in empty streets, it was quite another to sneak around outside someone's home.

In her excitement, she forgot to check where the soldiers were. Her room was a great vantage point, and she always checked before leaving, but it was too late now. She froze.

Imagine being caught right at the back door, she thought. There was no point worrying now.

She eased through the city, checking each corner as she went, staying a few blocks away from the waterfront. The streets there were quieter and darker, and it would be easy for her to hear anyone else who may be around as she retraced her path to the woman's home.

She crossed into the village and found her street.

Except for that house, the entire street was dark. The faint light of a candle showed through a window.

Very odd for this hour, thought Seraphina. *Maybe they forgot to blow it out before bed.*

She inched closer to the window and looked inside. Thanks to the candle, she made out a simple room; just some chairs and a table. She knew nothing about Hebrew homes, at least not that she could remember so she had no idea what to expect. Seraphina squinted into the back of the house.

That must be where they sleep, she thought.

She looked down the wall of the house. There was another window, on the other side of the doorway. She sidestepped, passing the doorway, wanting to take a look through the other window.

'You might as well come inside,' said a voice from inside the house. Seraphina jumped, and her heart stopped for a moment.

'Seraphina, did you hear me?' It was the same voice.

Her name! Whoever it was, knew her name! Her heart was now thumping in her chest, and she had absolutely no idea what to do next, so she leaned back against the wall. Then, sliding down, she sat on the ground.

This is silly, she thought, *I'm sitting on the street.*

The door of the house opened, and a pair of feet appeared next to her on the doorstep. She looked up, butterflies fluttering in her stomach. There was the woman again, with the same warm smile.

She extended her hand to Seraphina. Reassuring her, she told her to get up and come inside.

I might as well. I'm here now, after all, Seraphina thought.

The woman closed the door behind them.

Seraphina stood in the middle of the room, her eyebrows lowered, and her eyes narrowed. A man appeared from the back of the house. It was the same man she'd seen the first time. He introduced himself as Saul and asked her to sit. For now, she would do what they asked, she decided. The woman lit another candle and sat down with them.

'You look confused,' said the Hebrew woman. 'I am Yadira, and Saul here is my husband.'

Seraphina nodded, her hands gripping the arms of the chair to stop them from shaking. Her eyes darted back and forth between Saul and Yadira.

What the hell is going on?

Their faces were filled with kindness and warmth, so she relaxed a little. They looked at her as if they knew her, and the familiarity was unsettling. She took a deep breath and told herself to calm down. There was no danger, at least she hoped not.

'Very well,' said Seraphina. 'First things first. How do you know my name?'

Yadira smiled at Saul. 'I named you, Seraphina.'

Seraphina's eyes lit up. She stood and walked toward Yadira, her arms partially extended, but Yadira put up her hands.

'Oh. I'm sorry, but we are not your parents, Seraphina.' Seraphina retreated into her chair. 'Maybe I should have explained that first.'

Seraphina's face tightened. 'So, who are you?' she asked.

Yadira told the story. A long time ago, she and Saul had been close friends of Seraphina's parents. Josef and Rebekah. Yadira told her a little about her parents, and how they lived with her, here, in the Hebrew village.

Seraphina had always wanted to know their names, but she noticed something, and interrupted.

'You keep using the past tense. What happened to my parents?'

'I am getting to that, Seraphina. Maybe we are moving too fast here,' said Yadira.

'What do you mean?'

'When I saw you on the street the other day, I was shocked. I did not believe it was you straight away. There was something about you, something so familiar that reminded me of my old friend, Rebekah. It was not until that night, when I could see you properly, with no other distractions, that I was certain of the resemblance. I knew then that it was you.'

'How do you even know me?' asked Seraphina.

'I told you, we knew your parents. I was very close with your mother.'

'You said you named me?'

'Yes, in fact I helped you into the world. After you were born, I was there. Your mother and I were sitting together as she nursed you. We got to thinking of names. She did not like any of the ones that she and Josef had come up with. So, she asked me to think of some names. I suggested a few. When I said "Seraphina" she froze. "That's it" she said. She loved the name immediately. That is how you got your name.'

Seraphina absorbed the story, nodding as she did. She had no idea what to say, so she went with a simple 'alright.'

'Would you like to see where you were born?' Yadira held both hands out to Seraphina.

Her eyes lit up. 'I'd love to,' she said.

Yadira got up and went to the back of the house and Seraphina followed. The small house opened out into a courtyard. In the middle was a simple wooden table. Three chairs sat around it.

'The table,' said Seraphina. 'Is that where I was born?'

'On this table, yes.'

'But not here, in this house?'

'No. Not here,' said Yadira. 'After what happened, I moved the table here. I didn't know you were alive. I never imagined that I would see you again.'

'So, if the table wasn't here when I was born, where was it?

'In your parents' old house, just down the street.'

Seraphina looked at the table, then out towards the street. Why were they talking about a table? There was something far important to ask.

'Yadira, what happened to my parents?'

'The truth is I do not know. At least, not for certain. Ten or so years ago, we were having a big problem in this part of the city. At least it was a problem to us Hebrews. Women were disappearing, and we did not know why. The Romans then were not like they are now. They were terrible. Caesar is an ambitious man, but he is also civilised and because of him, the soldiers now have some discipline and decency that they did not have in those days. All the women who were disappearing were Hebrew. This meant that the authorities did not bother to investigate. The usual response from a soldier was dismissive. They would just guess that whoever it was had gone back to Israel, or maybe Judah. That was the end of the matter.

'We knew that wasn't the truth. Our lands are far away from here. No one had the means to travel such a long distance. We have camels and donkeys, but such a journey can only be made by boat. Hebrews here are not allowed to board Roman or Egyptian ships, and we have none of our own. Besides, women here would not just disappear and leave their families.

'We suspected foul play. Someone was stalking Hebrew women, attacking them. Many of those who disappeared worked in the city late at night and they would walk back to the village after work, so no one would be around to see if one was attacked. I heard the stories, but I did not know any of them personally. One night, a woman was in the village. She was crying. We found her badly beaten, but alive. Her name was Eliana. She told us what happened. A Roman soldier had approached her. At first, he was charming and friendly, asking where she was from, complimenting her beauty. Then he forced himself on her. Eliana was badly injured. She tried to tell us as much as she could. The soldier smelled like wine, she said. As if he had been drinking.

'Eliana had managed to fight him off. She had run away, then hid for hours. Once she was certain the soldier had fled, she came back to the village where we helped tend to her injuries. She was in bad shape. Now we knew for certain. It was a soldier attacking our women. There was no other explanation.'

Seraphina allowed Yadira's story to sink in. She shook her head, not wanting to know what happened to her own mother. 'So, this woman, Eliana. Did she identify the soldier?'

'No, it was out of the question,' said Yadira. 'She was terrified; certain that if he ever saw her again, he would kill her. It would be easy for him. He would accuse her of attacking him and that would be the end for her. She wanted to leave but we tried to convince her to stay.

Maybe we could do something about it, we said, but she wanted no part of it. Eventually, we managed to smuggle her aboard a ship to Caesarea and years later, her husband and son went to join her. Looking back, it was a good thing that we acted so quickly. After she was attacked, Roman soldiers were all over the village, patrolling, and making their presence felt. It was clear they were looking for something, or someone. Most knew the story. We Hebrews are a secretive bunch though. We gave no indication that anything was wrong.'

'What happened after that?' asked Seraphina.

'One night a few days later, two soldiers were roaming through the village very late. They were desperately searching for someone. The people stayed in their homes because the soldiers were not trying to be discreet and everyone knew they were there. It was obvious that something was wrong. I saw them run up and down this street at least three times. They went into a house a few doors up from here. They were in there for a long time.

'My parents' house,' said Seraphina. It was not a question.

'Yes, your parents' house. When they finally left, I waited. Then I went up to look. The place had been ransacked. That house is where you grew up with your parents, Seraphina.'

Seraphina nodded, urging her to continue the story.

'The soldiers were a mess,' said Yadira. 'To be honest, it surprised me how they acted. They did not even try to be quiet. They were not thinking clearly. That much was obvious. They had been in a fight. One had scratches on his face. The other had grazes on his arms and knees. I think he was bleeding. The one with the scratches matched the description that Eliana gave us. I feared the worst. The table and chairs had been left untouched. A few days later, I moved them here. I never saw your parents again.'

'How about the soldiers? Did you ever see them again?'

Yadira shook her head. 'No. It is not common for Roman soldiers to come here. That is why it was so odd. They swarmed the village after Eliana's attack. Then those two came the night your parents disappeared. On one hand, it was stupid of them. Then again, they knew we were powerless. What could a Hebrew do to a Roman soldier?

Their power over us is unchecked. They were not worried about any consequences. There is something you have to understand, Seraphina. Hebrews have been mistreated in this city for many years. The idea of a Roman soldier being punished for a crime against a Hebrew is laughable to most people. Whoever committed these crimes, knew this. They knew that no one would care. There was no way they would ever be held responsible.'

'They? You think it was more than one person?' Seraphina asked.

'There is no way to know. It could have been a group. It could have been a single soldier. We may never know.'

Seraphina let this sink in. It enraged her. Someone had killed her parents without giving it a second thought. She noticed the goose bumps on her skin, as her anger rose.

'Well, I want to know,' said Seraphina. 'Whoever did these things must be held responsible. It doesn't matter if they were Roman and their victims were Hebrew. It isn't right.'

Yadira nodded. She had the same thoughts. She looked at Seraphina and tried to help her understand.

'Seraphina, I am telling you these things because you deserve to know. They were your parents. We care about you and are happy we have found you. Remember how long ago all of this happened. Trying to find out who it was could be very dangerous. Your parents would not want you to risk your own life.'

'Doesn't it bother you, Yadira?'

Yadira nodded. A tear rolled down her cheek. 'Of course it does.'

'You said you weren't certain of what had happened to my parents. What did you mean?'

Yadira wiped her tears away. She told Seraphina that it was just her denial. She knew they had been killed. If they were alive, they would have come home at some point. They would have looked for you. No matter what. Seraphina just nodded. She saw this was opening up old wounds for Yadira. Inside, she raged. Surely there had to be some justice. For her parents. For the other women who were killed. Yadira looked at her. She could tell what Seraphina was thinking because she had thought it a thousand times herself.

'Seraphina, I understand how you must feel. I can only imagine how much this hurts. So many years have passed without you knowing. I just don't want to see you get hurt.'

'What if you were next, or someone you knew?' asked Seraphina. 'Or a family member perhaps?'

Yadira's head shot up, and her eyes widened. The attacks stopped after that night, she told Seraphina. There had been ten women attacked before then. Yadira's voice trailed off, and her eyes shifted away from Seraphina.

'What?' asked Seraphina. 'There's something you're not saying. What is it?'

Yadira hesitated.

The girl deserved to know, she thought.

She sighed. 'Tension here in the village had been rising. People were angry and frustrated. They were ready to do something. Then the attacks stopped.'

'What are you saying!' yelled Seraphina. She flinched for a second, jarred by her reaction. Seraphina put a hand to her chest and took a deep breath in. Then, in a softer tone, she asked 'if the attacks continued, someone might have taken action?'

'Possibly. It was so long ago, Seraphina. It's hard to know for certain. Even then, you must understand something. The men were angry because their wives had disappeared and were likely killed. Children had lost mothers. There was rage in the community. That rage figured into their thinking. When the attacks stopped, it was a blessing because if the men had risen up, they would have been annihilated. A complete massacre. Stories of how the Romans deal with enemies are legend around here.'

They should have at least tried, thought Seraphina. She sat there, taking everything in. It was surreal.

What am I doing here, she thought.

She looked around the house, and at Yadira and Saul. Everything in her body told her to run, to leave this house, and never return. Maybe in time, she could forget it all.

It was too late for that. Things would never be the same as they were before. She was sad yet energised. Talking about her parents had brought them to life for Seraphina. She had spent so long knowing nothing, and now, at least she knew a little bit about who they were. The three of them continued to talk. Seraphina wanted to do something. After all, they were her parents and she wanted to avenge them. Seraphina could see the concern on Yadira's face. She listened as Yadira spoke, but her mind was elsewhere. Just for that moment, she was consumed by vengeance. She began to hear Yadira's voice again and jerked out of her trance.

'I wish I could remember them. Wait, if you knew this is how I'd react, why did you tell me?' asked Seraphina.

'You deserve to know the truth,' said Yadira.

'I'm glad you told me.'

'It was the right thing, Seraphina,' said Saul.

Seraphina slowly circled the table. She asked what her parents were like. Yadira laughed, saying she could talk about them forever. Seraphina wanted to know everything. Maybe she could come back and learn more about them. She looked down at the table, running her fingers along its edge.

'I was born on this table?' she asked.

'Yes. Your father made it before you were born. Your birth didn't go exactly as planned. That night, we had been expecting help. An older woman who had helped with previous births. She was sick though. So, it was just your mother and Josef, and I came to help.'

Seraphina pressed her hand on the table.

'It's a beautiful table,' she said.

'You would do everything at this table.' Yadira chuckled. 'You ate, drank, wrote and played at it. Every night you sat at it and ate dinner with your parents. Do you remember any of this?'

Seraphina shook her head. She wanted so badly to remember. She looked at the table, thinking. There was something familiar about it, so maybe she would remember in time. Her thoughts started to drift away.

'If these soldiers were still in the city, they would be about ten years older,' said Seraphina, almost to herself. 'They would have risen in rank.'

'Yes, that's right. They would probably be senior officers by now. They would be more powerful than they were then. That is why you should not—'

'This is crazy!' shouted Seraphina. 'A man attacks and kills people for no good reason. All you are worried about is telling me I shouldn't do anything!'

Yadira was taken aback, jumping back a step. She collected herself and nodded, looking at the floor.

'I'm sorry, Yadira. I'm sorry I yelled at you.'

'It is alright, Seraphina. I understand. If I were in your shoes, I would feel the same way too, and part of me feels responsible for you.'

'I appreciate that, I really do.' Seraphina sighed.

'To answer what you said, I would love to find whoever did it. To bring him to justice. However, I tend to take the world as it is, not as I think it should be. The man who did this was a Roman soldier. His victims were Hebrews. It is a sad reality, but we couldn't have done anything then. Only those with some power could have. None of them cared enough.'

Seraphina saw the sense in her words. She liked what Yadira said about taking the world as it is. This was a wise woman.

'When the soldiers came into the village that night, they were searching for me?' Seraphina asked.

'I believe so. I assumed they had eventually caught up to you.'

'Then you saw me the other day.'

'Yes, and later that night.'

'Now, here we are.'

'Yes, so that man you were with the other day. He is the caretaker of the library, correct?' asked Yadira.

'How do you know that?'

'Darling, we Hebrews make sure we know as much as possible about the people around us. Besides, everyone knows who Afiz is, he looks after the library.'

Seraphina smiled at the mention of Afiz's name. She wondered what he would make of all this.

'So, Seraphina, where do you live?'

'That's a very long story, to be told another time.' Seraphina paused and thought for a moment. 'Can we go and see my old house?'

Yadira nodded. 'Yes, but next time. A new family lives there now. I know them well enough. I think we have to, how can I say this, disguise you a little.'

Seraphina gave her a curious look.

'Make you look a little more Hebrew.'

Seraphina looked down at her clothes. Growing up in isolation meant she knew little about fashion trends. Sure, Afiz had bought her some new clothes to make her look more Egyptian. Aside from that, she had no idea, and that night, she was dressed plainly.

'I'm out of style?'

Yadira laughed, and everyone relaxed. 'Even though I know them well, we should be careful. I don't want to start broadcasting your identity. It doesn't matter how much time has passed, there still could be some risk.'

Fair enough, thought Seraphina. She asked if there was something she could wear. Yadira reminded her it was getting late.

'Oh, you are right. I should be getting back.'

'To where? You did not say where you live.'

'Like I said, that is a very long story. I will have to tell you another time. I promise to come and see you again soon.'

She looked at Saul. He had stayed quiet for the most part. Every word had been absorbed though. He gave Seraphina a big hug. He was a big bear of a man, and Seraphina felt dwarfed. He smiled at her. 'Take good care of yourself, Seraphina. I am glad you came here.'

'Thank you, Saul.'

She turned to Yadira and hugged her tightly.

'Thank you, Yadira. I thought I was never going to learn the truth about my family.'

'It is my pleasure. Please be careful, Seraphina. Come see us again soon, and we will talk more.'

'I will.'

Seraphina eased back into the night and vanished down the street.

'Do you think we handled that the best way?' Yadira asked Saul.

'Yes,' said Saul. 'It was a surprise to see her, but she deserves to know the truth. We will have to see what happens next. Do not worry. Things will work out.'

He wrapped an arm around his wife, to comfort her.

'I hope so, Saul.'

ELEVEN

She gasped for breath, her small legs exhausted. The voices weren't far behind. She panted and willed her feet to move, almost falling over. The soldiers' voices again. Her eyes widened as they got louder. Their deafening whispers cut into her heart. Tears streamed from her eyes as she sprinted through the night. Her head jerked from side to side. A dark corner, an open doorway, anything. She was out of options. She felt his hands behind her, about to grab her.

Seraphina's body shot up. It was a nightmare. She was breathing heavily. Her heart was racing. She put a hand on her chest, took a deep breath, and her pulse began to calm down. She looked down and saw Maximus, panting and wagging his little tail.

She looked down at the mess around her. Seraphina had been studying with a vigour. Her thirst for knowledge had increased of late. She had been devouring scrolls daily. The philosopher from Valentia was due any day now and she thought about him often, and in her excitement, she had been reading roll after roll of parchment on all manner of topics. Forgiveness, morality in government, familial love, and many more.

She wanted to be ready for him. Afiz would not tell her his name.

She knew he would be staying in the library as there was a special living chamber on the ground floor only for visiting scholars.

Seraphina had seen the room only once as it was off limits to her, one of the few things that Afiz kept to himself. It hadn't stopped her from trying though. For years, Seraphina had searched for the keys without luck. Once he arrived, Seraphina would find a way to meet him and see the lavish chamber.

She was working on that plan. Surely Afiz could be persuaded. She wanted to have debates and discussions with him, just like she did with Afiz, but it would be tricky. Seraphina was very methodical with her plan, she laid out all the variables.

Obviously, no one knew she lived in the library. Except Afiz. Even if Imhotep knew, he didn't know what she looked like. The philosopher would speak to both Imhotep and Afiz each day.

Maybe she could pose as a friend of Afiz's, an old friend, who came to visit the library at night. She thought of whether Afiz might go along with this. Then again, why would a caretaker have a friend visiting late at night? Why would Afiz have a teenage girl for a friend?

Seraphina shook her head. Her plan needed some work, but she was determined. She vowed to come up with a better idea and get Afiz on board.

She got back to her reading. It was an ancient Hindu text on forgiveness. She had noticed something odd in her research. The Greeks and Romans had no notion of forgiveness. Not in the same way the Hindus did. The ancient Greek philosophers had a fairly narrow idea of forgiveness. They spoke of forgiving only if someone had not intended the offending action.

This was nothing like what the Hindus had in mind. They spoke about the importance of letting go. Reading on, Seraphina saw why they thought it so important. They say there is an impact of holding on to emotions. To use their words exactly, the baggage of negative and unresolved emotions. It talked about failing to forgive someone. The weight of those emotions could stay with you and affect your future. Seraphina saw the logic in that.

She thought of what Yadira had told her.

Could I ever forgive those soldiers? They made me an orphan and my parents are dead and gone.

The thought filled her with sadness and anger at the same time, but it did not feel good.

She considered the future. Imagine a lifetime of these feelings. What would that do to her? She shook her head. She didn't want to find out. Then again, forgiving those soldiers seemed impossible when they had taken her family from her.

She would think on it some more. More than anything else, Seraphina wished she could remember her parents. She had tried to meditate. It hadn't worked. Not since the first night she tried. That night by the water had brought back lost memories. She wanted more of that. She would try again soon, she decided.

Distracted again, she thought. She returned to the text. Why was this concept completely absent from Greek or Roman philosophy? Earlier that week, she had read a different text. It was also about forgiveness, written by a Persian philosopher. The Persians had their own perspective. To them, it was an act practised by kings that showed their glory. It was even described as a divine act. Seraphina was excited as she read. She would impress the philosopher, no doubt. She stopped and wondered. What if she could talk to him about forgiveness? Now that was an idea. Who else better to talk to than a philosopher?

She finished the scroll and put it away. She had been reading for hours, and it was nice to get back to her old routine, but she was soon distracted by a thought of Quintus. She wondered if she would see him again. She hoped so. The prospect made her smile.

She also thought about Yadira, and her promise to go back and visit. The first visit had been intense. There was no telling what the second might yield. She wanted to see her old house. Maybe it would jog her memory.

She looked at her bed, and the window above it. The sun had set a little while ago and its golden hue in the evening sky was fading. A star or two had appeared in the sky above.

My life is a little crazy at the moment, she thought.

Then she had a truly unique idea: to go to sleep at a reasonable hour. She lay down, but her imagination came to life, as it often did before she fell asleep like a candle's flame flickers brightest just before it fades to nothing. She saw herself travelling to distant lands. She would rub shoulders with brilliant scholars. She would write great texts, and many would read them. The thoughts made her smile and she fell asleep, thinking of her dreams becoming reality.

TWELVE

Afiz had befriended a few soldiers over the years. Generally, Roman soldiers did not interact much with locals. When they did, it was only if they had to, and even then, they showed little respect.

There were exceptions.

Thankfully, Afiz knew a few of the kinder ones. They gossiped with him occasionally, and now there was talk of the young king, Ptolemy. He had fled the city. Rumour was that he was amassing an army to drive Caesar and his soldiers out of the city. Cleopatra would also be a target. It was common knowledge that she had allied herself with Caesar, and Ptolemy was furious about the partnership.

All this was interesting, but Afiz was most concerned about a civil war which could easily spread out across Egypt. Egypt had been free of war for a long time, and no one wanted another conflict. The thought of soldiers battling in the streets was scary.

Afiz hoped it did not come to pass.

He would have to worry about it later. Afiz had a busy day today. Gisgo, the philosopher from Valentia, was due to arrive in the city. Everything needed to be perfect. Imhotep typically left Afiz to his own devices but a visiting scholar was a different matter.

He had asked Afiz the same questions again and again. Being honest, Afiz thought the curator's neurosis was amusing. Everything had been prepared and right then Afiz was as excited as Imhotep was anxious. There was nothing to worry about though because as usual, Afiz had thought of all the details.

Afiz's main worry was Seraphina.

The girl had not stopped talking.

She wanted to know everything about Gisgo's visit. Afiz had given her a few answers, but didn't tell her everything, including his name, for example, because Seraphina would have read every text Gisgo had ever written, then would have relentlessly questioned him. The thought was funny, but Afiz did not know Gisgo, and he couldn't risk offending the great philosopher. Then again, he wasn't even sure that Seraphina and Gisgo would meet.

That was the other thing. Seraphina had asked him about meeting Gisgo … many times. Afiz had yet to think of a way it could work. He wanted to say yes, but it was complicated because he didn't want Imhotep to find out about it.

If he were dealing with anyone else, it might be easier because, much as he loved Seraphina, she was a chatterbox. It's not as if Gisgo would meet her and then forget her. Seraphina would make an impression. Whether a good or bad one, Afiz did not know, but he couldn't risk Gisgo speaking to Imhotep about Seraphina. He didn't want to disappoint Seraphina; neither did he want to anger Imhotep.

Imhotep already suspected someone was living in the library and if he became certain, it could become a problem. Afiz thought about what would happen if Seraphina offended Gisgo. The curator's anger would know no bounds.

He'd have to figure out a way as it would mean a lot to Seraphina.

He'd just have to be careful.

Gisgo's story was a fascinating one. He had miraculously survived the Roman conquest of Hispania. In military conflicts, academics did not always fare well. The Romans could be particularly fierce toward them and Afiz had heard stories that annoyed him. The Romans revered knowledge, yet, they had no qualms about killing the purveyors of that knowledge.

Valentia had been razed to the ground. It was now a ghost town, but despite this, Gisgo remained there. Afiz was intrigued by the man, and he hoped to have many conversations with him about his unique history.

Afiz walked up to find Seraphina. He'd had an idea. It was time for a surprise. He knocked on the door, and Seraphina opened it straight away. She had been waiting, already dressed.

'Good morning, Seraphina.'

'Good morning, Afiz.'

Maximus rushed over to Afiz and sniffed his feet while wagging his tail.

'Good morning, Maximus,' said Afiz with a giggle. 'Hey, stop that, it tickles.' He asked Seraphina why she was all dressed up.

She spoke softly. 'I thought we might be going out this morning.'

Afiz smiled. 'I see, and where did you think we might be going?'

Seraphina smiled back. 'To the harbour … perhaps.'

Afiz feigned a look of curiosity and scratched his chin. 'Hmmmm, and why would we be going to the harbour?'

Seraphina tried her best to act nonchalant. 'I thought there might be a ship arriving this morning.'

'Ships arrive every morning, Seraphina.' Afiz was just messing with her now.

'Afiiiiiiiz'

'Why would this ship be so special?' Afiz was openly smiling now, thoroughly enjoying their little game.

Seraphina stamped her foot, ever so slightly. 'Come on, Afiz.'

'Come on, what?'

She put her hands on her hips. In a matter-of-fact voice, she said 'You know, and I know, that a certain philosopher from Valentia is arriving today. We both know that I have always wanted to meet a visiting scholar.'

He went back to rubbing his chin. He put his other hand on his hip, mimicking Seraphina. 'Yes, but how can you meet him without our curator finding out about it? You haven't really come up with any plan.'

She folded her arms across her chest. 'I know. It's annoying. I've got nothing.' She shook her head.

Afiz shrugged with his palms facing up. 'So, even if there was such a ship arriving, with such a philosopher, how could I be taking you with me to meet him?'

For once, Seraphina was speechless.

'Luckily for you, someone else came up with an idea. It relies on you being a little quieter than usual. Well, a lot quieter.'

'Tell me, Afiz.'

'Shouldn't we first discuss the brilliant person who came up with the idea?' Afiz rarely had this much fun, so he indulged in it.

'Afiz, you're killing me,' said Seraphina.

Afiz waved his hands. It was enough. 'Alright, alright. I'm sorry. So, it's no secret that I have an assistant. The whole city has seen you with me running errands. We have our whole story about you and where you live with your parents.'

Seraphina flinched at the mention of her parents.

Afiz noticed. 'What's wrong?' he asked.

'Nothing, please go on.'

'Very well, you can meet him,' said Afiz.

Seraphina leapt across the room and hugged Afiz.

'There is only one thing to worry about.'

Seraphina stepped back. 'What's that?'

Afiz looked serious now. 'Gisgo cannot find out you live here, Seraphina. It would be disastrous.'

'Gisgo!' exclaimed Seraphina.

Afiz covered his mouth with his hand. He could not believe he just let his name slip.

'Now, Seraphina …'

'I think I have read some of his texts. He considers things that many Roman philosophers have not.'

'Stop for a second,' said Afiz. 'He cannot find out you live here. Do you understand?'

'Of course. Not a problem. Come to think of it, I *have* read some of his work.'

'Seraphina, you are not to interrogate this man. In fact, you are not to ask him any questions, at least not to begin with. He is here to visit our library and meet local scholars. Do you understand me?'

Seraphina leaned against the wall. She had a big smile on her face. 'Come on, Afiz,' she said. 'You know me better than that. I would never do such a thing.' Sarcasm was heavy in her look and voice.

Afiz shook his head. 'No need for me to tell you to hurry up and get ready. You've obviously been waiting. Let's go, but I'm serious about what I said, Seraphina. Are you sure you understand?'

Seraphina lost the smile for a moment. 'Afiz, I would never do anything to embarrass you.' She meant it. Afiz looked her straight in the eye.

The smile was back. 'Come on, Afiz. We don't want to keep Gisgo waiting now, do we?'

Afiz headed for the stairs, and Seraphina followed.

I've never been so excited, she thought.

She followed him closely, tapping him on the back as they descended each step.

The playful child in her is alive and well, he thought.

It was the first time in over a week that she been her old self, and he liked it.

THIRTEEN

The city was back to normal. The festival was over, as were its celebrations. During the celebrations, she and Afiz would go out less, so as much as she enjoyed the festivities, she was always glad they were over, and she could spend more time outdoors.

She looked around at a glorious day. The sun was shining. Chariots and carts rumbled through the streets. Vendors made her jump, as they loudly shouted about their wares. The rich, earthy smell of spices and street food lay over the market like a blanket.

The sky was a brilliant blue, dotted here and there with a few milky, white clouds. Seraphina was struggling to contain herself. Once they were outside, she calmed down. She was on her very best behaviour. For Afiz's sake. For Gisgo, she would be the perfect example of good manners.

Afiz watched her. It made him happy to see her so excited; she was like a little kid again. Seraphina was half-skipping, half-walking along, oblivious to everything and everyone around her. He gave her a sharp, little look, gesturing with his hand for her to calm down a little although her enthusiasm was contagious.

Even Afiz had to admit it was a spectacular day. He walked along, thinking to himself. He wondered if Seraphina had forgotten about the Hebrew woman. Maybe things were returning to normal. He hadn't spoken to her about it for several days, so he made a mental note to ask her about it. It was important to Seraphina, so he didn't want to gloss over it.

As they approached the harbour, a unique-looking ship was nearing the docks. Its style and shape were different to the other ships in the bay. The harbour master was just ahead and all three of them watched the ship come in, recognising it as being from Hispania. Such a ship was rare. Like Gisgo, it had done well to survive the conquest of the region.

'Hello,' said Afiz to the harbour master.

'Good morning, Afiz.' They shook hands.

Afiz pointed to the incoming vessel. 'Is that the ship?'

The harbour master nodded. 'Yes. That's your visitor. Different type of boat, isn't it?'

Afiz nodded, not taking his eyes off the water. 'Yes. Have you ever seen one like it?'

'Once,' said the harbour master. 'A long time ago. I've spent some time to the west of here. Those Hispanians are some of the best ship builders I've ever met. I was always fascinated by their handiwork.'

Afiz nodded in agreement. Seraphina stared at the ship, smiling. It gave her a thrill, being out here on the edge of the dock. The only things in front of her were water, ships, and sky. Looking out to the horizon, she imagined being on a ship one day, going to some faraway place on an adventure.

The harbour master turned to Afiz. 'So, your philosopher? He is Hispanian?'

'Yes.'

'I do not believe I have ever met a Hispanian philosopher.'

'It's a first for me too, sir.'

'Well, they are about to dock. Let's go and welcome them.' The harbour master set off toward the dock.

Seraphina looked at the quayside and thought out loud. 'They build these quays so the bigger ships don't come too close to the shore and damage their rudders.'

'Very impressive,' said the harbour master. Seraphina looked up, startled. 'You have an interest in naval engineering?' The harbour master smiled at her.

Seraphina nodded. She had not intended to start a conversation.

'She is interested in most things,' said Afiz.

The ship dropped its anchor as Seraphina came to the very edge of the dock. The harbour master started talking to the captain. Seraphina looked at the crew coming off the ship. Suddenly, a very tall man stood up on board. He was thin and looked old, yet his movements were precise. He looked straight at Seraphina, and the stern look on his face gave way to a smile.

As he came onshore, Afiz offered him a hand.

'Now, now, there is no need for that,' said Gisgo.

'My apologies, sir, Gisgo. Welcome to Alexandria,' said Afiz.

'You can cut out the "sir" too, young man.'

Seraphina was amused. Afiz was far from young, although compared to Gisgo he was. Seraphina observed the elderly philosopher. He stood several inches taller than Afiz, with a bulky robe hanging from his thin frame. She looked down at his feet. She had never seen feet so long. Gisgo noticed the fascination.

'Hello, young lady,' he said.

Seraphina bowed her head then gestured for him to walk ahead. Seraphina smiled at Afiz, searching for his approval. Afiz nodded at her, and they both followed Gisgo who kept up a surprising pace for a man his age. Afiz struggled to match it as he wasn't the swiftest on his feet.

They came to the street and Afiz called out to a nearby cart driver and Gisgo's things were loaded, then the driver sped off.

'It is an honour to meet you, Gisgo.' Afiz offered his hand.

Gisgo shook it. 'Thank you, and your name is?'

'It's Afiz. My apologies. I am the caretaker of our library here in Alexandria.'

'Yes, I gathered,' said Gisgo.

Afiz turned and held his arm up to the buildings behind him. 'So, what do you think of our fair city?'

'It is very impressive. Seeing the lighthouse on our approach was a real pleasure. It is a splendid structure.'

Afiz nodded. 'Yes, one of the jewels of our city.' He started to walk, leading the way for Gisgo.

Gisgo walked alongside him. 'I can't wait to see the library,' he said.

'I'm sure you will love it,' said Afiz.

Gisgo looked back towards Seraphina as they walked. 'What is the young lady's name?'

'Seraphina,' said Afiz, smiling.

'Does she assist you in some way?'

'Yes, she helps me with my duties in the library. She is an excellent assistant.'

'Seraphina is a nice name,' said Gisgo.

Afiz nodded as they continued to walk. Seraphina beamed at the mention of her name, but she stayed quiet and well behaved much to Afiz's amazement. He was pleased … but amazed.

'Alexandria seems to be thriving,' said Gisgo as they walked through the city.

Wait until you see the marketplace, thought Afiz.

Gisgo asked about the library's collection. He had heard the rumours which Afiz assured him were well founded. Every text that comes into the city by ship is copied for the library. That system had been in place for many years. Given how busy the port is, the main challenge was finding space to store everything.

Gisgo laughed. 'A good problem to have, but how about scribes?'

'Well, that can be a challenge too, but we have no shortage of keen minds in this city. People come from far and wide. We get to choose from the best.'

'I suppose the library attracts all sorts of brilliant people.'

'It does, and has for hundreds of years,' said Afiz. 'Now more than ever.'

'Why do you think that is?'

'The Roman Republic is a vast civilisation. Education has spread like wildfire. The *pax Romana* has helped that. The library historically attracted minds from all of Egypt. Now it attracts minds from all of the Republic.'

Gisgo nodded. 'Makes sense.'

'What is Valentia like?'

'Very quiet, my friend. The *"pax Romana"* arrived some time ago. It wasn't so peaceful. I am one of a handful of people who remain.'

'I am sorry, Gisgo.'

Gisgo held up his hands. 'Think nothing of it. Times must change. Even the great Roman Republic will fall someday.'

They had arrived at the front entrance to the library where Imhotep was waiting for them.

'Welcome, Gisgo,' said the curator to his famous visitor. 'I am Imhotep, the library's curator. Welcome.'

'Thank you. It's a pleasure to meet you.' The two shook hands.

'I trust that Afiz has taken good care of you?'

'Yes, we have just been having a nice chat.'

They all went inside, and one of the servants showed Gisgo to his room. As he walked off, Imhotep looked down at Seraphina.

'Oh, Imhotep,' said Afiz, 'this is Seraphina. She is a young assistant I have recently employed to help me in the library.'

He looked her up and down. 'Nice to meet you, Seraphina. You are Egyptian?' he asked.

Seraphina nodded. 'Yes, sir.'

'Very well.' Imhotep's voice boomed out. 'I am sure if Afiz chose you, that you must be of great help to him.'

Seraphina smiled politely. Gisgo was back. He had been shown to his room, and now wanted to start to look around. He was mesmerised. There were endless walls of scrolls. The shelves were divided by majestic Greek columns which stretched from floor to ceiling. The main atrium disappeared into the back of the building.

'This is truly incredible,' he said.

'Thank you, Gisgo. We are very proud of it,' said Imhotep. 'The library is just one part of the museum complex although many aren't aware of that.' They walked as a group into the main atrium as Imhotep spoke. Gisgo marvelled at his surroundings while Seraphina was excited but trying not to show it. Imhotep gave the tour, and Gisgo asked questions.

'How big is the museum?'

'There are several buildings, surrounded by gardens,' said Imhotep. 'There are hundreds of scholars living there and we like to provide a relaxing space for our scholars to work. If you decided you would prefer to stay there, we can arrange it. I do think you will be more comfortable here.'

'I would much prefer to stay here,' said Gisgo.

'Wonderful. The museum includes a philosophy school and library. The scholars there keep themselves busy. They produce texts which are then transferred to this library. They also work by themselves and in groups. Of course, they carry out various experiments as well.'

Gisgo's eyes widened with excitement. 'It sounds fascinating. I am looking forward to my time here.'

Imhotep could tell he had impressed the visitor. He smiled and asked how long Gisgo planned to stay.

'A month or so.'

'You'll practically be a local.'

Gisgo laughed. 'Thank you for the warm welcome. Seraphina, why don't you show me the way back to my room? I think I'm already lost.'

'Certainly, Gisgo,' said Seraphina. She smiled at Afiz. He produced a key which Seraphina took eagerly. 'This way.' She led him down the corridor. Imhotep watched them as they walked away.

'So, you hired an assistant?' asked Imhotep, not even turning to face Afiz.

'Y … Yes.' Afiz composed himself for a moment. 'I apologise for not running it by you first.'

Imhotep turned around. 'Don't be silly, Afiz. That's unnecessary. You're the caretaker, and I have complete trust in you. You're free to hire who you please. But a young woman? How did you even meet her?'

Afiz saw that he looked calm, almost indifferent.

'A chance meeting when I was out for errands one day.'

'Hmmm. How is she settling in?'

'Very well. She loves the library and has a keen intellect. She is doing a great job.'

'Well, that's good to hear,' said Imhotep. 'Our dear Gisgo certainly seems to be taken with her.'

'Yes. I am sure she is thrilled to be meeting a renowned philosopher such as him.'

'She looked as though she had never heard of the museum. Why don't you take her over there when you go with Gisgo? If she is going to work here, she'll have to learn about the whole place.'

Afiz nodded. 'I have no doubt. I'll be sure to take her tomorrow.'

'Good. She might as well see everything this place has to offer.'

'I agree. Thank you, Imhotep. I will go and make sure Gisgo is properly settled in.'

'I shall see you later then,' said Imhotep.

FOURTEEN

Seraphina was in awe. The room was ten times bigger than hers. Fine tapestries adorned the walls. A huge four-poster bed stood in the centre of the room. Fine rugs lined the generous floorspace. Beautiful wooden furniture lined the walls. In a corner was a spacious reading area, with two large chairs and an empty set of shelves.

'Is this where Caesar stays when he comes to town?' Gisgo smiled at his own joke.

Seraphina gawked at the lavish room. 'I'm not sure, but he should definitely give it a try.'

Gisgo laughed. 'I like your sense of humour. So, tell me, Seraphina, what's your interest in the library?'

'I love to study. Knowledge is fun for me. I've always been that way. When Afiz asked me to work with him, I jumped at the chance. Although I spend most of my time working, I do get a chance to read. As you saw, the collection is huge.'

'I could spend a lifetime in there, reading,' said Gisgo. 'Have you been to the museum?'

'No. My duties are limited to the library.'

'Perhaps you will be able to come with me tomorrow.'

'Imhotep just suggested that, actually,' said Afiz as he entered. 'Tomorrow, the three of us will visit the museum complex. Gisgo, you will have the opportunity to meet many scholars across a range of disciplines. You can also visit as much of the museum as you'd like although I'd recommend a walk through the gardens. Totally up to you, of course.'

'Sounds like a perfect day,' said Gisgo.

Seraphina thought the same.

'Excellent,' said Afiz. 'Well, all your things are here.'

'Thank you, Afiz. It has been a real pleasure. Thank you for getting me settled in.'

'You are most welcome. We will let you unpack but please, just ring this bell if you need anything.' Afiz pointed to a small brass bell on the table near the door.

'You are too kind.' Gisgo bowed his head slightly in thanks.

Seraphina left the key next to the bell and she and Afiz walked back out into the main atrium. There were looks from the men working in the library. They didn't linger though and went back to their work.

'Quite a morning, wasn't it?' said Seraphina.

'Yes. Follow me,' said Afiz.

They walked in silence. Afiz took Seraphina to the back of the library, into one of the empty lecture halls where it was quiet. Seraphina looked out at the garden, daydreaming about the museum trip the next day. Afiz kept walking then slowed near the front podium.

He opened a small door to the left, and they climbed up a narrow staircase which led to another door. Seraphina was intrigued now. She had never been in this part of the building. Afiz looked back at her and smiled. He pulled a key out of his pocket and unlocked the door. On the other side was a landing. Seraphina came through the door then realised where she was. The door to her room was off to her right. She looked at Afiz with admiration.

Seraphina's head was a jumble of thoughts. She sat down on the bed. Maximus was sleeping in the corner, oblivious.

'That went well,' said Afiz.

'What do you mean? You planned all that?' asked Seraphina.

'I mean with Imhotep. I must say, I was impressed by your behaviour. It was almost like being with a different person.'

'Well, I try.' Seraphina giggled.

'I appreciate it, Seraphina. Thank you.'

'No problem. So, what else did you two talk about?'

Afiz told her about the conversation he'd had with Imhotep.

'Yes, that was a surprise,' said Seraphina.

'To be honest, I thought of it on the spot. I didn't expect him to be waiting outside for us. He said he'd be in his office.'

'Did he say anything after I left?'

'No,' said Afiz. 'He said I was free to employ who I wanted, and he asked how you were doing. He seemed unconcerned and pleased. It looks like it is your day for making good impressions.'

'Don't I always, Afiz?'

Afiz and Seraphina had both remained cool under pressure. Now that she was relaxed, Seraphina started interrogating him about the museum. She wanted to know everything. Her main gripe was that she had never been told what those buildings were. She listened eagerly to his answers, bouncing on the bed during the conversation. Tomorrow could not come soon enough.

'Are we really going to the museum? All these years, I've been wondering what those buildings were. I can't believe you told me they were guard houses.'

'Well, I had to keep you away from there. If someone had ever seen you, you would be very conspicuous. Plus, I knew how relentless you would be. Until today, it was important for your presence here to be a secret. Even now, always make sure you remember—'

Seraphina finished off the sentence. 'Even though I work here, no one is to know I live here. I know, I know.'

'Good, so we stick with the same story we've always had on that.'

'Yes. You know, one day, I might have to actually see Lake Mareotis.'

'I have heard it's beautiful.'

'My fictional home. One day, maybe.'

'That reminds me, Seraphina. I wanted to talk to you about something else.'

'What is it, Afiz?'

'What we talked about a few weeks ago. Where you come from, the Hebrew woman you saw, the questions you have about your past.'

'Ah, yes.' Seraphina sighed.

'I just wanted to check in with you and see how you had been feeling about all that.'

'I guess I haven't thought about it that much lately. I mean, it's still important to me, but I've been getting back into my study routine, which feels good. Plus, I wanted to be ready for Gisgo. You know how I've always wanted to meet one of these scholars. I still can't believe you never told me about the museum.'

'Seraphina, I'm sure you can understand why. Aside from the endless pestering I would have had to endure, it was for your safety. Could you imagine? I would probably worry about you sneaking out of the library into the museum.'

Seraphina's jerked her head around to look at him.

Does he know?

'Is everything alright, Seraphina?'

'Yes, why?

'Just looked like, I don't know, maybe you flinched.'

'Afiz, you are imagining things. It must be your age, old man,' she said, imitating Gisgo.

'Very funny, young lady. So, everything is alright with you then?'

'Yes, Afiz. Maybe we can talk about it again some time. There are still lots of unanswered questions.'

'I understand. I hope you feel you can talk to me about these things. I know you're not my daughter, but I love you as though you were. I don't know how good a job I did, but I feel as though I helped raise you. What I'm trying to say is that I'm here for you.'

Seraphina watched him falter over his emotions. He was such a good man.

'Afiz, you did raise me, and I love you too. You will always be the one who took me in and looked after me. I have often thought about that night, and that me coming here was somehow destiny. Granted, there is a lot about my past that remains a mystery, but no matter what, I am grateful for what you've done for me.'

Afiz sighed with relief. 'I'm so glad to hear you feel that way. I better go now, but let's talk more tomorrow.'

He went to walk out, and Seraphina stopped him. She gave him a big hug for a few seconds.

There was no one like Afiz. He had always looked out for her.

Before he left, he reminded her of the new routine.

'Don't forget that from tomorrow morning, you are to act as if you work here. You'll need to come and go from the front entrance every morning and evening.'

Seraphina saluted him with a mocking smile. 'Got it, Afiz.'

Afiz hesitated for a second.

Seraphina grinned at him. 'You want to know where my secret passageway is, don't you? You want to know how I get in and out of the library without using the door?'

'No.' Afiz shook his head.

'If you say so. I guess I'll see you tomorrow then.'

Seraphina felt bad. She hadn't lied but felt dishonest nonetheless. Especially when he had asked about Yadira.

I have to see Yadira and Saul again, she thought.

Then she would talk to Afiz and her main concern was that she'd have to confess about sneaking out.

She put her worry aside.

Tonight, she just wanted to get out of the library. To run free and feel that liberation she always did while sprinting through the night.

Worry could wait for a day, she thought.

Seraphina's thoughts drifted towards Quintus again. A slight smirk came to her face. She had considered him a lot the past few days, mainly about how they had met. She had never met a stranger like that and connected so well. Seraphina closed her eyes and made a little wish that she would see him again.

She indulged in a little fantasy, imagining running through the night with him. Maybe they could sit together at the edge of the waterfront at her favourite place. What would she wear? She normally wore loose clothes. They were best for running, but now she wasn't sure. After all,

Quintus had seen her in an elegant dress.

She laughed at her own silliness. Could this be the love she had read about so many times?

No, she thought. *It couldn't be.*

She didn't really know him, but there was definitely some attraction. He was handsome, and she liked his voice. He was tall, just a little taller than her. She remembered his thick hair. The peaceful look of his eyes. She liked the way his lips moved when he spoke, and the flash of his smile when he had laughed.

Her mind turned to her learnings on the subject. The phenomenon of attraction. That's what this was, she decided. Seraphina didn't know what to think, but she was excited when she thought of Quintus; she felt good.

Then, there was also uncertainty. Maybe there were some things the scrolls couldn't explain.

Calm down, she thought.

She thought practically. She might never see this boy again, but if she did, Seraphina wanted to get to know him better.

She felt a warm glow in her chest at the thought.

It was still the middle of the day, and she had reading to do. Tomorrow was a big day. She would spend it with Gisgo, and she would see the museum.

Those grand buildings, she thought. *Bastions of intellect and knowledge.*

She might even meet other scholars, talk to them, see their experiments. See a scroll being written first-hand that would go on the shelves and be studied by many in the years to come. So many possibilities.

Suddenly, her mind was far away from Quintus.

There was no time to waste. She wanted to read everything Gisgo had ever written, plus, all the philosophy scrolls she could get her hands on. She noticed Maximus with a funny look on his face. She had been pacing her room for over an hour. Seraphina stopped, swooped down, and picked him up.

'Oh Maxi,' she said, 'isn't it all so exciting?'

Maximus just kept wagging his tail and tried to lick Seraphina's face. She ran out of her room and traced her route back to the library.

I'll be coming through here a lot from now on, she thought.

Down the stairs, out of the lecture hall, and she was in the library. She spotted Imhotep. He had seen her too. He was watching her. She headed for the shelves.

Everything is fine now, she thought.

There were plenty of people studying. They'd given her a few looks earlier. Now, they were already ignoring her which was fine by Seraphina.

It took her some time, but she found a few of Gisgo's scrolls in the philosophy section. By tomorrow, she would know them back to front, but she kept looking, wondering what topics would impress the philosopher, deciding in the end that there was no way to know. It didn't matter, because if nothing else, she would come across as well read.

Then she saw something that made her smile.

The place of the cure of the soul

It was inscribed above the shelves. She said the words again in her mind, and they rang true. She looked around at the place that was so special to her.

The Great Library of Alexandria.

She was blessed as she had grown up here, after all. She wondered if anyone else had but decided probably not. She could learn about any topic she desired, from the world's greatest minds.

This was her home.

The largest collection of knowledge in the world.

Her home.

As she looked around, it occurred to her that this was the only home she had ever known, at least the only one she remembered.

She thought of her parents, Rebekah and Josef. The names didn't jog her memory, at least not yet. Then again, what six-year-old knows her parents by name? They would have been simply 'mother' and 'father' to her.

She thought of Yadira, and her promise to return and see her and Saul. She wasn't sure if it was a good idea to keep uncovering the past.

Life is here and now, she thought. *That's the past. Maybe I should let it be.*

That was Yadira's advice. There could be danger, and she worried about Afiz, in particular. If she did anything that jeopardised his safety, she would never forgive herself. Afiz had done too much for her, so she decided to take things one step at a time. It was the best plan for now.

Seraphina looked down at the table. There were quite a few scrolls. She picked them up to take them back to her room, but there were too many. Undeterred, she slowly stacked them on her arms then she inched forward carefully. The last thing she wanted was to drop them. Some of the scholars watched with great amusement. What was this girl doing? The scrolls were piled so high that they blocked her vision, and on top of that, she wasn't so much walking as she was shuffling her feet, so with each step, the drag of her feet could be heard.

I did not think this through. Why didn't I just take a few now and come back for the rest?

Meanwhile, Afiz, Imhotep, and Gisgo had stopped talking, and were watching Seraphina intently. She was now so conscious that everyone was looking at her that her steps became more tentative. A bead or two of sweat formed on her brow.

Great, she thought. *I knew I was having too good a day. I met a philosopher, the curator believed our story, and I don't have to hide during the day anymore. Yet, here I am, about to drop a stack of scrolls and the whole library is watching me.*

She heard a voice behind the pile of scrolls. 'Why don't you let me help you with those?'

She peeked around to see Gisgo standing there and gave him a little smile.

'Oh, thank you so much, Gisgo,' said Seraphina.

She handed a few to him, and they walked together. Thankfully, Gisgo's writings were at the bottom of her pile. If he'd seen them, it would have been embarrassing.

'So, where are you going with all these?' asked Gisgo.

'To the records room. It's that one over there.' Seraphina indicated with a nod of her head. She could see that Imhotep and Afiz were still watching her, so she ignored them. He took half the scrolls she was carrying and followed her. Seraphina laid hers down on a table and breathed a sigh of relief. Gisgo put his down and looked around.

'So, what happens in here?'

'Well, this is where we keep records of all the texts in the library,' said Seraphina. 'Whenever new texts come into the library, we record them here. This way, we have a full catalogue of all the items in the library.'

He pointed to the scrolls they had just put down. 'So, these are new texts?'

'No,' said Seraphina, shaking her head. 'I'm just updating their condition in the catalogue.'

'Good thing you didn't drop them back there then.' Gisgo chuckled.

'Exactly. Thank you so much for helping me.'

'You are welcome. Shall I leave you to your work?'

'That would be great. Thanks again.'

'It's my pleasure.'

Gisgo looked around as he left. He was an observant man, and the library seemed to fascinate him. That he had helped her showed he had a soft side too. She liked him, she decided, even with the stern air he gave off. She watched him until he was out of sight.

Seraphina was proud of her quick thinking. She had never even set foot in the records room, though she did know its purpose. It occurred to her that she should not go into the library during the day and take scrolls as she pleased. Afiz was probably furious. Nevertheless, she'd been savvy enough to answer Gisgo's questions without arousing suspicion. She moved the pile of scrolls to the back of the room and looked out into the library, but no one was watching her anymore. She saw a crate in the corner of the room, and carefully placed the scrolls into it. She checked one last time to make sure she wasn't being watched, then hustled into the back of the library.

FIFTEEN

She'd never looked at candlelight so intently.

It took so many different shapes that fascinated her as she gazed but also calmed her mind, allowing her to focus on the flickering yellow flame.

I'm getting pretty good at this meditation thing, she thought.

Her mind felt clear, and her body felt light, and a calm smile was spread across her face as she sat there.

She hoped the Hindu scholars would be proud. She had been gazing for at least an hour now and one thing she was starting to love about meditation was the power it gave her over her thoughts.

It wasn't about clearing the mind of all thoughts.

Rather, it was about letting thoughts just be.

Most passed away after a fleeting moment, and the same applied to feelings. She could feel or think anything, and all she had to do was not wrestle with that particular emotion or thought. In a matter of moments, it had passed.

Happy with her progress, Seraphina began to make a game of it.

She brought her attention back to the flame and took another deep breath. She remembered the table Yadira showed her.

Her table.

She let her imagination wander.

A little girl playing while her parents are busy in the kitchen. The girl was having a wonderful time, crawling around the base of the table. She looked at its legs and saw a pattern and she scampered around the legs at one end of the table then she moved towards the diagonally opposite leg on the other side and repeated the motion. Over and over.

Her mother called to her. 'Hey, what are you doing? You're not a baby anymore. You shouldn't be crawling on the floor. It is dinner time, so you go and get ready.'

'What are we having, Mama?'

'Liver stew.'

'Yuck.'

'Enough of that!'

The girl sulked, both because she had to stop playing, and because they were having liver stew for dinner. She hated liver. The girl's mother came out of the kitchen to find the little girl still playing under the table.

'Seraphina, I said to get ready for dinner.'

Seraphina jolted out of what felt like sleep. The candlelight was right in front of her.

It was a memory!

She was about to have dinner with her parents.

She had heard her mother's voice, its tone and pitch but her father had not been in the memory, although she had sensed his presence nearby. Seraphina closed her eyes again. She wanted to get back there, but there was nothing.

It was gone for now.

She clenched her fists in frustration, for just a few moments ago it had felt so real. A clear memory of her mother, and their old home. There had been chairs around the table. She counted them in her mind - one, two, three. Just like she'd seen at Yadira's house. In that memory, she hated liver, and she always had.

It was a genuine memory.

Seraphina sighed. The thought of food made her hungry, so she decided to eat before going out. Given that Gisgo was visiting, there was bound to be some delicious food lying around. She walked downstairs. It was late, and no one was in the kitchen. Afiz would be meandering about, and Gisgo was probably asleep by now. This was her favourite time of day, when the whole world was asleep.

She felt free.

Today had been a great day. The liberty to wander the library alone during the day was an entirely new experience. People had seen her and not been bothered. She had not needed to hide. Though there was her minor debacle with the scrolls which may have angered Afiz. She had not seen him since, so she didn't know if it had been of any consequence.

She smelled something delicious and followed her nose to the kitchen.

No one was around.

It looked as though Afiz and Gisgo had already eaten, but Seraphina was used to helping herself after living there for so long.

Having dinner with Gisgo, now that would be a treat. Maybe it could happen while he was staying. She thought she smelled oxen, and opened the pots hopefully, and there it was, her favourite food with plenty of bread and vegetables too. Living in the library came with its perks, and the food was one of them. Imhotep had a lavish appetite, and there was always plenty.

Seraphina fixed herself a generous plate. She ate in the records room. It was so peaceful. Rows and rows of scrolls stared down at her from the shelves above. She ate and savoured the delicious flavours. Afiz appeared at the far end of the library, near the now closed entrance. Seraphina didn't see him at first, but as he got closer, she saw the worried look he had on his face. Seraphina was chewing a big mouthful of food and dipped another piece of bread into the sauce. She wasn't sure what Afiz was going to say, so she decided to let him speak first. He sat down next to her.

'I think we need to work on your table manners next, Seraphina,' he said.

'Very funny.' She could only manage a muffled response.

Afiz chuckled. 'Seraphina, please don't talk with your mouth full.'

She swallowed and wiped her mouth with the back of her hand. 'Sorry, Afiz. Did you come here to discuss dinner etiquette with me?'

'No.'

'Is everything alright? I'm sorry about this afternoon and the scrolls. I was just thinking about tomorrow. I'm so excited to spend the day with Gisgo and see the museum for the first time that I just wanted to make a good impression.'

'I'm sure you will. Are some of those scrolls written by Gisgo?'

'Yes, but I am reading some texts written by other philosophers as well.'

'Very well,' said Afiz. 'I am happy for you to make a good impression, but please do not ask him endless questions about his own work. Remember he is here for a visit to enjoy Alexandria, and to see the library and the museum. He might also want to meet other intellectuals while he is here. There may be ideas he wants to exchange. He might even pen a scroll while he is here, which would be added to our collection of course.'

'I promise to be on my very best behaviour, Afiz.'

'I appreciate that.'

'So, what *are* you worried about?'

Afiz told her about his conversation with Imhotep. Especially that his reaction was unexpected. Seraphina lowered her eyebrows and focused on Afiz.

'When I told Imhotep I'd hired you, he wasn't surprised at all. He was quite indifferent, actually.' Afiz still looked slightly puzzled to Seraphina.

'That's good, right?

'I suppose, but I found it a bit unusual. He is a pedantic man to say the least. I think it's very strange. He didn't ask for any details - when I had employed you, why I had chosen you, what your skills were, to name but a few.'

'Did you bring any of that up at all?'

'I apologised to him for not getting his approval before I "hired" you.'

'What did he say?' Seraphina asked.

'He said it wasn't a problem. He told me that he trusted me and that I was free to find anyone I needed to help me in the library.'

'That seems quite reasonable.'

'Yes, but I know the man, Seraphina,' said Afiz crossly. 'Trust me, it doesn't fit. He's never relaxed about anything.'

'Fair enough, but is it at all possible that he meant what he said and it's just not a big deal to him?'

'Possible, but I'm not buying it.'

'You worry too much, Afiz,' she said.

'And your optimism is sometimes misplaced, Seraphina.'

'Good point, but I still like my optimism.'

'I do too, but for now, try to keep a low profile around the library. Walking into the main chamber and trying to carry twenty scrolls out by yourself is not the best way to be inconspicuous.'

'Another good point. I'm sorry, Afiz. I was a little excited today. That's all.'

Afiz understood. It was nice for them to have a long chat. It felt like it had been a while. Seraphina shared with him the feeling of freedom in walking around the library. She didn't have to hide. After all, it was the first time she was in her home and allowed to be seen. Afiz had never thought of it that way. It had been a big day for her. He still wanted her to lay low.

'You've got yourself a deal, Afiz. I will keep that in mind from now on. I'll definitely try not to make such a spectacle of myself.'

Afiz laughed at her. 'It was rather funny.'

The same mischievous grin was back. 'Were you laughing on the inside? When you and Imhotep were looking at me?"

'I was. I was almost shaking from holding in the laughter. I thought you would trip up and fall down at any minute.'

'While you were busy enjoying the comedy, Gisgo was the only gentleman in the room.'

'Yes, it surprised me when he went over to you. I think he is quite fond of you. Remember this, Seraphina. Gisgo seems to be an exception. The men who looked at you and did nothing are the norm.

The more traditional types.'

'What are you trying to tell me?' she asked.

'Well, to them, a woman has no place in this building. Especially a young woman. Even more so-'

'What?' Seraphina felt a rush of anger coursing through her. 'That is outrageous. How dare they! How can they even justify such a backward point of view?'

Afiz gave her a moment to calm down.

She lowered her voice and continued. 'Wait, you were saying … even more so. Even more so what?'

'Hmmm, I'm not sure I want to tell you now.'

She raised her eyebrows at him. 'Just tell me.'

Afiz leaned forward and rested his chin in his hand. 'If they observe you closely, they might suspect you are Hebrew. People we pass in the streets are one thing. People in here are quite another. Besides, you are usually wearing typical Egyptian clothing when we go out.'

'I wore the same today,' said Seraphina.

'Yes, but here the same people will see you every day. They will observe you more regularly. They also talk amongst themselves, and with Imhotep every day. Do you see where I am going with this?'

'I suppose, but it seems very unfair.'

Afiz nodded in agreement and put his hand on her shoulder. 'It is, my dear. Life is not always fair. I don't like it either, but you are dear to me, and I want to keep you protected. In such situations, I prefer to take the world as it is, and not as I think it should be.'

Seraphina cocked her head and looked at Afiz. Wasn't that exactly what Yadira had said? In those exact words? How odd.

Afiz waved his hand. 'Seraphina? Are you still with me?'

'Sorry, Afiz.'

'What happened there? I feel like I lost you for a moment.'

Seraphina stretched her arms and yawned. 'Just tired. Big day. I zoned out for a second.'

Afiz nodded. 'Very well,' he said.

'I do understand what you are saying, Afiz. I still think it is ridiculous. Being female does not make me less capable. Being a

Hebrew does not make me less capable. These men are supposed to be intellectuals. They're not very progressive.'

Afiz pictured Seraphina scolding a room full of elderly scholars. The thought made him smile. 'As I said, I agree with you. Just stay on the safe side.'

Seraphina nodded. 'I will, Afiz.' She watched his face. He didn't make direct eye contact with her. 'Is there something you are not telling me?'

'No,' said Afiz. 'However, I do think that there is something that Imhotep isn't telling me. Until I figure out what that is, caution is the best way forward. Agreed?'

Seraphina agreed and thrust out her hand. 'Agreed.'

Afiz shook his head and laughed at her antics. They shook hands.

'I hope some of these traditional views change,' said Afiz. 'I believe they will in time. I am sure it is something you can read about when you find the time.'

'Afiz, you and I both know that I always find the time to read about the things I am interested in.'

Afiz laughed. 'Yes, that is a certainty in life that we can always count on.'

They laughed together for a few seconds. Seraphina then thanked him.

'For what?'

'For always being patient with me. For listening to my point of view. For caring about what I have to say. I know I can sometimes be a pest, so I want you to know how much I appreciate all of it.'

'Sometimes?' Afiz laughed behind his hand.

'Hey! I'm not that bad.'

'No, you're acceptable. Most of the time. Now, I will leave you be, so you can finish your dinner.'

'Goodnight, Afiz.'

Afiz turned his chair back and moved as if to get up. He hesitated for a moment and remained in his chair.

'Is there something else?' asked Seraphina.

'I saw something outside a little earlier,' he said.

'Oh, and what was that?'

'I was checking the front entrance was locked from the outside. I do this every night. When I turned around, I saw an old Hebrew woman. She was trying to hide, but I spotted her. She didn't notice me at the first. Her attention was on the library. Once she saw me, she vanished.'

'Weird,' said Seraphina.

'Yes, I thought it was too.'

'Someone admiring our grand home, perhaps?'

'Actually, I thought this might be our mystery Hebrew woman,' said Afiz.

'I hadn't considered that. You think it was her?'

'I'm not sure. That was the first thing that came to my mind, so I thought I would ask you.'

'It's possible, I guess. There's no way for me to know without seeing her.'

'I wish I'd seen her the first time. Then I would know if it was her.' Seraphina shrugged.

'Anyway, it just felt a little odd when I saw her. Alright, it is very late. Sorry for interrupting your dinner.'

'No need to apologise, Afiz. I am glad we got to talk.'

The two wished each other goodnight. Seraphina watched Afiz as he got up and walked away looking burdened. There was something weighing heavily on his heart, and Seraphina felt terrible. That was twice that she had lied to Afiz. She considered it and decided to stick with her plan. It was important to her to see Yadira again and talk to her. Then she could talk to Afiz. She remembered Yadira's warning to be careful. Of course, she trusted Afiz, but for now she wanted to follow her instincts. For now, lying to Afiz was a necessary evil.

Stop worrying, she told herself.

She looked down at her plate. The stew was getting cold. She wolfed down what was left and thought of Quintus. She hadn't talked to many people in her life. There was really only Afiz. A short chat here and there to someone on the street when running errands. Come to think of it, her exchanges with the harbour master and Gisgo had been some of the longest in her life. Her chance meeting with Quintus had been different. There was an ease and comfort there. She could've talked to him all day.

My life is odd, she thought. *I live in a library, I have spent most of my life hiding from people, and I have only one friend. Well, two, including Maximus. Maybe that is all about to change.*

These thoughts didn't upset Seraphina. She quite liked being different.

SIXTEEN

It was late. Quintus came to a halt, looking up at the library. He hadn't been able to sleep. On a whim, he snuck out of the house and decided to take a walk. There was no destination in mind, and he had kept walking. His thoughts consumed him.

As he gazed at the library, a tear trickled down his face. Then his jaw and fists clenched. How could his father be so obstinate? He could see the future of his dreams slipping away. The thought of being a soldier made Quintus sick. He leaned against the library wall, folded his arms, and shook his head. Then his gaze dropped to the ground; the same place his father had shoved him down.

His kept his eyes fixed on the ground as his brain churned.

It was hopeless, he thought.

Quintus pushed himself off the wall and took a few steps to his right. It was time to go home. Almost immediately, something moved in front of him. He collided with whoever it was, and they both fell to the floor.

He looked up and saw a young woman with a small, grey dog next to her.

'Seraphina?'

She was dressed in loose trousers and a shirt, both made of simple cloth. It was quite the contrast to the elegant dress he had last seen her in. She looked up, her eyes wide with alarm. Her hands moved behind her body, pulling her away from Quintus.

Quintus raised his hands and smiled. 'It's me, Quintus.'

Seraphina stopped moving and tilted her head. Her heart slowed down as she recognised the man before her.

'Hello. I'm very sorry about that.'

'That's alright,' said Quintus. 'I wasn't looking where I was going.'

He stood and helped her to her feet.

'What brings you out so late at night?'

Seraphina began to relax. As she looked at Quintus, she felt her cheeks flush a little. Her heart started beating a little faster, this time for a different reason.

'Just felt like a walk, actually,' she said.

'So, this is where you live?'

He watched as Seraphina tightened up for a moment. Her eyes went upwards to the sky, and then the library. Her gaze came back to Quintus, and she gave him a little simper. He decided to let it go.

Quintus crouched down to Maximus. 'So, who's this?'

'Oh, this is Maximus. So, what brings you here?'

'I couldn't sleep. Thought it might clear my head to take a walk.'

Quintus watched as her head bobbed in response. She was clearly shy, and a little uneasy, but despite that, he enjoyed being around her.

On their first meeting, she had captivated him. She was so cheerful, and they seemed to share a curiosity for each other, and even if she was a little awkward, there was still a certain confidence in the way she held herself, and her intelligence was evident from the way she spoke. Seraphina's exquisite beauty had not been lost on him either. She was as tall as him, with long dark hair, and eyes he could lose himself in. More than anything, he remembered her smile. It radiated a warmth and joy that Quintus had never seen in another human being.

Even in her shy state, he could see and feel that warmth.

He couldn't believe himself. He had met this girl once, for a few minutes. Yet here they were, meeting again and his mind was racing.

He wondered what his father would think. He had no doubt the great Rufio would be furious. Sneaking out of the house would be bad enough. If he knew he was with an Egyptian girl, his fury would know no limits. Was she Egyptian though? Quintus thought about it. She dressed and behaved like an Egyptian, but her facial features were more Hebrew.

'What are you thinking?' asked Seraphina.

'Nothing, except … do you want to go somewhere?' he asked.

'Like where?'

'Maybe we could take a walk together.'

'Maybe. Yes, alright,' said Seraphina.

'Actually, don't soldiers patrol the city at night?' asked Quintus.

'Yes, but a few hours after dusk, they all congregate near the palace.'

'Sounds like you know a lot about it. Come out at night much?'

'Maybe. So, do you like to run?'

Quintus gave her a curious look. 'Yes, I suppose I do.'

'Well, Maximus loves to run.'

'So, just how fast can you run, Maximus?' he asked the dog.

Seraphina laughed. 'You know you're talking to a dog, right? To answer your question, he's the second fastest here.'

Quintus pulled himself upright and returned the steely look that Seraphina gave him. 'Sounds like a challenge.' Quintus grinned.

'So, are you ready?'

'For wh—'

Quintus never even finished the question. Seraphina dashed off, disappearing into the night, with Maximus following at her heels. She looked back at him, smiling that beautiful smile. That was all the encouragement he needed. Quintus chased after her.

She was fast. Quintus could just keep her in sight. He didn't catch up. After a few corners, they were heading down a long street.

This goes to the harbour, he thought.

He still was a long way behind. He pumped his legs harder, and she looked back. She could see him, only just. Quintus could have sworn she grinned at him. She was getting further and further away. Quintus was going at full speed and was not catching up.

Seraphina soared into the air. She flipped, jumped, and somersaulted. Her feet bounced off walls, ledges, barrels and carts. Anything that was around. The gymnastics didn't slow her down. Quintus watched in awe, but kept running.

Who is this girl, he thought.

A few moments later, he saw her waiting for him at the end of the street.

He slowed down, catching his breath.

'Where did you … learn to do that?' he said between panted breaths.

'You looked like you had trouble keeping up there.' Seraphina giggled. 'Even Maximus outran you.'

Quintus shook his head. 'I had no …' he panted, 'what happened? You're so fast …'

'You had no what?' asked Seraphina.

'I had no idea what I was up against.'

They both laughed at this, just like they had on their first meeting. Their eyes met for a moment, and Quintus looked out over the water.

'It's beautiful here,' he said. 'I don't think I've ever been to this part of the city before.'

She nudged him with her elbow. 'Not quite what you're used to? The lavish quarters of Roman soldiers?'

He turned to face her. 'I'm not a Roman soldier.'

'Maybe not, but you live with one.'

'How do you know that?'

She smiled. 'Well, it was a guess to be honest. Now I know I was right.'

Quintus nodded and asked her how she had guessed.

'You have a certain way about you. You stand tall, good posture, very formal in the way you act. Though I'm not sure you would make a good soldier.'

Quintus raised his eyes at this.

'You're far too slow.' Seraphina giggled.

'I'm glad you are finding amusement in my inadequacies.' Quintus chuckled. 'So, enlighten me. Where are we exactly?'

'This is the north-eastern edge of the city. The Hebrew districts begin just over there,' she said as she pointed. Then, with heavy sarcasm, 'This, of course, is what we call the harbour.'

He rolled his eyes at her and laughed. 'Very funny.'

She bowed in mock deference. 'My pleasure. You don't know your own city?'

'I guess not as well as you do.'

She nudged him again. This time she lingered close to his body, just for a moment. 'Slow in more ways than one, huh?'

She could feel the smile on her face and beamed as he smiled back. Seraphina watched as Quintus gazed into her eyes. Then, he looked away. Seraphina saw the muscles in his face relax as he looked out over the water. She was surprised at how relaxed she felt around him.

'What are you thinking?' she asked.

'Only that I need to work on my sprinting.'

'Really?'

'No.' He sighed, just a little sigh, but enough to make him look sad to Seraphina.

Quintus felt a few beads of sweat on his forehead. He looked over to her. Seraphina's eyes waited for his response. He took her hand. Gently.

'I was thinking that I have never met someone like you before, Seraphina.'

'Oh. Well, I have never had someone hold my hand before.' She felt herself blushing.

'Then I am honoured to be the first,' said Quintus.

'I don't think I could have chosen a better candidate.'

Seraphina threw her hair back, feigning drama. Quintus laughed at her theatrics. His eyes locked onto hers, and he tingled as her smile widened. Quintus raised Seraphina's hand and kissed it softly. He felt her quiver. Then everything in his body seemed to freeze, as she stepped closer to him. They were so close that he could feel her breath against his face. He was mesmerised. Then Quintus felt her hands grab his shirt, and her arms pulled him close as her lips met his.

Their lips massaged each other's without parting, and they

embraced. Seraphina's arms around Quintus' neck. His arms around her waist. They stood there for what seemed like an eternity. Quintus finally broke the silence.

'That was a surprise.'

'A good one, I hope?'

'Yes, a very good one.'

'You know, I have never kissed a boy before.'

'You seem to know what you are doing.'

'Beginner's luck, I guess. You should be feeling pretty lucky too,' she said.

'Yes, lucky and slow. That's me. What are the chances we would meet like this?'

'Who knows? Some believe that all things happen exactly as they are meant to.'

Quintus nodded.

'Besides, I'm a night person, so that probably slightly increased our odds,' said Seraphina.

Quintus laughed. 'Well, however it happened, I'm glad it did.'

'Me too, though there is a lot you don't know about me, Quintus.'

'That's true, but I can be patient. I don't mind waiting to learn everything about you. I'll enjoy it, getting to know a bit more each time I see you.'

'Each time you see me? Who said I wanted to see you again?'

'My apologies for being so presumptuous,' said Quintus. 'If you want to see me again, I'd like that.'

'I am joking. I would love to see you again.' Seraphina gave Quintus a hug. 'Come on, sit down. This is my favourite place, especially at night.'

They sat next to each other on the wall, looking out at the vast sea.

'Have you ever wondered what it might be like on the other side of these waters?' asked Seraphina.

'I think about it a lot. More so these days,' said Quintus.

'Why is that?'

'To begin with, we are facing Rome right now.'

Seraphina looked out. 'Really? Rome? Amazing.'

'I imagine so.'

'You've never been?'

Quintus shook his head. 'No, but I want to.'

'Me too. Then again, I want to go everywhere.'

'Everywhere?'

'Yes, everywhere.' Seraphina held out her arms wide.

'That could take quite a while.'

'I am young, I have plenty of time.'

Quintus laughed. 'You are right about that.'

'So why do you want to go there?'

Quintus told her of his plans to study in college. He loved the sciences. Maybe he would become a mathematician, or an engineer. Seraphina joked that at least he'd have something to fall back on.

'Fall back on?'

Seraphina grinned at him cheekily. 'You have no future as an athlete, that much is for certain.'

Quintus shook his head, still smiling. 'Not going to let that go, are you?'

Seraphina started to giggle. 'Did you see how far I outran you by?'

'Yes, I had plenty of time to notice as I tried to catch up.'

'Alright, I will stop reminding you.'

'As memorable as that was, it wasn't my favourite part of the night.' Quintus glanced at Seraphina's lips.

'Oh really? What was?'

Quintus leaned forward and gave Seraphina a gentle kiss.

'Ahhh, I see,' said Seraphina.

'That is the first time I have ever kissed a girl.'

'Interesting. That is the first time I have ever been kissed by a boy.'

He put his arm around her. 'We're even now.'

'Yes, we are.'

Seraphina rested her head on his shoulder. Together, they looked out over the water. She wasn't quite sure how this had all happened. There was a wonderful feeling inside of her. She'd never felt like this before. It was odd - excitement, nerves, the desire to jump and dance all over the place, all topped off with a deep joy. It was tough to contain herself.

She thought of Rome, all those miles away. She caught herself imagining all types of adventures. Faraway lands, learning from brilliant minds, different cultures and tasty new cuisines. She could feel it. Almost as if it was within reach. She felt Quintus next to her and thought maybe she could share all of that with him.

I'm getting ahead of myself, she thought.

She didn't care though. The feeling was exhilarating. She wanted it for as long as it would last.

Quintus too had a million thoughts running through his head. He was overjoyed that this beautiful young woman was sitting next to him. He'd never thought much about romance. Other things kept him busy. He worked hard in school and his main plan had been to go to Rome and pursue an education. After his father's ultimatum, Rome did indeed seem to be his destiny. Not for education though, but to wear a uniform.

There was no way he would spend a single day wearing the uniform of the Roman army. He had yet to figure out how he would sidestep his father on that. He brought his thoughts back to the beautiful girl next to him and pulled her closer.

'This is nice. The most fun I have had in a long time,' he said.

'I feel the same.' Seraphina sighed.

'So, are we destined for more twilight dates? Or do I get to see you during the daytime?'

'I'll think about it,' said Seraphina, sitting up straight. 'Where do you live?'

'Further east of here, along the coast. There is a Roman camp there. That's where I live.'

'A Roman camp? A military camp, you mean?' asked Seraphina.

'Yes.'

Seraphina was intrigued now. 'How interesting. There are homes in those camps?'

She was an inquisitive type, no doubt about it. Quintus nodded. 'Yes. Officials and soldiers all live in the camp, and some have their own houses.'

'So, what are you? A lieutenant?'

'Very funny. I am not a soldier.'

'Your father is.'

'How did you know that?'

Seraphina shrugged her shoulders. 'The only logical conclusion, really. Plus, I saw you and him talking the other day. Just before I came and spoke to you near the library.'

'Ahhhh, yes. I remember now.'

'Was everything alright that day? I know I asked you at the time, but something seemed amiss.'

Quintus grimaced, just for a moment. 'Is it alright if we talk about that another time?'

'Of course. I didn't mean to pry.'

He put his hand on top of hers. 'I know. It's no problem. How about you, where do you live?'

Seraphina thought for a moment. 'Hmmm, is it alright if I give the same response?'

'You live in a Roman camp too?' He laughed at his own humour.

'Quite the comedian, aren't you? No, I don't live in a Roman camp. What I meant is, do you mind if we talk about that another time?'

Quintus smiled at her. That warm, sincere, beautiful smile of his. 'Of course.'

She got lost in him for a few moments. After a little while, she came out of her trance. 'It is getting quite late.'

'I hadn't noticed,' he said.

'Well, that's because you've been having such a good time.'

'I won't deny it.'

'I should go for now. Did you sneak out of your house to come here?'

'Yes, why do you ask?'

'It can't be the easiest thing to sneak out of a fortified Roman military camp. Especially at night.'

Quintus nodded.

'Very impressive,' said Seraphina. 'Please don't get caught. I want to see you again.'

'So, when do you want to see me again?'

'How about a week from now?'

'Same time? Same place?'

'How about we meet here this time?' Seraphina watched him with raised eyebrows.

Quintus looked out over the water. He had an idea. 'Sounds great to me,' he said.

They said goodbye. She kissed him again on the lips, lingering a little longer this time. Quintus opened his eyes just in time to see her fade into the night with Maximus in tow.

What a girl.

SEVENTEEN

Imhotep had been summoned to the palace. He would rather be showing his visitor around, but when Cleopatra summoned you, you showed up. Besides, Afiz would take care of Gisgo.

Imhotep was bored. It was a routine visit to meet with the queen's advisors. They were supposed to be academic men, but they were, in reality, favoured cronies of the previous king who drew exorbitant salaries and lived in extravagant homes. Academia, the library, and the museum were the furthest things from their minds, but, on a day like this, they showed up and looked interested.

Imhotep played along too, even though he despised the exercise. The last woman to sit on the throne was a queen named Berenice. She had been a firm believer in the importance of academia, but her father had come back from exile in Rome and beheaded her. It was a perfect metaphor in many ways; he didn't value the academic arts at all. The same was true of his spoiled daughter, who now sat upon the throne.

It didn't matter to Imhotep. The library's importance was undisputed. The museum attracted brilliant minds from all over the world and his tenure was not in jeopardy. Yet, it was wise to keep the queen happy.

So, he waited.

Cleopatra was famous for this. She would summon important officials for a meeting, then keep them waiting for hours. He sat in the foyer of the palace, admiring the huge alabaster columns then he heard steps behind him, and turned to see who it was.

'Imhotep, is that you?

It was Rufio. Imhotep stood up as the veteran soldier approached him. They shook hands.

'Hello, Rufio. How are you?'

'Imhotep, curator of our great library. Well, not our library,' said the general. 'I am very well. Have you not heard my news?'

'No, Rufio. As I am sure you can imagine, I don't mix much in military or political circles.'

'Caesar has appointed me as the commander of all his forces in Egypt. I also have the responsibility of governing the entire region.'

'Congratulations, that is quite an honour,' said Imhotep. 'So, where does the fair queen Cleopatra fit into things?'

'She is the ruler of Egypt so far as the public is concerned. On an official level, I am here to support her and carry out her wishes. Caesar has given me absolute authority though, so truthfully, all Egypt is under my control.'

'I see.'

'I am surprised you have not heard,' said Rufio with a sneer.

'I have some news that may also surprise you.'

'Oh, what is that?'

'Do you remember how we met, Rufio?'

'Of course I do,' said Rufio. 'You were in the wrong place at the wrong time.'

'What you mean is I saw you attack a woman, then kill her and her husband with another soldier.'

'Yes, that is what I meant. Very good memory. Do you also remember what I said to you back then?'

'You threatened to kill me and my entire family if I ever breathed a word of it to anyone.'

'Have you kept your side of the deal, Imhotep?'

'It wasn't much of a deal for me, Rufio, but yes, I have.'

'Oh, I don't know about that. You were only helping the curator in those days, so time has served you well. If my memory is accurate, that curator died not a year later. You managed to wrangle your way into his position. Ever since, you have served as the curator of the greatest library this world has ever known.'

'I earned every bit of it,' said Imhotep.

'If you say so, but the fact is that you could have lost it all. You have stayed silent all these years, and things have worked out well for both of us.'

'Yes, I can see that.'

'Besides, it would do you no good to break our deal now. With the power I have now been given, an old accusation would be of no consequence.'

'I am aware of all this, Rufio.'

'So, why do you bring up the past?'

'If you recall, there was a second element of the deal we made.'

'Yes, the girl. The daughter of those wretched Hebrews.'

'Wretched, Rufio? The woman was walking the streets, minding her business. You decided you wanted her and attacked her. Her husband came to help her. Then you and your accomplice murdered them both in cold blood.'

'Well, Benedict did not know the full story.' Rufio chuckled.

'I could tell. He came to protect you, and you made him a murderer without him even knowing.'

Rufio let out another sinister chuckle. 'You know, he never found out about that. We're going to keep it that way, aren't we?'

'I will never speak a word of it, Rufio. You know that. As you say, it wouldn't do any good now. I'm not keeping your secret out of loyalty, or friendship. You are a ruthless, vile man. I am only keeping up my end of the bargain out of fear.'

Rufio smiled as this man lavished insults upon him. To him, they were compliments.

'Why bring up the girl, Imhotep?'

'Do you remember her name?'

Rufio thought for a moment. 'Come to think of it, no. I don't. It has been a long time.'

'Does the name "Seraphina" ring a bell?' asked Imhotep.

Rufio shook his head. 'I don't think so. Do you think this is the girl?'

'I doubt it. She might be though. My caretaker has just employed her. There is something distinctly Hebrew about the way she looks.'

'That isn't much to go on, Imhotep.'

'I'm telling you because of our agreement. What would you do if it turned out to be her? If you found out later that I had met her and that I had not told you?'

Rufio put his hands upon Imhotep's shoulders and looked into his eyes. He spoke slowly. 'You're right. That would not work out well for you.'

'Exactly,' said Imhotep, pulling away.

Rufio mocked him. 'You're a coward, great curator. You accuse me of all manner of things, yet you would put this girl in danger when you are not even sure if she is the one.'

'A deal is a deal. I might be a coward, but I am wise enough to know who to ally myself with.'

That made Rufio smile. He loved the power he had over others. 'That works for me. Thank you. Leave it with me, I will get to the bottom of it.'

'Please do not thank me. How will you find out if it is her?'

'Benedict. The man does not forget anything. We spent days looking for her after that night. He will remember, without a doubt.'

'Just leave me out of it, alright?'

'I am a man of my word. Whatever I am, you can always count on that. Seraphina, Seraphina.' He said the name out loud to try and jog his memory.

One of the queen's servants came out to call Imhotep.

'I must go, Rufio. Goodbye.'

'It is never goodbye, dear curator. I will see you, perhaps sooner than you think.'

Rufio watched him as he walked up the stairs into the palace.

Could it be, he thought. *Could it be that the girl had been under his nose this entire time? Living in Alexandria?*

The thought sent his head spinning. It had been years now. A long time ago, he had come to a decision. That night forced him to rethink things, so after that night, he stopped taking Hebrew women for sport. For him, it was a minor sacrifice, and once that had paid off well, as he had realised his ambitions.

His mind turned to the girl. Was it necessary to pursue this? As he'd said to Imhotep, it would make no difference now. She would be a teenager now, almost a woman. Still, she was a Hebrew. No one of importance would take her side over his. He knew the answer to his question. It would have to be taken care of. He was a cruel man and did not believe in loose ends. Nor did he leave anything to chance. He would have to pay a visit to his old friend Benedict.

EIGHTEEN

Ptolemy was the thirteenth, and the most recent in a long and successful dynasty. The young king was only a boy, but, despite this, he had a maturity beyond his years. He had surrounded himself with able soldiers and strategists. Of these, Pothinus was the most important, and he was the real power behind the operation. Everything had been going to plan. He had been successful in turning the young king against his older sister, but then along came Caesar.

Pothinus had not anticipated Cleopatra's guile, and he resented that she had allied herself with the Romans. They were outsiders.

It had been a brilliant move on her behalf. Her seduction of Caesar had left her all but invincible on the throne. Pothinus knew that Caesar was pulling the strings, but the bottom line was that Cleopatra sat on the throne, a situation he was keen to remedy. Ptolemy was helpful for his young age, but he was still a boy. Thankfully, the young king knew his limitations, and was content to have others do his bidding. Pothinus came up with the strategy. Achillas, a talented general, built their army and sourced weaponry.

Caesar had arrived in Alexandria at a time when Cleopatra and Ptolemy were bickering. Cleopatra wanted to respect her father's wishes. She had reached out to Ptolemy and offered to rule together, side by side. Just as their father had intended. By then, it had been too late. Pothinus had been manipulating the king for months. Ptolemy told his sister that she had no business being on the throne, and that he had no desire to share.

Pothinus used his influence over the city, and the people were on their side, but Cleopatra orchestrated her coup, and she soon had Caesar in her corner. Pothinus had tried to incite the people against them, but Caesar had proven too clever. He had given a credible speech about the wishes of the late king and turned the crowd.

There was a small consolation in all this. Caesar had been slow to act. They had taken advantage. Achillas' soldiers had moved to secure their fleet. Naval strength was imperative for the attack they were planning. Pothinus and Achillas had been plotting the attack for a while. They had thought of everything. It was time to meet with the king and present their plan. They found him alone, finishing a grand lunch.

'King Ptolemy,' said Pothinus. 'Might we have a moment of your time?'

'For what, Pothinus? Are we ready to attack those traitors or not?' said the king.

'Yes, we are,' said Achillas. 'Everything is prepared.'

'Well, don't keep me in suspense. What is your plan?' asked Ptolemy.

Achillas gave his report. 'Our fleet is hidden in the heads to the north east of the city. Behind the Roman camp. Our soldiers are dispersed in their battalions near our current position. When we sound the attack, two forces will attack on land. One will swarm the streets of the city and head towards the palace. The other will head straight to the Roman camp. Our fleet will set sail, with several ships attacking the camp. The remainder will proceed to the city's harbour. There, they will cut off Caesar's fleet.'

It was an impressive plan. Ptolemy said as much. He questioned Achillas' confidence though. Overthrowing the Romans would not be so easy. He asked Pothinus if he saw any flaws in the attack.

'Not at all, your majesty. Our scouts have been busy for weeks. We have checked the numbers of soldiers in the camp east of the city. After we did that, we counted the numbers in each force.'

'What do you mean, each force?' Ptolemy sounded confused.

'Throughout the city, there are three main groups of Roman soldiers,' said Pothinus. 'The biggest is at the fortified camp at Columbarium. There is a second force at the barracks near the Temple of Artemis. The third force watches over the fleet in the harbour.'

'Do your plans provide for each of these forces to be overwhelmed?'

'Yes, your majesty,' said Pothinus.

'Are there any contingencies we need to be prepared for?'

'At any given time, there are soldiers scattered throughout the streets in the city.'

'What are your plans to neutralise those soldiers?'

'They are mainly patrolling in the day time in pairs,' said Pothinus. 'Where our forces meet these patrols, they will be overwhelmingly outnumbered.'

This was music to the king's ears. He relished the thought of Roman soldiers being cut down in the city streets.

His streets.

Pothinus could tell they had lost the boy's attention. He finished anyway, saying 'we have determined that an attack just after sunset will be the optimal time to strike.'

'Very well. That all sounds in order. Is there anything else, gentlemen?'

'Yes,' said Pothinus. 'While we are ready to attack now, there is one other factor we should include in our thinking.'

'What is that, Pothinus?'

'The presence of Caesar in the city.'

'I do not follow. Are you saying we should attack when Caesar is in the city, or when he isn't?'

'When he isn't,' said Pothinus.

'Why is that, Pothinus?'

Pothinus explained his theory. 'The Roman troops are loyal to Caesar, but they also fear him. Their attack would be a crushing blow.

Like any good soldiers, if they know they are defeated, they will retreat. Caesar despises deserters, so If Caesar is still in the city, the Romans are more likely to fight to the death. If he isn't, they are more likely to flee.'

'Interesting theory. Do you agree, General Achillas?'

'I do,' said Achillas. 'We've talked a lot about this, and it's a fair conclusion. Our men have fought the Romans before. They know what they're talking about.'

The king looked at the two men. He gave their words some thought for a few moments.

'I admit I lack experience in these matters, however, I am not convinced. Whether Caesar is in Alexandria or not will be of no consequence. You say our forces are poised to overrun the Romans. I believe we will be successful, but I also believe in prudence. If we can gain even a slight advantage in Caesar's absence, then we will wait. My understanding is that we have one chance to attack. That is what Pothinus has led me to believe. Therefore, we cannot afford to fail. I am happy to wait until the conditions are perfect. Well, as perfect as they can be.'

'Wonderful, your majesty,' said Achillas.

Ptolemy glared at the insolent soldier. 'I am not finished yet, General.'

'My apologies, your majesty,' mumbled Achillas.

'As I was saying, I don't want to wait too long. As soon as we know Caesar is leaving the city, you must be prepared. Are your scouts keeping watch at the Roman camp and the harbour?'

'Yes, your majesty,' said Pothinus.

'Very well, then. We will know once Caesar has left the city. Then we will take back the palace and the city from my treacherous sister. Make all the necessary preparations, both of you.'

'Yes, your majesty,' they said in unison.

NINETEEN

Seraphina had been in and out of sleep all night. She was grateful that she had got some rest, but the excitement was just too much for a full night's sleep.

Today she would spend the day with Gisgo, Afiz and Imhotep. They were to show the great philosopher around the museum. Seraphina was elated. She couldn't remember the last time she was this excited, and she waited impatiently. Afiz had given her specific instructions. She was to wait until sunrise, and then enter the library from the front.

Patience had never been one of Seraphina's strong suits. Maximus was still in deep sleep, as was most of the city. The only sound was the tapping of Seraphina's foot on the floor.

Finally, the sun rose in the distance. Seraphina leapt off the bed, and a few moments later, she was in the back alley, with a big smile on her face, walking along the side of the building. She felt like she had forgotten something and looked back. The stone from the wall! She had left it on the street, along with a big gaping hole in the wall of the library.

She dashed back and laid the stone back in place. Looking around, she did not see anyone which was lucky. She walked through the front entrance where not a soul was in sight. Maybe Afiz had a point about 'arriving' so early. As she walked through the main hall, Seraphina could hear voices toward the back of the building. The voices were coming from the kitchen where she found Afiz and Gisgo and said good morning.

'Afiz has just been telling me about what we will be doing today,' said Gisgo. 'It sounds like we are in for a treat.'

'Shall we get started?' Seraphina couldn't wait.

'Would you like some breakfast first, Seraphina?' Afiz smiled at her excitement.

'No, thank you,' said Seraphina. 'I ate at home.'

'Very well. Gisgo, are you ready?' Afiz looked over to the old man.

'Most definitely,' said Gisgo.

'Let's go then,' said Afiz.

The front entrance to the library faced the street. The trio walked out, turned left, and Seraphina was stunned. All those years living here, and she had never been to this edge of the library before. Then again, she had only started using the front entrance a few days ago.

That was the first time I had been in the library during the day, she thought.

She saw the lecture hall from the outside, and the adjoining garden. She couldn't believe it. All this had been here, right under her nose. She looked at Afiz who was telling Gisgo everything about each building they passed. He looked at Seraphina for a moment with a grin on his face.

It was hard to tell who was having more fun. Seraphina was enthralled but also in disbelief. Gisgo had never seen anything like this in his life. Afiz enjoyed giving the tour. Imhotep would usually be doing it, but the curator had been called away at the last minute.

They entered the first building, a huge study hall. 'Scholars study here in their free time,' said Afiz. 'Sometimes impromptu lessons are given by senior scholars. There are areas of the hall set aside for this. Scientists also conduct their experiments in this building.' Afiz pointed to a series of rooms along the side of the hall. As Afiz spoke, Seraphina spotted an elderly Egyptian man in the room at the end.

Gisgo and Afiz wandered through the hall, discussing various matters. Seraphina walked away from them, drawn towards this man.

Perhaps he is a scientist, she thought.

No one else was in the study hall, as it was still quite early. He looked up at her for a moment, then returned to what he was doing. As Seraphina got closer, she could see he was writing, and that on the table lay wooden triangles and circles, in various shapes and sizes. They looked like toys. He would play around with them repeatedly then scribble something. Seraphina wondered if he was crazy. Nevertheless, she was fascinated and kept moving closer, standing at the entrance to the room, watching. The man paid no attention to her and continued working.

'I was wondering where you were,' said Afiz.

'Me, Afiz?' said the elderly man. 'Or are you talking to this young woman?'

'My apologies, Khay,' said Afiz. 'I was talking to Seraphina. Have you met?'

'No,' said Khay. 'I am working on something here and she was watching.'

'I hope she did not interrupt you, sir,' said Afiz.

'She did, in fact. Never mind. How are you, Afiz? Where's Imhotep today? Haven't been promoted to curator, have you?' Khay chuckled to himself.

'I am well, thank you. No, there has been no promotion. Imhotep has been called away on official business today.'

'I see. Who's your friend?' Khay gestured at Gisgo.

'This is Gisgo, a visiting scholar from Valentia. Gisgo, this is Khay. Khay is one of our most renowned scientists.'

'Nice to meet you, Gisgo. Valentia, that is a long way from here. When did you arrive?'

'Just yesterday, actually,' said Gisgo.

'What is your expertise?'

'Philosophy. How about you? What are you working on here?'

'This particular experiment is concerned with trigonometry. My main areas of study are astronomy and mathematics. Geography is also an interest of mine.'

'I thought as much,' said Gisgo. 'Not many people from this part of the world have heard of Valentia.'

'I imagine it to be a fascinating place,' said Khay.

'You could say that.' Gisgo looked down at the wooden shapes on the table. 'So, these are calculations using the angles of the triangle?'

'That's right,' said Khay with a smile.

'Khay studied under the great Hipparchus,' said Afiz. 'He visited the library and studied here at the museum before my time.'

'Hipparchus the astronomer?' Both Gisgo and Seraphina spoke at the same time.

They all laughed at this, and Khay turned to Seraphina, raising his eyebrows.

'You have heard of my mentor, then?'

'Yes, his work is fascinating,' said Seraphina. She cast a sideward gaze at Afiz, then back to Khay.

'Why do you find it fascinating?'

'Well ...' Seraphina hesitated.

'Go ahead.' Gisgo encouraged her with a nod and a smile.

'He used geometry in his studies of astronomy,' said Seraphina. 'Through his experiments, he discovered the calculations that are the foundation of trigonometry.'

The room was silent. Afiz was used to Seraphina's brilliance, and Gisgo was already very fond of her. Khay's frown and grimace moved into raised eyebrows and a smile.

'This girl knows what she's talking about, Afiz. Is she also a scholar?' asked Khay.

'Well, not quite. She helps me take care of the library, and does a brilliant job of it.'

'Well, maybe you can join us in the hall some time, Seraphina.'

'I would be honoured, sir,' said Seraphina.

'We will leave you to your work, Khay,' said Afiz. 'I would like to continue showing Gisgo around.'

'I should get back to this anyway.' Khay gestured to the mess of props and parchment on the table. 'If you happen to be around at lunchtime, come and find me. Seraphina and I can discuss the latest in the world of mathematics. Nice to meet you, Gisgo. Are you with us for some time?'

'Likewise, Khay. Yes, I am here for a month. I will no doubt see you again.'

'Enjoy your visit.'

Seraphina beamed at Khay as they left. His question about her being a scholar had made her day. She knew he had been joking. Still, it was a huge compliment.

'So, do you charm everyone you meet, my dear?' asked Gisgo.

Seraphina was daydreaming and barely heard the question, shrugging her shoulders in response.

'I see a bright future for you,' said Gisgo.

Afiz nodded. The two of them walked ahead, with Seraphina following. She gazed in awe at the vast buildings as they went through them. It felt surreal. Her other dreams started to feel within her reach. She'd been a bit worried when Khay had first looked at her, but luckily, it hadn't deterred her.

When the opportunity came, she had impressed him. Her steps had a light bounce to them, as she followed the two men.

They continued meeting scholars and others who worked throughout the museum. Introductions were made, and Seraphina spoke to more people than she had in her entire life.

They sat in the gardens and listened to debates.

They walked through the grand halls overlooking the harbour.

They even shared lunch with Khay.

Everyone had a wonderful time. They discussed all manner of topics—philosophy, astronomy, geography. There were lively debates and plenty of laughter, and Seraphina was enthralled. It felt as if she learned more in that single afternoon than she would in an entire day of reading scrolls.

Throughout the day, there had been a few odd looks. Aside from a few servants, she was the only woman in sight. She remembered what Afiz had said about traditional thinking. So, it made sense to her. She wondered if anyone could tell she was Hebrew which played on her mind a little, but she didn't worry too much. After all, she was having the best day of her life. The sun set, and it was time for the day to end.

They had seen every building and garden in the museum.

They had met countless scholars.

Many meetings had been set up for the remainder of Gisgo's visit. Seraphina had even been invited to a few.

Gisgo and Afiz were exhausted, but Seraphina did not want the day to end. After dinner, Gisgo and Afiz both retired for the night. Sleep was the last thing on Seraphina's mind. She grabbed a bundle of scrolls and took them to her room, finally beginning to doze off hours later. She thought of Quintus and couldn't wait to tell him all that had happened today. It would be so wonderful to see him again. That was her last thought as she drifted into sleep.

TWENTY

Seraphina kept watch from her window. There were a few Roman patrols out tonight, but most had returned to the barracks. It had been a quiet day, after the excitement of yesterday.

Seraphina had spent the day reading and being distracted, of course. Yesterday had been amazing, and she wanted more. She wondered when she would get to go back to the museum.

Other than that, she thought of Quintus.

Beautiful, charming Quintus.

That night, though, there was another priority. She focused on the evening's adventure which would need to be stealthier than usual. She wanted to visit Yadira and Saul again. Tonight, she was going to see her parents' house.

She still had not told Afiz although she felt guilty, keeping things from him. She was a little worried about his reaction, scared it would break the trust they shared. Maybe he would understand. For now, she put it out of her mind. She had to focus and make sure she was not seen by any of these soldiers. They looked like mice in a maze from her vantage point. Some scurried in pairs through the labyrinth of streets and alleys, others congregated around the palace and idly chatted.

It was time to go. Maximus couldn't come tonight. There would be no sprinting or somersaulting. She thought of Yadira's words, and vowed to be extra cautious. Her agile frame crept out of the library in silence.

She looked both ways at the end of the back alley.

The coast was clear, so she proceeded with care, checking each intersection which took her a lot longer than usual.

She saw something out of the corner of her eye.

She froze, then in a flash retreated behind the building next to her.

Peeking around the corner, she saw two soldiers walking along the waterfront. They were oblivious to her presence.

That was close, she thought, her heart racing. She waited until they were gone, and proceeded to Yadira's house without further incident.

'Hello, Seraphina,' said Yadira. 'Please, come inside.'

'Thank you, Yadira. It is nice to see you again.'

Seraphina entered the house and familiarised herself with it again, the building seeming much less odd to her the second time around. Saul appeared from the back of the house. He had a younger man with him. Seraphina tensed up. Another stranger.

'Hello, Seraphina,' said Saul. 'Meet Joshua, our son.'

Joshua extended a hand to Seraphina, which she shook as she breathed a sigh of relief.

'Nice to meet you, Seraphina.'

'Nice to meet you too, Joshua.'

'Let's all have a seat,' said Saul. 'Seraphina, after you came to see us last time, we told Joshua.'

'Ahhh,' said Seraphina, looking at Joshua.

'There is nothing to fear,' said Saul. 'Joshua knows how to keep a secret. A day or two ago, Joshua told us something that may be cause for concern. He has heard whisperings around the village. There are some Romans looking for a young woman named Seraphina.'

'Some Romans? Soldiers?' asked Seraphina.

'These are no ordinary soldiers,' said Joshua. 'These are members of the general's private guard.'

'How do you know that?' asked Seraphina.

'Their uniforms bear a special insignia.' Joshua ran his fingers through his hair. 'I grew up here. Over the years, I have learned about the various types of soldiers.'

'Why would they be looking for me?'

'We do not know for certain that they are,' said Yadira. 'Seraphina is not a rare name, and I personally know of three or four.'

'Did you tell anyone what we spoke of? The last time you came to see us, I mean,' said Saul.

'No,' said Seraphina. 'Not a soul.'

'Has anything unusual happened since we last met?' asked Yadira.

More than a few things, thought Seraphina.

'Before I answer that, let me ask you something,' said Seraphina to Yadira. 'Did you come to see me at the library?'

'I did, Seraphina. I am sorry.'

'It made Afiz very suspicious. Please don't do that again. You were the one telling me to be careful, Yadira.'

'You are right,' said Yadira. 'That will not happen again.'

'So, can you think of anything unusual that has happened?' asked Saul.

'Just a moment,' said Seraphina. 'Yadira, why were you looking for me at the library of all places?'

'Well, I made a few assumptions,' said Yadira.

'What do you mean?'

'When I first saw you, you were with Afiz. He is the caretaker at the library. I assumed you were not friends, because, well, that would be a bit strange. Then I thought of how you could know him. When you were here last time, I asked where you live. You told me it was a long story. So, I came to the most logical conclusion.'

'And that was?'

'That you live in the library.'

Seraphina was in shock. That was her greatest secret. Only Afiz knew, and yet this woman had put it together. She thought of denying it, then looked up. All three faces were fixated on hers. Everyone in the room knew the truth.

'Well, I guess everyone here knows I live in the library,' said

Seraphina.

Some light laughter cut the tension for a moment. Seraphina was trying to process everything. Saul moved to the seat next to her. He took her hand in his and reassured her.

'Tell us what you are thinking,' said Saul.

'A couple of days ago, a visitor to the library arrived. He is a philosopher from Valentia.'

'Valentia, where is that?' Joshua looked puzzled.

'A long way away. Anyway, I went down with Afiz to meet him at the harbour. So far as anyone knows, I am Afiz's assistant. I help him with various tasks in the library. Accompanying him to greet a visiting scholar is routine. When we got back to the library, the curator was waiting for us at the front of the library which was unexpected. At least Afiz thought so.'

'Do you think this could be connected to why people are looking for you?' asked Yadira.

'I have no idea. Afiz was quick to think. He introduced me as his recently hired assistant. The curator's name is Imhotep. Afiz said Imhotep's reaction surprised him.'

'Why?' said Joshua.

'Afiz seemed to think that he was too relaxed about it. He apologised for hiring me without approval to which Imhotep was indifferent.'

'Seems reasonable to me,' said Saul.

'I thought so too, but Afiz was convinced something was off,' said Seraphina. 'He said to keep a low profile until he figured things out.'

'Has he spoken to you since then?' asked Yadira.

'Afiz? Or Imhotep?'

'Afiz,' said Yadira.

'Not about that,' said Seraphina.

'I don't really see how meeting Imhotep could be related to these Romans who are looking for you,' said Joshua.

'Remember, we don't know for sure that it's this Seraphina they are looking for,' said Saul.

'True,' said Joshua.

'Is there anything else you can think of, Seraphina?' asked Saul.

The only thing Seraphina could think of was Quintus.

He couldn't have anything to do with this, she thought. *Could he?* It was unthinkable.

'No, that's it.'

Seraphina felt uneasy. She had now placed more confidence in these people than she had in Afiz. They were still only strangers to her. Her mind turned to the Hindus, writers of some of her favourite scrolls, and their teachings about feelings. The impact of holding on to emotions, she recited to herself. It was too much for her. As soon as she could, she would tell Afiz everything. Afiz had always been understanding. Whatever happened, she was sure things would be fine. She hoped so, anyway.

'Alright,' said Saul. 'I think the best thing to do is keep as low a profile as possible. Talk to Afiz as soon as you can to see if he has come to any conclusion about Imhotep. In the meantime, Joshua, can you try to see what else you can find out? Without arousing suspicion, of course.'

'I will do my best, father.'

'Thank you, Joshua,' said Seraphina.

'Seraphina, can I ask, how is it you have come here twice now, late at night?' asked Joshua. 'Aren't you afraid of being seen?'

'I know these streets very well, and I am always careful.'

'Just know that the Roman soldiers who patrol at night are not always the most honourable.'

'I think I know that better than anyone, Joshua.'

'I am sorry, Seraphina. That was insensitive of me.'

'It's fine,' said Seraphina. 'I appreciate the concern. Yadira, there is a reason I came here tonight. I want to see my old house.'

'Where your parents and you used to live?' asked Yadira.

'Right,' said Seraphina. 'Can we go?'

'Is that why you're wearing … that?' smirked Yadira.

'Yes. It was the most, uh, Hebrew looking outfit I have.'

All three looked at Seraphina with great amusement.

'I have something that might be more suitable,' said Yadira.

Yadira took her into the back of the house where to the side of the courtyard, there was a small entryway Seraphina had not noticed last time. Inside was a small bedroom with Yadira's clothes all over the bed. Seraphina had to duck to avoid hitting her head on the doorway.

'Yes, be careful there,' she said. 'You're so tall.'

'Were my parents tall?'

'Your father was a huge man, tall and strong. I never thought of Rebekah as tall, but I guess she was. She always looked so tiny next to Josef.'

'I wish I could have known them more.'

'They loved you very much, Seraphina.'

Seraphina sighed. Then she looked down at the bed. 'So, what is all this?' she asked, gesturing towards the clothes.

'A few different things. You can wear this if you like.' She held a dress up to Seraphina's shoulders. 'It belonged to your mother.'

Seraphina took hold of the dress, keeping it pressed against her shoulders. She looked down, and the length was just right. She held the dress for a moment, almost hugging it. Then she smelled it.

'How many of my mother's things do you have?'

'Only this dress, and one other thing.'

Yadira turned around, and found what she was looking for. She presented it to Seraphina. It was a simple necklace, a worn, flat silver ring on a chord.

'Your father gave this to your mother when they were married,' said Yadira.

Seraphina squinted at the ring. She saw some writing. 'There is something carved on here. An inscription.'

'Yes, it is written in Hebrew.'

'I can see. "Our love"?'

'You can read Hebrew?' said Yadira.

'Hebrew, Latin, Coptic, some Greek.'

'I suppose living in a library has its benefits,' said Yadira.

Seraphina smiled. 'It certainly does, and I love to study.'

'Your mother would be so proud. She was a big believer in the importance of education. I am sure she would be glad to know you ended up there.'

'I bet she would. I can learn anything at the library. Just yesterday, I was helping Afiz guide a philosopher and we met a mathema—'

Yadira interrupted. 'Seraphina, I want to hear all this, I really do. It is late though, and if you want to see the house, we should go.'

'Yes, of course. I'm sorry. I get sidetracked easily.'

'No apologies,' said Yadira. 'I can tell there is a lot of passion in you. It is a wonderful thing. Very much like your father.'

'One day, I hope we can sit down and talk. For hours, days, weeks. You can tell me everything about them.'

'One day. For now, let's take things one step at a time.'

'Yes, time to see my old home, I guess,' said Seraphina.

'Let's go.'

Seraphina tied the dress around her waist. She admired herself. Even she thought she looked like a Hebrew. They rejoined Saul and Joshua in the front room.

'Your mother's dress,' said Saul. 'You look like her, you know. Don't you think so, Yadira?'

'Yes, I had not thought of it. Now you mention it, I can see it.'

'Really?' said Seraphina. She had a huge smile on her face.

'Yes. Now come on, let's go,' said Yadira.

'Just us?'

'Yes, Saul and Joshua will stay here. We don't need a whole caravan of us going over there. We're keeping a low profile, remember?'

'Right,' said Seraphina.

They stepped out on to the street. It wasn't so foreboding at this hour. A few candles were lit in the windows lining the streets. Men sat on the stoops of their homes. Seraphina had let her hair out and looked like quite the local. The men didn't even look up at the two women. As they neared the house, Seraphina saw a man standing in the doorway. He was holding a small child. It was a little girl. Yadira chatted with him as Seraphina looked at this beautiful child. She couldn't have been more than three or four years old. She looked at Seraphina with her wide brown eyes and smiled.

'Come in, Seraphina,' said Yadira.

The man explained that they were turning in for the night, and he asked them to blow the candles out when they left. The little girl kept smiling at Seraphina. Seraphina waved at her, as she disappeared into the bedroom with her father. The house was like Yadira's. The front room was rectangular, a kitchen sat at the back of the house, a couple of rooms could be seen to the left, and the back entrance was to the right. Seraphina walked around, taking in every detail. Yadira watched in silence. The young woman touched a wall. She pressed her hand against it.

Firmly.

She began to cry.

Her head sank, and she held her forehead with her other hand.

'My parents,' she whispered.

Yadira watched Seraphina. She felt her breath get deeper, and her chest hurt. She shared the girl's grief.

Seraphina thought of all she had missed by not growing up in this house.

Having memories of her parents.

Knowing who they were.

Living as a family.

She had always been a happy girl, grateful for her life, but right then, there was an emptiness. Part of her wished to go back to the way things were, although she knew it could never be like it was.

Maybe she would remember more in time.

Maybe that would only deepen the hurt.

She shook her head, and felt her anger rising.

'Something has to be done,' she said, wiping her tears away.

'Like what?' Yadira looked suddenly concerned.

'I don't know. My parents were murdered though. There has to be some justice for them.'

'Seraphina, I do understand how you feel, believe me, and trust me when I say this, but it is your pain that is talking right now.'

'Maybe, but whoever did this is now looking for me. At least it seems that way. What do you think will happen if they find me?'

Yadira had no response. She looked away from Seraphina.

'That's what I thought,' said Seraphina. 'They want to get rid of me too.'

'There is something you can do.'

'What's that?'

'You could leave,' said Yadira.

'Leave? As in, leave Alexandria?'

'Yes. We have friends who can help. You could go to Israel, or Judah.'

'Like Eliana did? Just run away?'

'At least she saw the reality of the situation,' said Yadira.

'And I don't? Because I want to give my parents some measure of justice?'

'I do not want to argue with you, Seraphina.'

'I am sorry, Yadira.'

The two stood in silence for a moment, both unsure of what to say.

'I really am sorry,' said Seraphina. 'Until recently, I had no idea where I had come from. It has been a crazy few weeks. Despite everything, I am glad I know who my parents were. I am glad I got to see this house. I just don't know what is going to happen.'

'Think about what I said. There is no shame in starting afresh. Somewhere safe.'

'This is my home, Yadira. Well, not this house anymore. This city is. I don't want to leave it behind.'

'I understand, Seraphina.' Yadira sighed.

Seraphina looked around the house again. She began to pace.

'You know, I remember this room. I have a memory of playing underneath the table. Here, in this very spot. My mother was in there,' she said, pointing to the kitchen. 'I asked what we were having for dinner. It was liver. I hate liver, I always have. I said "yuck" and mother told me off.'

Seraphina kept looking at the floor.

'Then I went to the back to look for my father ...' she trailed off as she went to the back of the house.

They were outside now.

'This was where he made furniture, wasn't it?' she asked, pointing to a corner. It had a makeshift roof over it. A wooden rack had been built to the side of the workspace.

'Yes, that's right. You remember?' asked Yadira.

'I do now. He would keep his tools on that rack?'

'Yes.'

'I came out and talked to him. I was complaining about having liver for dinner. I have never remembered him before now.'

'What did he say?' asked Yadira.

'He told me liver is good for me. He said that my mother had cooked after a long day of work. We should eat it with gratitude, he said.'

Then, the rest of that night's memories came to Seraphina. Her knees gave way, and she fell to the floor.

'Seraphina, what's wrong?'

'It's my fault, Yadira.' Her voice was raspy.

'What do you mean? What's your fault?'

Seraphina was struggling to breathe. Her words came out as barely a whisper. 'Oh my God, Yadira. I did this. I did all of this.'

'Seraphina, what are you talking about? Seraphina?'

Seraphina did not answer. She had fainted.

TWENTY ONE

She woke up, unsure of where she was. For a moment, she panicked. Yadira was there. She took Seraphina's hand to calm her. Seraphina breathed, and noticed the smell of a candle burning. She looked up at Yadira. Her warm smile and gentle touch soothed her.

'What happened?' asked Seraphina. Her voice was still a little scratchy.

'You fainted, Seraphina.'

'How long have I been here?'

'Only a few minutes,' said Yadira. 'Saul came and carried you back here. How do you feel?'

'A little woozy. I think I am alright.' She sat up in the bed.

'Just take it slowly, Seraphina.'

Seraphina shook her head in disbelief. 'I remembered everything, Yadira. It all came back to me.

'Being back in that house must have triggered it.'

'It must have. I have never had those memories before.'

'What did you remember?' asked Yadira.

Seraphina told her everything. The argument at the dinner table. Her running through the city. Seeing her parents attacked. Hearing their screams as they died. It was all with her now. Everything she had always wanted to know. She wished she could forget it all in a second. That would never be. It was forever a part of her now. Perhaps it always had been.

She told Yadira how she had run from the soldiers, then, hearing their footsteps, she had hidden. Then she made a dash for the library. A stranger had opened the door and taken her in. The next day, her life in the library had begun.

It was strange. Afiz knew nothing about the moments before he had met Seraphina. Yet they were some of the most defining of her life.

Afiz. The only family she had known for most of her life. He had raised her, fed her, taught her. At that moment, she wanted nothing more than to see Afiz; to tell him everything. She looked around the room she was in. There was nothing but pain there. The village was her first home, but she would never live there again. Too much had changed.

All her life, she had yearned for memories of her past. To know what was back there. Now she had too much of what she had wished for. The smell of those candles, the coarse walls that held up their small home; the same walls she had touched that very night. Her father's workshop. Her mother's kitchen.

She had to get out of there.

'I have to go, Yadira.'

'Seraphina, are you going to be alright?'

'Yes. I just can't be here right now.'

'I understand. How are you feeling now?'

'Good, I think.' She got out of the bed and stood up. She gazed at the candle's flame.

Trataka meditation, she thought.

It had worked without fail.

The memories of a previous life were now fused with her present reality. The aroma of the candle filled the room. 'I'm alright,' she said to Yadira, though it was more to convince herself.

Yadira took Seraphina's hand and held it in hers.

'Please be careful, Seraphina. Talk to Afiz and see if he has learned anything. Try not to do anything rash. If anything happens, or you need to talk, we are here for you. This is a safe place.'

'Thank you, Yadira.'

She came out of the bedroom. She looked at Saul and Joshua and nodded at them.

It felt like she was in a trance, and she moved at a slow pace. There was no one on the streets. It was very late now. The houses were dark, their candles having been blown out. All that remained of their light was the faint scent of smoke.

Seraphina did not rush home.

She did not feel like running through the streets.

Dream running, she had once thought.

That was the best way to describe it. That's how this had all started. Distracted as a child, running through the streets. Instead of just sitting and eating her dinner. Of course, her parents had followed her.

She shook her head and tried to tell herself it wasn't her fault.

Her parents were gentle people. What could they have done? Nothing, she decided. It must have been the same soldier that Yadira had spoken of. Attacking Hebrew women because no one would care. Seraphina could speculate forever, guessing what might have happened. It didn't matter what happened because they were gone.

Those soldiers were responsible. Seraphina had no idea what she would do, only that she would do something.

It was late when she got back to the library. The sun would be up in a few hours. As she smelled the fresh, sea air, Seraphina wondered if she would ever shake the guilt she felt.

TWENTY TWO

Benedict, like Rufio, had remained in Alexandria.

Their days together as soldiers were now distant memories. He no longer wore the uniform. He had made the decision years ago that the military life was not for him. His former counterpart had aided in that decision. Many years ago, he had seen Rufio talking to an Egyptian woman in the marketplace. That, in itself, was odd. An interaction between a Roman soldier and a local woman was a rare thing.

As he came closer, Benedict saw a fearful look on the woman's face. Her eyes pleaded with him. Benedict had interrupted something. As they walked away, Rufio quipped about Benedict 'ruining his sport.' Benedict shrugged it off as nothing more than a cryptic joke.

A week later, Benedict saw Rufio dragging the same woman into an alley late at night. Benedict had no idea what Rufio had planned, but he intervened.

The woman had been saved from a terrible fate. Rufio was intoxicated, and the next day the two soldiers spoke. Rufio's memory was hazy so Benedict told the story. He framed it so Rufio believed he had saved him from serious trouble. Rufio thanked him for his loyalty, and the two never spoke of the incident again. Shortly afterward,

Benedict's service was up, so he could be discharged, if he wished.

He did and decided to stay in Alexandria.

That incident had sealed Benedict's decision to leave the army. Rufio had no idea.

Benedict had been thinking of leaving for years but the two remained friends. In his younger days, Rufio had been different. He had saved Benedict's life twice in battle. Benedict was also close to Quintus, and the young man saw Benedict as an uncle.

If Benedict had known the true extent of Rufio's crimes, there would be no friendship. In fact, he would have made sure Rufio was charged for his crimes because, between the two, Benedict was the man of integrity.

The two men were polar opposites in terms of their values.

The passage of time and Benedict's bond with Quintus made their friendship easier as did the fact that Benedict no longer had to serve with Rufio as a soldier.

His old friend had appeared at the front gate, the general looking over the quaint farm, taking in the beautiful scent of the flowers that bloomed in these hills, carried by the light breeze from the sea below.

'Rufio, hello!' said Benedict by way of a greeting.

'How are you, old friend?' asked Rufio, walking down the path to meet him.

'I am well. What brings you here?'

'I thought of you the other day and realised we hadn't seen each other in quite some time.'

'It has been a few months,' said Benedict. 'Where's Quintus?'

'Not with me today. I wanted to come alone to see you.'

'Is everything alright?'

'Yes, in fact. Things are wonderful. Caesar himself has promoted me to be general over all of Egypt.'

'Quite the promotion,' said Benedict.

'Thank you. It has been many years since you and I were patrolling the city streets at night.'

'It certainly has.'

'You seem to be doing well,' said Rufio. 'The farm looks wonderful.'

'Thank you, Rufio. I enjoy living up here. It's peaceful and I enjoy the solitude.'

'I know you do. Remind me, why did you never get married?'

'Who knows, Rufio.' Benedict chuckled. 'Maybe there is still time for me.'

'Maybe.' Rufio laughed. 'Maybe. Shall we go inside and sit?'

'Yes, please come in. Have a seat.'

'Thank you.'

'So, what really brings you here today, Rufio? I'm happy to see you as always. The promotion is great news. I can sense something is on your mind though.'

'You're right. A detail from our time together as soldiers.'

'You know I don't like to talk about those days. They are long behind me.'

'I understand, Benedict. It's a minor thing.'

'So, what do you want to talk about?'

'Do you remember we were on patrol one night, and I was attacked by a Hebrew woman? Totally unprovoked.'

Benedict shook his head. 'No, how long ago are we talking here?'

'Ten, maybe eleven years ago.'

Just before I was discharged, Benedict thought.

'That's going back a long way, Rufio.'

'Come on, Benedict. You have the memory of an elephant.'

'I never did understand that expression, you know,' said Benedict.

'The attack, Benedict. Do you remember? There was a man with her. A beast of a man.'

'Maybe.'

'The two were attacking me, then you saved me.'

'I remember. Yes, the man resisted fiercely. He was strong. Why did they attack you?'

'I had no idea at the time. I still don't.' Rufio did what he did best and lied.

'Rufio, I'm glad I was there to help you that night. They were attacking you. We defended ourselves. It was a long time ago though. I don't care to spend my afternoon talking about civilians we killed, however justified it was.'

'Remember the girl?' Rufio raised his eyebrows.

'The little girl. Their daughter. Yes, of course I do.'

'Do you remember her name?'

'No, Rufio. She didn't stop to introduce herself, if you remember.'

'Very funny.'

'There's nothing funny about this, Rufio. In fact, it's quite upsetting to talk about after all these years.'

'Why?' asked Rufio.

'Why? Because I haven't been a soldier in a long time. Because they were human beings, regardless of what they did. I never felt right about that night. In that moment, it was a desperate situation. So, I did what I had to do. It is hardly my proudest moment as a soldier, or as a man.'

'You did save my life, you know.'

'You are right,' said Benedict. 'I am glad I was there. I haven't forgotten the times you saved my life.'

'All in a day's work. Besides, they were only Hebrews.'

This irritated Benedict, and it showed. 'What do you want to know about the girl, Rufio?'

'Still sensitive, I see.'

Benedict shook his head. 'I am asking what you want to know.' He wanted to get this conversation over with.

'Her name, Benedict. Do you remember her name?'

'How could it be important after all these years?' said Benedict sharply, his voice rising. 'Remind me, why were we looking for her in the first place?'

'You mean, aside from her parents attacking two Roman soldiers?'

'Yes, aside from that.'

'We had to question her.'

'Right.' He didn't believe Rufio. Not now, not then. Benedict folded his arms. 'Well, I don't remember her name.'

'Does "Seraphina" sound familiar?'

'No, not at all.' Benedict's eyes flickered, just slightly.

Rufio noticed and was quick to question his old friend further.

'That was quick. You didn't even think about it, Benedict. What is going on here?'

'Nothing is going on. You asked me a question and I answered.'

'I thought I could come here and talk to an old friend,' said Rufio. 'It's an important matter to me.'

'You can always talk to me. I simply don't remember. I also don't see the importance after all these years.'

'Well, it would be important to tell the girl what happened that night. Don't you think?'

'I thought you said it was to question her,' said Benedict.

'Back then, we would have questioned her as to why her parents attacked us. We also would have told her what happened. That we acted in self-defence.'

'I suppose. So, what happened? Did you find the girl after all this time?'

'Possibly.'

'Possibly?'

'There is a girl working at the library. The curator says his caretaker hired her. That she looks distinctly Hebrew. It seems like too much of a coincidence. A girl passing herself off as Egyptian, who looks Hebrew, living in the Great Library.'

'That's where her parents died,' whispered Benedict.

'Yes, the woman attacked me near the library.'

'It never made sense to me. What were they doing in that part of the city so late at night?' asked Benedict.

'Waiting for a Roman soldier to attack, obviously.'

'It seems odd to say the least.'

'So, you can't remember her name? For two days afterwards, we looked for her. Through the Hebrew village, around the harbour, on the edges of the city. I thought you would remember her name.'

'I don't.'

'Benedict, I am now the governor and protector of this region. I consider it a great responsibility. When that woman attacked me all those years ago, I had no idea why. It pained me that both she and her husband had to die, but I do believe we did our duty. That girl may have no idea what happened, and I would like to explain it to her. It is never too late to do the right thing, old friend.'

'That is very noble, Rufio.' He knew that whatever Rufio's intentions for the girl, they were not noble.

'Are you sure that "Seraphina" wasn't her name?'

'It really was a long time ago. I do recall her name began with an 's.' It was a long name. Seraphina, Seraphina, it could be.'

'Are you sure?'

'No,' said Benedict. 'As I said, I don't know. The name could be familiar. We searched for two whole days, but it was so long ago.'

Rufio decided to quit. 'Thank you, my friend. I'd hate to trouble the wrong person. If it is her, maybe she'll appreciate finding out the truth.'

'Maybe. I hope it goes well.'

'It was good to see you. Take care of yourself.'

'Let's do this again soon. I would love to see Quintus.'

'Yes, I live at the camp now. No longer in the barracks. I'll be sure to invite you. Goodbye for now.'

He walked up the path and out of the small farm.

Benedict is still soft, thought Rufio.

He knew his friend had not wanted to confirm Seraphina's name, but he was easy to manipulate. Benedict had the weakness of hoping for the best in people. It made him unfit as a soldier, and it was a good thing he had left the army, but he had proven very useful in this instance.

Now Rufio had to arrange a meeting with this Seraphina.

It was a meeting he had waited eleven years for.

TWENTY THREE

The Hindus had a lot of wisdom to share. She had found another scroll. This one spoke of the importance of forgiveness and empathy. It was fast becoming one of her favourite topics.

This is brilliant stuff, she thought. *Why have I never read this stuff before?*

She had always focused on Greek and Roman texts, which was common.

Some value was placed on Egyptian teachings.

The works of Hindu and Persian minds were harder to find in the library. Seraphina had never been taught by anyone, except maybe Afiz, yet the very layout of the library had influenced her education.

Seraphina read rapidly. The importance of forgiveness was a new fascination. She had never considered the notion of forgiving oneself but today, it was pertinent.

Often, she had found herself reading a scroll that was relevant to her state of mind. Years ago, she had read about divine order. The idea of divine order was that everything happened as it was meant to. Seraphina had dismissed it at the time but after her memories returning, it almost seemed obvious.

She continued to read.

The conflict within her was palpable. On the one hand, the idea of forgiving herself gave her relief, but on the other, the thought of forgiving those soldiers repulsed her. Maybe that was selfish. Is one person more deserving of forgiveness than another? Are some acts unforgivable?

Seraphina didn't know the answers to these questions. She only knew how she felt, but that was of no help, though. As Yadira had said, that was her pain talking.

Seraphina knew the importance of letting emotions go. She was also wise enough to know that acting on emotion was not always the best course of action.

If forgiveness is so important, then surely everyone deserves it? What about people who feel no remorse for the things they do? Seraphina stopped herself.

She could sense an eternal stream of questions arising. That would get her nowhere. She wondered what other seventeen-year-old girls were doing right then. Living a family life, looking after their community, helping their parents.

She doubted any of them were considering such deep questions, and in that moment, she yearned for a simple existence.

Seraphina shook her head. She loved learning, and the way her mind worked.

She had no idea what other seventeen-year-old girls were like, and she did not care.

Other people could live their lives as they wished, but Seraphina had big dreams, and was determined to pursue them.

I will ask Gisgo, she thought. *After all, he is a philosopher. He will be able to shed some light on this.*

She had to talk to Afiz too, but not about this. She was worried about that conversation, but it was important. Hiding the truth from Afiz was another thing she would have to forgive herself for.

She continued to read, and saw a word she had never previously seen.

Mudra

According to the text, mudras were first used as a part of chanting ceremonies then their importance extended to cultural and religious occasions, until they were eventually adopted into meditative practices.

As she read, she saw descriptions of different mudras which seemed to be a way of holding and positioning one's fingers; a hand gesture that was held during meditation.

It said that such gestures enhanced the flow of energy throughout the body, improving the effect of meditation. Each mudra had a different focus. She scanned the text, looking for one for forgiveness.

Seraphina had come to enjoy meditating, and a new style might be interesting, especially with a new focus.

The text spoke mainly about sitting in certain positions and regulating the breath. Some of the seated positions sounded funny to her, but she was willing to try.

There it was! A mudra for forgiveness. The thumb extended over the middle finger, to form a ring. All the other fingers remain extended. She made the shape with her hand, but it felt awkward.

It is worth a try, she thought.

She wondered how much focus she would get, sitting in an odd position with her fingers oddly crossed.

There is no time like the present, Seraphina thought. She kept the text in front of her, reading it for guidance. She sat on the ground and folded her legs into position.

I am tilted backwards.

She had to use her hands to pull her buttocks into a proper sitting position.

There.

Now, the hands. She made the same shape with both hands, extending her other fingers. The mudra made a small circle in each hand.

I am sitting here, cross legged and cross fingered. Imagine if Imhotep or Afiz walked in right now. They would either be very confused or fall over laughing. Maybe both.

If I want to be a scholar, I must conduct experiments. I guess this is one of my first.

Seraphina started to breathe.

Wait, what am I meant to do now?

She opened her eyes and looked back to the text. Breathing techniques were described in great detail. She started to read again. She was very uncomfortable, so she unfolded herself and sat back on the bed, continuing to read. It seemed that breathing was the most important thing in meditation.

This will involve a lot of practice, she thought.

As she continued, it was apparent to her that meditation was the union of several practices: breathing, sitting in a certain way, mudras. It was all so alien to her, but she was riveted.

The Trataka meditation had worked so well, after all.

It would be good to try this. The guilt had been weighing on her. She could rationalise, tell herself it was not her fault, but it wasn't that simple.

Seraphina believed in cause and effect.

If she had not run out of the house that night, her parents would be alive. She could point to countless other factors: she was six years old, the soldiers had killed her parents, she had not intended anything bad to happen, but in the end, it all came down to that simple fact. Cause and effect. There was no escaping it. Maybe in time, she could learn to forgive herself.

Forgiving those soldiers might be a part of moving on.

She finished the text and decided to try one more time, so she got back into a seated position called an *asana*, according to the text. Such odd words. Then she got her fingers positioned for the forgiveness mudra. Next, the breathing technique. *Pranayama.*

Seraphina began to breathe according to the technique. After a few minutes, her body felt relaxed. She no longer felt awkward in the seated position. More breathing. The hand position started to feel natural. She thought of her parents, and that six-year-old running through the night. Hiding there in the street, afraid of the soldiers.

This doesn't feel good. Maybe I should stop.

She persevered. Her body was still relaxed, the breathing still flowing. She imagined being back there, in that dark alley.

Alone. Scared. Crying.

She told herself it would be alright.

I forgive myself.

The thought soothed her. She felt as though she was in two places. In that room, high above the library and in that alley, all those years ago.

I forgive myself.

My parents loved me.

I forgive myself.

She felt lighter. Her shoulders relaxed. It felt like she took in more air with each breath. She sat taller.

I forgive myself.

It was not my fault.

I forgive myself.

Her body started to feel different. Like it was in a rhythm. It was a new sensation. Each breath seemed to energise both her body and the room around her.

I forgive myself.

I forgive myself.

I forgive myself.

I forgive myself.

I forgive myself.

She saw herself in that alley. Her steady breathing continued. The state of relaxation was now total. She could still see her younger self. However, now it felt peaceful. She could think of that moment and know that everything was going to be fine.

She opened her eyes. She felt at ease for a few moments. A feeling of worry returned to her.

Things aren't going to go away that easily, but it's a start.

Suddenly, she was distracted.

An aroma had crept into her room.

Cinnamon. Turmeric. Cumin.

Afiz was cooking! She loved it when Afiz cooked, and it had been a while. He only cooked at night, when it was just the two of them. Well, three, including Maximus. The pup, who was always hungry, would often score a bone or a small bowl of broth to feast on. She jumped up off the floor and put the scroll away, her excitement waning for a moment. It was time to have that conversation with Afiz. She could not put it off any longer, so she walked downstairs slowly, thinking of what she would say.

TWENTY FOUR

Afiz stirred the chicken in the clay pot. The aroma was delicious, and it reminded him of his mother. She had cooked this dish for him as a child, and many years ago, he had asked her how to make it. The memory of his mother teaching him to cook was among his fondest of her. He smiled as he prepared the meal. Cooking his mother's recipes was something that always brought him joy.

He heard Seraphina's footsteps before he saw her.

'Seraphina, come in here,' said Afiz. 'I am making one of your favourites. Spiced chicken.'

'I smelled it,' said Seraphina. 'I am starving.'

'How was your day?'

'Alright.'

'Is everything alright? You're very quiet.'

Seraphina nodded.

Afiz put down the plate in front of her. 'Alright, here you are.'

Seraphina looked down at the plate. It was laden with bread, vegetables, and a generous serving of Afiz's delicious chicken.

'This looks amazing,' she said.

'I thought you might like it. My mother's finest.'

'What was your mother like, Afiz?'

'A gentle, loving woman. Full of grace.'

'I would have loved to have met her.'

'She would have adored you, I'm sure.'

'I have something to tell you, Afiz,' said Seraphina.

'What is it?'

Seraphina sighed. 'I'm just going to come out and say it. I have been sneaking out of the library at night.'

Afiz didn't visibly react. 'I see. How long has this been going on?'

'You're so calm.'

'It's one of my finest traits,' said Afiz.

Seraphina giggled. Afiz had surprised her. 'It is. Very well. It has been going on for years.'

'Your secret passageway?'

'Yes.'

'If I remember correctly, you found that passageway not long after you started living here.'

'That's right.'

'All that time,' muttered Afiz.

'Yes.'

'Eleven years?'

'Give or take.'

'I have a question,' said Afiz.

'Only one? You are taking this very well.' Afiz was a constant source of surprise to Seraphina.

'Why are you telling me this now? If you have been doing this for over a decade, why the sudden need to confess?'

Seraphina looked down at her food but couldn't find the words to reply.

'Not hungry?' said Afiz.

'It's not that. I'm so sorry, Afiz,' said Seraphina, now crying.

Afiz came around the counter and sat next to her. He placed a hand on her shoulder.

'Come on, Seraphina, tell me what's going on. You're not giving me the full story.'

'It will take a while.'

She sobbed.

'We have plenty of time.'

Seraphina took a deep breath and started to tell the story. She began with her night-time adventures as a child. She told him how she would wander the streets, making sure to avoid Roman patrols. She told him about the harbour and its peacefulness at night. She shared with him how she explored the city and knew nearly every street and building. He asked her if there was anything else she had to tell, so she continued, telling him about seeing Yadira that night. She told him about going back to where they had followed her. Then she mentioned her house, as well as Saul and Joshua. Finally, she told him about visiting her childhood home.

He listened with concern when she mentioned breaking down and fainting. She shared with him about her lost memories, and how they had come back to her. Hesitating for a moment, she told him about Quintus. She described how they had met, and their twilight meeting. She decided to hold back the part about the kiss.

Afiz sat in silence and ate his meal. Seraphina felt like a weight had lifted from her, having told him everything. She had expected a reaction though. She ate too, and enjoyed the warm, tasty food.

'Are you going to say something, Afiz?'

'I am thinking,' he said between bites.

'Alright.'

They both finished their meals. Afiz took the plates and walked to the other side of the counter. He set them down next to the clay pot. He then took a seat opposite Seraphina.

'Firstly, thank you for telling me all this. I know it wasn't easy. I can only imagine what you have been going through.'

'Is that it?'

'I am upset, Seraphina. I won't lie to you. I wish you could have told me some of this sooner.'

'I should have, Afiz. I am sorry.'

'I accept your apology. We have to think of what to do now.'

'What do you mean?'

'Well, you are not a child anymore. This isn't a matter of me giving you rules to follow. You never were much for rules anyway. My concern is for your safety. The Hebrew woman and her family, do you trust them?'

'I do,' she said. 'They were friends of my parents.'

'How do you know for sure?'

'She saved things belonging to my mother. There was also a table.'

'A table?'

'Yes. I remember playing underneath it as a child and sitting down to dinner with my parents.' Seraphina began to weep again.

'We don't have to talk about everything right now,' said Afiz.

'I want to.' She sobbed then continued once she calmed down. 'I have felt so terrible, holding all this back from you. It feels good to get it out.'

'You poor thing.'

'They are good people, Afiz. Yadira told me a lot about my parents. She told me about attacks on Hebrew women. The disappearances that happened.'

'What?'

'Around the time my parents were killed, a lot of Hebrew women were disappearing. She told me a story about a woman who had escaped with her life. She was attacked by Roman soldiers.'

Afiz stopped breathing for a moment. He remained silent and could hear his heart thumping in his chest.

'What is it, Afiz?'

'Nothing, I think,' said Afiz. 'It was so long ago.'

'What?' Seraphina opened her arms wide.

'Maybe I know why Imhotep was acting so strangely.'

Seraphina's eyes widened. 'What do you mean?' she asked.

'Remember the other day, when I introduced you to him?'

'Yes, you said you were surprised at how well he took it.'

'I was. It was very unlike him.'

'And now?' she said.

'A couple of days after I first took you in, I was clearing some shelves. Imhotep was closing the library doors. A pair of Roman soldiers arrived. They had a long conversation. The soldiers seemed agitated. An argument erupted, and the soldiers wanted to search the library. I had no idea what they could be looking for. As I walked towards the front, Imhotep gestured for me to stay back.'

Seraphina leaned forward. 'So, what happened?'

'The soldiers left. One of them seemed to threaten Imhotep before he went. I couldn't hear the conversation.'

'The soldiers were looking for me?'

'Maybe.' Afiz held his chin, as a thin layer of sweat began to form on his forehead.

'Maybe? What else could it have been about?'

'I don't know. This all seems so surreal.'

'Imhotep thinks I am the girl they were looking for. That's what you think?' Seraphina stared down at the table, deep in thought.

'That is quite farfetched.'

'Maybe not,' said Seraphina. 'There were Roman soldiers looking for me in the Hebrew village recently.'

'What did you just say?'

'Joshua told me. Not just any soldiers either. According to Joshua, they were the general's private guards.'

'Why would a general be looking for you? Especially in the Hebrew village.'

'I have no clue. Did Imhotep ask where I lived?'

'No,' said Afiz. 'So far as I know, he thinks you're Egyptian.'

Seraphina's head dropped. She held the top of her head with her hands. Roman soldiers. Generals. Shadows from the past. Her memories, and the guilt that came with them.

'What do I do, Afiz?'

Afiz shook his head. 'I don't know. For now, I think you have to keep as low a profile as possible.'

'Do I go back to hiding?' Seraphina didn't like that idea so soon after gaining a little freedom.

'No, that would be too suspicious. Continue to work in the library as you have been. The scholars have been complimenting your work. They love how you keep everything in order.'

'Well, that's nice, I suppose.'

'You are doing a great job, Seraphina.'

'Thank you. I wonder if my days here are numbered.'

Afiz shook his head. 'Nothing is going to happen to you, Seraphina. If you leave here one day, it will be because you choose to.'

'What do you mean?'

'Well, do you want to live in a library forever? Even one as grand as ours? I just think there are bigger things waiting for you. A bigger life.' He threw his arms wide as if he was trying to catch the whole world.

'I hope so.'

'I have no doubt.'

The two smiled for the first time since the conversation began.

'So, I keep working in the library as if nothing is wrong?'

'Yes,' said Afiz.

'What if I run into soldiers for any reason?'

'Hopefully that does not happen.'

'And if it does?'

'Speak to them only in Coptic or Latin.' Afiz nodded, his eyebrows raised. 'Stick with the story we have always had. You work in the library and you live on the other side of the lake.'

'I suppose that's all I can do, right?'

'Right, but it won't come to that, Seraphina.'

'What makes you so sure? Yadira said I should run away.'

'To where?'

'To Israel, or Judah. She said I would be safe there. Maybe I could go back to Valentia with Gisgo.' She smiled at her own joke.

'I am sure he would love that.'

'Very well. I'll stick to the routine here at the library.'

'Good. Can you manage to stay inside at night too?'

'I think so.'

'Seraphina, this could be serious. Please, promise me. No wandering the city at night.'

'I thought you said no rules.'

'I said you wouldn't follow them anyway. Will it do me any good to forbid it?'

'I was dreading this conversation, you know.' She stared at the table again.

'I can imagine.'

'You didn't react how I thought you would.'

'What did you think I would do?'

'I don't know. Yell. Be angry.'

'That's not like me, Seraphina,' he said.

'I suppose not.'

'As I said, your safety is my concern. So, what are you going to do, and how are you going to be safe about it?'

'I've never been spotted once at night.'

'That you know of.'

'Right.'

'Yadira spotted you that one time.'

'Right again, but she was looking for me. Does that count?'

'I think so.'

'What do you want me to say, Afiz?'

'I want you to be able to talk to me,' said Afiz. 'You are like a daughter to me. I would prefer to know what is happening. That is far better than you hiding things from me.'

'I love you, Afiz.'

'I love you too, my dear.'

'I'll be honest, Afiz. I want to go back and talk to Yadira and her family. I will be very careful. You know how well I know the city. I won't be seen.'

'What about Quintus?'

'I want to see him again.'

'He is a Roman, correct?'

'Yes.'

'I think it's dangerous, Seraphina.' Afiz didn't want to lecture her but needed to express his fears. 'Especially with everything that's going on at the moment.'

'I know. I will be careful.'

'It's not just that. There is a lot of tension in the city. Rumours are spreading that civil war may break out any day now. There are likely to be more Roman soldiers on the street.'

'I will be extra careful.' She looked back up at Afiz, so he could see the determination in her face.

'You are practically an adult, Seraphina. I will not tell you what to do. Please promise me one thing.'

'What is that?' she asked.

'Consider what I have said to you. Seriously.'

'I promise I will,' said Seraphina.

'Thank you.'

'You are welcome.'

'Very funny. Well, I suppose one of your wishes has come true after all these years.' Afiz allowed himself a chuckle.

'Which one is that?'

'You are making plenty of new friends.'

'I suppose you're right. Speaking of which, when can I go back to the museum with you and Gisgo? Maybe we could see Khay again?'

'Before I know it, you'll have charmed an entire generation of scholars.' Afiz laughed louder this time.

'What would be so bad about that?'

'All I will end up doing is making appointments for you.'

'Like I said, what would be so bad about that?'

'I'm glad to see your sense of humour hasn't been lost in all this.'

'Never,' said Seraphina.

'So, this Quintus, what is he like?'

'A lovely young man, Afiz. I am sure you would like him.'

'Hopefully I will get to meet him,' he said.

'Do you think things will blow over? I would love for everything to go back to normal. Well, not everything.'

'You'd like some things to go back to normal. Then for others to remain as they are now. Is that about right?' he asked.

'Exactly.'

'Maybe it will work out the way you want it to. Then again the world doesn't usually work so smoothly.'

'I can always hope,' said Seraphina.

'True. It's getting late. Did you have enough to eat?'

'I did. Thank you. For everything.'

'No problem. Let's make sure we talk if anything else comes up, alright?'

'I promise.'

'Goodnight. Sleep well.'

Seraphina left the kitchen feeling much better. It was a good thing Afiz had called it a night.

She had a date.

TWENTY FIVE

Quintus sat in the small boat. His body swayed from side to side, and the edge of the boat knocked against the wall. He took a deep breath, and the sea's saltiness invaded his nostrils. His eyes were fixated on a spot along the wall, his foot tapping against the floor of the boat.

Quintus closed his eyes and relived the memory of Seraphina kissing him. He smiled and sighed. The thought soothed him. He couldn't wait to surprise her.

Imagine if his father could see him now. In a stolen fishing boat, waiting for a girl in the middle of the night. An Egyptian girl, at that. He would hit the roof. It wasn't so ridiculous, he reasoned to himself. He was only borrowing the boat, not stealing it.

She appeared at the water's edge and was easy to spot. She looked so beautiful. He started to row the small boat, the sound of the waves covering his approach. Seraphina sat on the wall and looked up to the sky. He wondered what she was thinking. She looked so peaceful. He continued to row, until he was practically at her feet. She didn't notice him. She was engrossed in the stars above.

'Psst. Down here,' whispered Quintus loudly.

Seraphina looked down with great amusement. A smile formed at the edge of her lips.

'Surprise,' said Quintus.

'Hello there. Am I supposed to get in?' she asked.

'Of course. I am taking you for a romantic boat ride. A perfect night for it, wouldn't you say?'

Seraphina dropped into the small boat, landing on her feet with ease. She draped her arms over Quintus' shoulders and gave him a soft kiss.

'I certainly would.'

Quintus wrapped his arms around her waist. He brought her body closer to his and kissed her back. It was a natural reaction. Distracted, he let go of the oars. He scrambled as he grabbed one, nearly falling into the water in the process. Seraphina caught the other one with ease.

'A tad clumsy tonight, aren't we?' she said.

'Sorry. My attention got diverted.'

'That's understandable. I don't really blame you, you know,' she said, laughing.

That smile. It is magnetic, thought Quintus.

She had a great sense of humour too.

'One thing is for sure,' said Quintus.

'What's that?' asked Seraphina.

'We'll never need to worry about your confidence levels.'

'I take that as a compliment.'

'Glad to hear it. Now, are you ready?'

'Absolutely. Where are we headed, Captain?'

'You will see.'

Quintus rowed and the two of them talked. He took her further to the east, where the city ended, and the countryside began. She admired the beautiful moonlit landscape which was all new to her. She looked at Quintus, who was rowing and talking. Their eyes met, and they smiled at each other.

'Thank you,' said Seraphina.

'For what?'

'All of this. The surprise, showing me things I've not seen before. This is only the second time I've been on a boat.'

'Is this better than the first time?'

'I'd say so. The first time involved a trip to buy some spices.'

'Spices?' Quintus looked puzzled, screwing up his eyebrows.

'It's a long story.'

They laughed, and Quintus continued to row. He would point out various things, and Seraphina listened with fascination. She sat and watched it all pass by because, at that moment, she felt like she didn't have a care in the world. As they continued, a large wall appeared in the distance. They got closer, and Seraphina saw what looked like a fortress.

'What is this place?' asked Seraphina.

'This is Columbarium.'

Seraphina shook her head, needing more of an explanation.

'The fortified Roman camp.'

'Oh. This is where you live?' she asked.

'Yes. Speak a little softer. There are sentries who keep watch at night.'

'Sorry,' Seraphina whispered.

She looked at the camp. It had an eerie feel to it, silent, yet foreboding. It was vast, bigger than any structure she had seen before. The thick wooden logs that formed its wall were imposing, each one ending in a sharp spearhead. The camp was quiet, but it exuded strength and power.

They were far enough away that no one could hear them, although a curious soldier might spot them, but no alarm would be sounded for a harmless fishing boat. Seraphina wanted to get out of there.

Quintus sensed her discomfort. 'Come on, there's something else I want to show you.'

He rowed away, towards the horizon. Before long, the coastline was far off in the distance. They were surrounded by water and sky.

'It's beautiful here,' said Seraphina.

'I know. I have come out here a few times before, always alone. After I saw you last time, I knew I wanted to share this place with you. Only you.'

Seraphina smiled and leaned over to him. Her hand grazed

the side of his face, and she kissed him. It was a long kiss, gentle yet passionate. She turned her body so her back faced his chest and rested against him.

'Is this comfortable?' she asked.

'Sure is.'

They sat in the cradle of the boat, looking up at the sky and talking. Seraphina pointed out constellations. Quintus listened with interest. He was in awe of her mind. She would talk about a star. Then she would speak about the science of astronomy. The topic would then shift to the way that waves worked. As he listened to her, their fingers intertwined. Then he wrapped his arms around her.

Seraphina's cheeks flushed. It felt so nice, sitting there in his arms.

'Is this comfortable?' he asked.

'Sure is.'

The two laughed in unison. It was becoming a habit. Quintus sighed with pleasure, and for a while they sat there in silence. Seraphina took it all in: the rocking of the boat above the soft waves; the sky in all its brilliance, lit by the moon and stars; the warm embrace of this beautiful young man; the fresh scent of the night air.

She could feel his breath against her neck. It was a pleasant sensation. She squeezed his hands. Seraphina had never been so happy.

Divine order, she thought. *This is exactly where I am meant to be at this moment.*

'Are you glad you met me, Quintus?' said Seraphina, turning to face him.

'Of course,' he said. 'How about you?'

'Yes. I don't think I have ever been this happy.'

'Me neither.' He sighed.

'So, do you remember the unanswered questions from our last meeting?'

'I do. I think I was meant to tell you what my father and I were arguing about, and ...'

'I was meant to tell you where I live.'

'So, who goes first?'

'I probably should. Before I answer the question, I want to tell you some things. There has been a lot going on in my life recently. Unexpected things, some good, some not so good. The point is that you have been a bright spot during a difficult time. So, is it alright if I take it slow in sharing certain details with you?'

'Of course,' said Quintus.

'I'm so relieved you said that.'

'You were worried, huh?'

'I was.'

'You don't need to be. I'm glad you asked.'

'Are all Roman boys so understanding and wonderful?' Seraphina said.

'No. I'm a rare breed.'

'Lucky me, I guess.'

'You guess?' he said.

Seraphina laughed.

'So, you were going to tell me where you live?' said Quintus with an encouraging squeeze.

'Yes. I live in the library.'

'What do you mean, you live in the library?'

'I was orphaned as a young child, and that is where I ended up. I have been living there ever since.'

Quintus was still, his mouth wide open.

'Hello?'

'Uhhh…' he said.

'Some of the things I mentioned are related to how I became an orphan. Those are the things I can't tell you about just yet.'

'Very well, but why?' said Quintus.

'All I can say is that it is very complicated. I promise to tell you everything when the time is right.'

Quintus gave her hand a soft squeeze. 'That's good enough for me, my dear.'

She hugged him tightly. She felt her body relax as they held each other.

'Thank you for understanding.'

Quintus sensed a lot was happening. Maybe it was best for him not to know for now. He was very curious, but would not pry. Her honesty was admirable, after all she didn't need to tell him anything. The fact she had told him any of it showed that she trusted him, and he felt he could trust her too.

This young woman is remarkable, he thought, not for the first time.

'So, you were going to tell me …'

'About what my father and I were discussing,' he said.

'Yes.'

'I'm about to finish my studies here in Alexandria, and I want to go to Rome to study. There are excellent colleges there, and I am also interested in learning directly from a scholar, someone who could be a mentor to me. I am fascinated by the sciences, engineering in particular.'

'That all sounds amazing.'

'It would be. My father has great connections through the military, and he knows lots of influential people. I was talking to him to see if he would contact colleges for me. I was hoping to visit Rome and see these places, maybe even meet a renowned scientist, or an engineer. He could open those doors for me.'

'What did he say?'

'He listened for a while, but he was just pretending. There is only one thing he has ever wanted me to do.'

'What's that?'

'Become a Roman soldier, of course.' Quintus grunted his annoyance.

'When you could go and study? That seems like such a waste.'

'That's what I said.'

'The idea of having a scholar as a mentor.' Seraphina sighed. 'That would be a dream come true.'

'For me too.'

'Sorry, I interrupted. You said he was pretending?'

'The entire conversation was a manipulation. He only acted like he cared. He guided the conversation towards my views on the military. He then accused me of being closed-minded. He said I did not appreciate the benefits of the military to society.'

'Many great minds have written of its importance,' said Seraphina. 'The military stabilises a situation after an armed conflict. Strong armies keep the peace as a deterrent to war. There are other benefits, but none of them matter if you know what you want to do with your life.'

Quintus was speechless again.

'What?' she asked.

'Your mind. I'm not sure I can keep up. You're brilliant.'

Seraphina smiled at the compliment. 'Why thank you. Will you take me with you to Rome? We can study together.'

'I love that idea,' said Quintus.

'That really would be a dream come true.' Seraphina shook her head. 'Sorry, I interrupted again.'

'It's alright.'

'How did the conversation end?'

'He insisted that I go to a training camp for six months. After that, we would talk about my future.'

'A camp like Columbarium?'

'Yes. You didn't like it, did you?'

'No. It's a spooky place.'

'A little less so in the daytime, but I know what you mean.'

'Do you like living there?' Seraphina shook her head anticipating the answer.

'No. That is one of the reasons I was excited about leaving.'

'What will you do?'

'Sail away with you, of course,' said Quintus. 'In fact, that is why I brought you here.'

'Really?'

She knew it was a joke, but part of her wanted it to be true. How nice that would be. To run away with Quintus and leave all this behind. It was a fanciful idea, but she knew she couldn't leave. Not before everything in Alexandria was resolved.

'Maybe one day.' Quintus laughed.

'Maybe. Seriously though, what will you do?'

'I'm not sure. One thing I do know is that I will never, ever enlist in the Roman army.'

'You obviously feel strongly about this. Why is that?'

'My father. I do love him. He raised me and taught me a lot. I will always be grateful for that, but he is not a good man. He looks down on people. Thinks that Romans are superior. He has always been a military man. I think those views represent the worst instincts of the Roman army. I do not want to be part of any of that.'

'That must be difficult.' Seraphina held him tighter.

'What's that?'

'To feel so conflicted about someone whom you love.'

He raised his eyebrows. She had articulated exactly how he felt.

'It is,' said Quintus. 'My destiny lies on a different path to his. He just refuses to accept that.'

Seraphina smiled at him. 'I like the sound of your path.'

'Oh, do you now?'

'Yes. In fact, I think you have copied some of my ideas. Are you a mind reader, Sir Quintus?'

'I might be,' he said. 'Do you feel like your mind is being read right now?'

'Maybe.'

'Like I can tell what you are thinking at this precise moment?'

'I don't know. Why don't you tell me, so we can find out?'

He leaned forward and kissed her. It was a deep kiss, the touch of his hands on her face gentle, his lips pressed just hard enough against hers.

'That you want me to kiss you,' he said, breaking away, but keeping his face close to hers.

'That is some good mind reading, young sir.'

'Now, sit back, beautiful Seraphina. This night is not over yet.'

'More surprises?' She fanned herself, imitating a dramatic actress.

Quintus laughed at her theatrics. 'Just one more.'

He began to row again, back towards the city. As their boat cruised the waters, they continued to talk. About everything. Constellations, places to study, things they knew about the city. They joked with one another and teased each other. On this night, on that very sea,

Seraphina and Quintus were falling in love. They both felt it, but neither would speak of it.

Not just yet.

Quintus neared their destination. He waited for Seraphina's reaction. She was laughing, and then he saw it. She froze and looked in awe at what was in front of her. Quintus turned the boat and sat next to her. He wanted to share this moment with her. They looked upon the majestic Pharos Lighthouse, its light shining out over the water.

'This is incredible, Quintus,' said Seraphina. 'I have never seen it like this, from the water.'

'A bit different from this angle, huh?'

Seraphina nodded. 'That's an understatement.'

'Do you know how it works?' he said quietly.

'No, actually.'

'A gap in your knowledge?' Quintus laughed. 'I'm shocked.'

'Just tell me how it works.'

'Very well. Can you see that fire burning in the tower?'

Seraphina nodded.

'Inside there is a large bronze plate. It turns to reflect the light of the fire out into the sea. That light guides ships coming in and out of the harbour at night.'

'Incredible,' said Seraphina.

'Why thank you.'

'I was referring to the lighthouse. Your explanation was excellent also. You will be a great engineer.'

'I'm flattered. If I am to be an engineer, what will you do?'

'Who knows, I have many talents,' said Seraphina with the slightest giggle to show it was meant as a joke rather than braggadocio. 'Perhaps I could be a great philosopher.'

'Interesting. Have you ever even met a philosopher?'

'I have, actually.'

'I forgot. You live in a library. What's that like?'

'It is wonderful. In so many ways. It's a long story though, and one I will have to tell you next time we meet.'

'You are right. It is very late. I should be getting back.'

Quintus rowed the short distance from the lighthouse to the dockside.

'Thank you for such a wonderful evening, Quintus,' said Seraphina.

'My pleasure. Here we are.'

'Will you be alright from here?'

'Of course,' said Quintus.

She pulled him close for a goodnight kiss. Then she hopped out of the boat, climbing up the wall with ease. Like an acrobat.

'Goodnight. Thank you again.'

'Sweet dreams, Seraphina. When can I see you again?'

'How about three nights from now? We can meet at the same place.'

'I'll be there,' said Quintus.

TWENTY SIX

Rufio listened as his guards gave their report. It was boring. He had asked them to find out as much as they could about the girl working in the library. They hadn't learned much. She was there every day. She worked with the caretaker. These things Rufio already knew. They had asked around the different parts of the city and had learned nothing.

'Different parts of the city!' Rufio interrupted. 'What parts of the city do you mean?'

'The centre of the city, where the Egyptians live. We questioned some people in the streets near the library. We learned nothing new. We even went to the Hebrew vill—'

'The Hebrew village!' Rufio yelled. 'Why on earth would you go to the Hebrew village?'

'I thought you said the girl was Hebrew,' said one of the guards with eyes wide with fear.

'Yes, you said she was Hebrew,' said the other.

Rufio shook his head at the guards. 'This shows that neither of you listened to my instructions. I said that there is an Egyptian girl working in the library, and that her name is Seraphina—'

One of the guards interrupted. 'Seraphina is a Hebrew name.'

'That's right. A Hebrew name,' said the other.

Rufio was furious. He stared deep into the eyes of both men, one after the other, then said in a quiet voice that was heavy with menace. 'It is bad enough that you are incompetent. Now you dare to interrupt me while I am speaking.'

'Sorry, sir.'

'My apologies, general.'

Rufio glared at both men again, just to make sure they understood how close to the line they had come. "As I was saying, there is an Egyptian girl named Seraphina working in the library. I said she might be Hebrew, but that I did not know. Did you see anything that made you think she was not Egyptian?'

'No, sir,' said the first guard. 'She spoke Coptic and Latin whenever we observed her. The people we spoke to who had met her were mostly vendors from the marketplace. They said she spoke perfect Coptic. Her clothes are typical for an Egyptian woman.'

'So, what compelled you to go to the Hebrew village?'

The guards were silent.

'What if she is a Hebrew?' asked Rufio quietly again, feeling his temper coming to the boil. 'Did it cross either of your thick skulls that going to their village would be a terrible idea?'

'I do not follow, sir,' said one of the guards.

'They would tell her we are looking for her!' yelled Rufio, finally exploding.

'Who would, sir?' asked the other guard, while shaking in his boots.

Rufio was exasperated. 'The Hebrews you spoke to!' he shouted.

The guards said nothing in response.

'I take it from your silence that you idiots understand now.'

'Yes, sir. We apologise.'

'We are very sorry, general,' said the second guard. 'We were just trying to find out as much as we could.'

'Your incompetence is equalled only by your stupidity. Get out!' he yelled at the top of his voice.

The guards retreated without another word and as quickly as they could before they felt the full force of the general's ire.

'Fetch Cato for me. Now!' yelled the general to a nearby servant.

'Yes, sir.'

A few minutes passed. Rufio heard footsteps and looked up to see a tiny man entering the room. Rufio, now relaxed, had his feet up on the table. Cato was one of Caesar's finest spies. Caesar had ordered he remain in Alexandria under Rufio's command. It was a show of great respect for the new general. It also underscored just how important Egypt was to Caesar.

'Cato, how are you?'

'I am well, sir. How are you today?'

'Frustrated, Cato. I need your help.'

'What can I do for you, sir?'

Rufio gave Cato his orders. He trusted the spy. For simplicity's sake, he stuck to the same story he had given Benedict. Cato listened as the general spoke. He knew of Rufio and his ruthlessness, and he knew Rufio did not care about telling this girl the truth about her parents, especially over a decade after what happened. Cato didn't care though. He was a spy, very good at what he did, and his job was to take orders and provide information, and because he had done his job well over the years, Caesar had rewarded him well. Cato knew that Rufio was a man who valued loyalty. He would do his duty and give the general what he asked for.

'She is not to be harmed in any way,' said Rufio. 'Is that clear, Cato?'

'Yes, sir,' said the spy.

'I need to know for certain that she is the girl I have been looking for.'

'I will not let you down, sir.'

'Thank you, Cato. Is there anything else you need from me?'

'No, sir. I will go to work, and report back soon. You will have what you need, I assure you.'

That was music to the general's ears. He wanted to take care of this little problem from the past, once and for all. He had far grander ambitions to pursue.

TWENTY SEVEN

Gisgo was fixated on the scroll in front of him, scribbling notes as he read, although he never took his eyes off the scroll. The 'notes' were illegible scrawls, a mishmash of his thoughts. Seraphina approached him, but the old philosopher did not see her, only noticing her once she had sat down in front of him.

'Seraphina, how are you?' said Gisgo, not looking up.

'Things are wonderful, Gisgo. How are you?'

'I am reading at the moment, Seraphina,' he muttered.

'Sorry. I will leave you to it.'

'Come back,' he said. 'Sit down. What is on your mind?'

'A few things, actually.'

'Well, start with one of them.' He pushed his scroll and notes to one side and clasped his hands on the table in front of him.

'Have you read much about the notion of forgiveness?' said Seraphina.

'The notion of forgiveness? I have read as much as you have, probably. Maybe more.'

'So, it is of interest to you?'

'Of great interest,' said Gisgo.

'Why?'

'Philosophers from our part of the world are yet to consider its importance. The ideas I have read about come from the lands to the east of here. There are also several fine philosophers from the Persian traditions who speak of forgiveness.'

'Yes, I have been reading a number of Hindu scrolls on this topic.'

'I have read some of those same texts,' said Gisgo.

'So, what do you think?'

'I believe forgiveness is important. It is a virtue not given much weight in the Roman world. The Hindu teachings make very good points. The Persians glorify the idea of forgiveness. Perhaps too much, to the point where they miss its essence. I have often thought of it from a scientific perspective.'

'What do you mean?' Seraphina creased her brow.

'I have read of experiments using magnets. How they will attract or repel depending on the way they are rubbed or held together. Aristotle has written a lot about his observations of nature. He talks at length about the motion of objects, gravity, and many other natural phenomena.'

'I am not sure I understand, Gisgo. What does any of that have to do with forgiveness?'

'My point is that everything in nature has a counterbalance. It may be an opposite, like water is to fire. It could be a contrary force, like gusts of wind that meet in a valley. Herbalists speak of the mutual relationship between plants and soil. There has always been injustice in our world. I believe forgiveness is its counterbalance.'

'I have never thought of it that way,' said Seraphina. 'So, you believe forgiveness is the natural way of things?'

'Yes, but it is not always so simple.'

'How do you mean?'

'Well, forgiveness involves human willingness. A willingness to forgive. We are creatures of instinct though. Our emotions, our reactions. Forgiveness is essential to the harmony of nature. That does not mean we will always forgive. Our tendencies as individuals, our human nature, can sometimes be to honour our emotions over our wisdom or knowledge.'

'So, what you are saying is that forgiveness is the right thing to do,' said Seraphina. 'But that we won't always do it because our emotions may get in the way.'

'Precisely. Injustice can hurt our feelings. It is not always so easy to forgive.'

'Can't you just look someone in the eye and say, "I forgive you"?'

'This is where the Hindu teachings are particularly valuable,' said Gisgo. 'They speak of the importance of releasing emotion. The simple speaking of words does not do that. I believe forgiveness is more important for the forgiver than the forgiven. The forgiver is released from those emotions. He, or in your case, she can move on. However, for there to be true forgiveness, you must mean it. Truly. In your heart. Then you can forgive, let go, and continue on the journey that is your life.'

'I see.'

'There is another aspect of forgiveness as well, Seraphina.' Gisgo locked on to Seraphina's eyes with his gaze.

'What is that?'

'The forgiveness of oneself,' he said.

'I have read about this.'

'It's more important than forgiving others.'

'Why?'

'Because our criticism of ourselves is always the harshest. We all fail from time to time. That is natural. We do not always accept it as a simple failure and move on, however. Often, we make the mistake of seeing ourselves as failures. That can compound over time. Do you remember the part about baggage? The baggage of unresolved emotions?'

'Yes.'

'That relates to our feelings about ourselves too,' said Gisgo.

'Very interesting. I have a question.'

'What is it?' The old scholar readied himself to be tested by her question.

'Well, most of the time I know if I am feeling a certain way about someone else. I always know if I feel wronged by someone. How would I know when I need to forgive myself for something?'

'An excellent question,' said Gisgo. 'I think the easiest way to know is if you feel bad about something you did. Or didn't do. Does that make sense?'

'Yes, I think so.'

'There is an easy way to do that.'

'What is it?' Seraphina sat up straight. An easy solution to such a difficult problem was an enticing thought.

'Well, typically in those situations we start telling ourselves how stupid we've been. We might feel regret, or even try to start fixing what has happened. Do any of those sound familiar?'

'Definitely.' She nodded.

'Good. Whenever you notice any of that, recognise what is really going on. Then, try to develop the practice of forgiving yourself instead of being hard on yourself.'

'So simple.'

'It is once you get used to it. Did I answer your question? I'm sorry if I started babbling.'

'Yes, you did,' said Seraphina. 'I mean, you did answer my question. You weren't babbling.'

'Good. Is anything else on your mind?'

'No. Thank you so much for taking the time to speak with me. I feel as though I learn so much more in a conversation like this than I do from reading a scroll.'

'You are always welcome. If that's the case, you should come join me in the museum some time.'

'Really? I would be honoured.'

'Of course. Khay was asking about you. I think he enjoyed meeting you.'

'I would love that.'

'Great. I'll let you know when I am going.'

'Wonderful. I shall see you then. Thanks again.'

'My pleasure.'

TWENTY EIGHT

Caesar and Cleopatra sat with Rufio as he gave them a report.

This meeting was unnecessary, Caesar thought.

It was for Cleopatra's benefit. She was worried about Ptolemy. She was convinced he was planning an attack on the city, but even if he was, Caesar knew that any such attack would be a failure, because his forces outmatched any that Ptolemy could amass.

He reclined on the luxurious chair and listened. His apathy irritated the young queen, who listened to the general's every word. Rufio gave a detailed summary of the Roman forces in the city including the Egyptian forces that remained loyal to Cleopatra.

He ran through the various scenarios for a possible attack and in all of them, their soldiers in the city would repel the attackers with ease. Cleopatra peppered him with questions. Rufio was forced to admit there were gaps in the intelligence they were working from. They didn't know how many men the young king commanded. However, they had a good estimation. Rufio kept saying that. It infuriated the young queen.

'An estimation!' she yelled. 'What you are saying is that you're guessing.'

'It is more complicated than that,' said the general.

'Do you even know where his forces are stationed?'

'No. That is to be expected though. It is only natural that they would hide.'

'That doesn't exactly fill me with confidence, General,' said Cleopatra.

'Why are you so worried?' asked Caesar. 'There is no need to give the general such a hard time. He knows what he is doing.'

'A hard time!' shouted Cleopatra. 'This man is charged with defending our city. If I do not ask questions of him, who should I ask? You?'

'I think you should remain calm,' said Caesar. 'I have every confidence in Rufio and our soldiers. They will do their job.'

'I think you underestimate Ptolemy's ambition.' Cleopatra fired the angry words across the room. 'It is fuelled by those vile henchmen of his. I may despise them, but they are veteran soldiers. They know these lands far better than you Romans.'

'In that case, the good general should not be here answering questions. He should be preparing our defences, wouldn't you say?'

'Fine. Please make sure you take every precaution, General. This city is important to me, and so are its people.'

'Of course, your majesty,' said Rufio. 'Farewell, Caesar.'

'Goodbye, Rufio. I shall see you on my return to Alexandria.'

Caesar sniggered at Cleopatra's comments. She cared for nothing but her throne. She spoke of the danger of her brother's ambition. It was her ambition that Caesar feared. He knew that she had not just taken him as a lover. It was a political alliance. One of Caesar's great gifts was foresight, and he knew what Cleopatra desired most. Like him, it was power. Truth be told, it was one of the things he loved about her, but he still had to be wary. Caesar could always see the good in any situation. This uprising, if it happened, would keep Cleopatra busy. Her other ambitions would be put on hold.

'You don't see Ptolemy as a serious threat?' said Cleopatra. It was more of a question than a statement.

'I do not.'

'Maybe Ptolemy is not, but Pothinus and Achillas are ambitious, capable men.'

'I have no doubt,' said Caesar.

'Yet you dismiss them as well.'

'I do.'

'Why, Caesar?'

'Because they are no match for me.'

'Your arrogance is a weakness in your thinking.'

'Interesting you say that. My thinking has served you well so far, has it not? You sit alone on the throne, don't you?'

'I apologise, Caesar,' said Cleopatra. 'I am just worried.'

'I understand. Perhaps I should explain what I meant. Pothinus is an excellent strategist, and Achillas may be an even better general than Rufio, so they may even overthrow the city. However, they cannot defeat the might of the republic. Even if they somehow took the city, they would not hold it for long. The trade that comes into the city would cease under their rule, and there would be instability. The city's economy would dry up. I would return with forces and take the city back. That would result in more bloodshed, and more lost wealth and who ultimately pays that cost? The people. Those people know the city is better off as it is. Even your father recognised the use of Roman influence. The city is thriving, it attracts a huge amount of sea trade, and it is a centre of knowledge and education. The lighthouse is known around the world. Ptolemy may want to go to war over your throne, but doing so will be damaging to the city and its people. Ultimately, we will prevail.'

'That was a good speech,' said Cleopatra.

'Thank you. You see my perspective now.'

'I do. It makes sense. There could be a lot of bloodshed though.'

'There could,' said Caesar. 'I hope to avoid it, but the decision lays with your brother and his men. I hope he does not seek to destroy a city out of pride, because if he does, we will defend it and its people.'

'I hope it does not come to that.'

Cleopatra could see why the man was revered. He always had a long-term strategy. He had gained control of the vast Roman Republic, and his abilities and methods could not be doubted. She didn't believe the part about defending the city and its people. She knew, just as Caesar did, the strategic importance of Egypt. Its resources and location were of huge benefit to Rome.

She did not care about his motives. She only cared that he would do what was necessary. Cementing her position on the throne was her priority, and in time, that would happen. She did not believe her brother capable of taking the city. Once he was captured and his forces eliminated, she would sleep much better at night.

Until then, she would trust Caesar and hope for the best.

TWENTY NINE

Cato was a chameleon. One of his gifts was that he could blend into any scene. His skin was dark for a Roman, and in Alexandria he could pass for an Egyptian. He was dressed as a common man and loitered near the library. He enjoyed Alexandria. It was a welcome change from the cutthroat environment of Rome. The centre of the republic was worse than usual these days. Senators fighting for power, factions within the military, it was ugly, and he was happy to be away from it all.

It was an odd mission he had been given. He never questioned orders though. It was not his place. Caesar had given Rufio the power to command him, so as far as Cato was concerned, Rufio's orders were Caesar's orders.

He chatted idly with a vendor on a street corner.

My Coptic is still good, he thought, as he spoke to the vendor in the local language.

Cato spoke a dozen languages, and always stayed in character.

He had followed the girl for a couple of days now, and there was nothing unusual for him to report although he would be patient, for if there was something to be discovered, he would know it in time.

Seraphina came out of the alley, a bag slung over her shoulder.

The caretaker was with her. They chatted as if it were just another day. She was tall. Not thin, but lean with a look of strength about her. To the unobservant, she was just another Egyptian woman walking on the street. Her clothing, her speech, the darkness of her skin, even her mannerisms — all were Egyptian without a doubt. It was her facial features that gave Cato some doubt. She looked Hebrew, and then again she also looked Egyptian. Cato guessed there was some mixed blood in her.

It helped her disguise.

Cato followed the pair, staying within earshot where possible. There was little to listen to, as Seraphina and the caretaker spoke of mundane things. They were out in the marketplace to run some errands.

He feigned interest in various items. He chatted with vendors. As he watched Seraphina, he noticed something dangling from her neck. It reflected the sunlight, silver, perhaps. He cut around the block and approached a corner, and the girl and the caretaker were only a few feet away. They were talking about something, but the noise of the marketplace muffled most of their words. He made out some of Seraphina's words. There was 'village' and 'soon.' Detecting tone was much easier. He could tell that the caretaker was worried about something.

Just then, a caravan passed. Cato moved to cross the street. He waited for the camels to pass. As he paused, he got a good look at Seraphina. She was only inches from him. He examined the necklace and noticed the Hebrew words engraved on it. Cato caught Seraphina's eye and he offered a friendly smile, and once the street was clear, he continued on his way.

Seraphina thought nothing of it.

THIRTY

Things were tense in the city. The rumours of the royal feud had spread. The siblings were fighting, and the young king had fled into the countryside. Some had chosen a side, but all agreed on one thing. They did not want a war.

Seraphina was uninterested in politics. She knew very little about Cleopatra, or Ptolemy, or even Julius Caesar. She, like others, feared the possibility of bloodshed in the city's streets. It made her think of the fearsome Roman camp, and she shuddered at the thought.

She wanted to clear her mind. She picked up Maximus off the ground and petted him. He had not received nearly enough attention of late. He rolled around on Seraphina, playful as ever. Seraphina smiled at the small dog. She had an idea.

'Want to go for a run, Maximus? Do you?'

The answer was always yes. His wagging tail only confirmed it. She grabbed him and before they knew it, they were sliding down the wall of the library. She poked her head around the corner. It was a few hours before midnight, but the sky was already black with just a faint moon to light the streets.

Perfect for a dash through the city, thought Seraphina.

She scanned the streets, and the coast was clear, so she gave Maximus a look, and he bolted first.

The two sprinted and leapt through the streets. Their steps were light, almost silent. Seraphina thought of Quintus and yearned to see him again. Tomorrow night was the night, and the thought of him brought a big smile to her face.

She saw a crate to her right and, stepping up with one foot, she pushed off it with the other, soaring into the air, somersaulting.

Whatever that feeling was, when she thought of Quintus, it filled her with awe. It was unlike anything she had ever experienced. It must be love, she thought. Love. I am in love. The thought sent her spinning into a series of cartwheels. Maximus ran alongside her, watching her roll down the street like a tumbleweed in a heavy wind.

They arrived at the waterfront. It was as still as ever. Seraphina looked off to her right, in the direction of Columbarium, thinking of her dear Quintus. Part of her wanted to run over there and see him.

Then she looked to her left where the lighthouse was in the distance, its bright light shining into the sea. It took her back to that evening, sitting next to him, looking up at the majestic structure.

The thought gave her goose bumps.

Everything felt at peace when she was with him.

It was a great feeling.

It was also a welcome one, given all that was going on. She thought of her parents. Did they ever come here? She hoped so. It was so beautiful. The thought of them sitting together on the wall made Seraphina smile. Wherever they were now, they were together. She believed that.

She took her mother's necklace in her hand, pressing her thumb against the silver. She ran a finger across the writing. Our love, she thought. She had remembered more about her parents, a little more came to her each day. Her mother, stern. Her father, playful. Both were loving. She hoped for a memory every day, for the rest of her life, but she knew they were gone, and only lived on now in Seraphina's memories.

She pressed the necklace between her hands, and a tear ran down her cheek. A thought crossed her mind, that she would have to let her parents go at some point, but she did not want to, when she had only just got them back.

The tears were now streaming down her face, and Maximus crawled up to her lap, licking her face with affection.

It made Seraphina giggle.

'I can always count on you, Maximus.'

Her gaze shifted away from the water to the streets. The Hebrew village. So much had happened in the last month. She could almost see Yadira's street from where she sat.

Seraphina got up and walked away from the harbour, entering the now familiar streets, inching past each house with hesitant steps. It was not fear, but uncertainty that she felt.

Maybe because I fainted last time I came here, she thought.

Maximus took her cue and followed at her heels.

The flames from the candles lit the street. Seraphina breathed in the familiar aroma. A few people sat outside their homes, enjoying the night's fresh air. Saul stood in his doorway and welcomed the unexpected guests.

'Come in,' he said.

'Thank you, Saul.'

'And who is this?'

'That is Maximus.' Saul had picked up the dog, who looked tiny in his massive hands. 'He likes you.'

'I like him too.'

'Hello, Seraphina,' said Yadira. She walked in from the back of the house. 'This is a nice surprise.'

'How are you, Yadira?'

'I am well. How are things with you?'

'Interesting, as usual,' said Seraphina.

'Let's sit down,' said Yadira.

The three sat, and Maximus busied himself by taking in his new surroundings. He sniffed the edges of the walls, tracing his way through the house. They watched him in amusement.

'Why have we never had a dog, Saul?' asked Yadira.

'There are plenty of strays on the street. You can take your pick,' said Saul.

She shook her head at him. 'Where did you get him, Seraphina?'

'In the alley behind the library, actually. He had been in a fight. I took him inside and looked after him, and he has been with me ever since.'

'How sweet of you. How are things at the library?' asked Yadira.

'Fairly normal. It has become routine in fact. I do my work, and everyone has got used to me being there.'

'Did you learn anything more from Afiz?'

'I did.'

Seraphina told them about the conversation she'd had with Afiz. The part about the soldiers in the library was chilling to Yadira. That they had threatened the curator was of no surprise.

'This happened two days after Afiz found you?' asked Yadira.

'That is correct.'

'I wonder if Afiz could describe the soldiers,' said Yadira.

'That wouldn't help much.'

'What do you mean?'

'It would just confirm they were the same soldiers searching the village all those years ago. What we need to know are their names.'

'I suppose you're right,' said Yadira.

'She is,' said Saul. 'I think we can safely assume they were the same soldiers. Two soldiers canvassing the city for a young Hebrew girl. Even if they were not the same soldiers, I'm sure they shared the same motive.'

'Have you thought about my suggestion?' asked Yadira.

'I have, Yadira. I have thought about it a lot. I will not leave Alexandria, at least not to flee. If I leave this city one day, it will be on my own terms. I will not run away from my parents' murderers. I don't care that they are powerful. I don't even care what they might do to me. I have to find out who they are.'

'Then what happens when you do find out?' asked Yadira.

'I don't know. There must be justice for my mother and father. I will tell who I can. Surely someone will care that innocent people were murdered?'

'They will not see it that way, Seraphina,' said Yadira. 'The story will never be that Rebekah and Josef were murdered. The soldiers will say whatever they need to. They attacked the soldiers. They were stealing and there was a struggle. I have seen it happen time and again. Besides, this was over ten years ago. There is no way to know if they are even still here.'

'Then why would Roman guards be looking for me?'

'Good point. So at least one of them is still here. Those guards were private guards to the general. Whoever is looking for you is a person of power.'

'How many generals are there in Alexandria?' said Seraphina.

'I have no idea. At least a few, I would guess.'

'Joshua might know,' said Saul.

'By the way, where is Joshua?' Seraphina looked around in case she had missed him.

'He's not here tonight. He lives near Lake Mareotis, where he has a farm,' said Yadira.

A mischievous grin was on Seraphina's face. 'Ahhh, I see. That is where I am supposed to live.'

'What do you mean? Where you are supposed to live?'

'Years ago, Afiz came up with a story,' said Seraphina. 'My cover story. Until recently, I never set foot in the library during the daytime. I often have gone into the city with Afiz to run errands, since I was quite young. So, if anyone ever asked me, or if I was discovered in the library, we had a story ready.'

'And that story is?' asked Yadira.

'That I live with my family on the other side of Lake Mareotis.'

'I see. Have you ever had to use this story?'

'No.'

'And now part of the story is that you work at the library?' asked Yadira.

'Yes, that's right.'

'So, what happens at the end of the day? When you are meant to go "home"?'

'That is one of my secrets.'

'I understand.'

'I'm joking, Yadira. I mean, it is a secret, but I trust you and Saul.'

Yadira and Saul both laughed and wanted to know.

'I have a secret passageway in and out of the library.'

'No!' said Saul. 'Really?'

'Yes. I leave the library through the front entrance. Then I go into the back alley behind the library. Then I use my secret entrance, and go up to the room I live in.'

'You've never been seen?' asked Yadira.

'Only the end of the alley is completely visible from the street. The rest is obscured. To notice me going in and out of the library, you'd have to be looking straight at me. I am very careful when coming in and out. Even if someone saw me go into the alley, they would think I am using the back door. Afiz and I come out of the back door when we go to run errands.'

'Unbelievable,' said Yadira.

'About a week ago now, I actually made a mistake, and I left my secret entrance uncovered. I was lucky, because no one was around, so I quickly ran back and closed it.'

'Sounds very lucky.'

'It was early in the morning, and the place was deserted. You are right though, I was very lucky. That could have been a disaster.'

'So, what brought you here tonight, my dear girl?'

'I hope I am not imposing, Yadira.'

'Not at all. I'm just curious.'

'I wanted to get out of the library and clear my head. A lot has been happening. The spot where you found me that night, it is my favourite place in the city. I like to sit there and think, look up at the stars, and relax. It has been a while since I took Maximus out for a run too.'

'You've always come to that spot at night?' asked Yadira.

'Yes, I have for many years. I have always felt drawn to that place.'

'I am sure you now know why.'

'I do.'

'So, at night, you sometimes sneak out of the library and go running through the streets with Maximus here?'

'Sometimes.'

'And to get out of the library, where you live, you use a secret passageway?'

'That's right.'

'It sounds like your life was fascinating even before all this happened.'

'That's true, but it was a lot calmer back then.'

'I hope I did the right thing in telling you.'

'Telling me what?'

'Everything.'

'You did, Yadira. I never could have imagined all that I have learned. I am still making sense of a lot of it, but I am glad I know. I have spent most of my life remembering nothing about my parents. Now I feel at least a bit connected to them.'

'They are with you. They always will be.'

'I hope so. I remember a bit more each day.'

'It was such a horrific thing, and you were so young. It's no wonder that your mind blocked your memories of the past.'

'Thank you for helping me through this.' Seraphina smiled at her.

'I don't know how much help I've been, but you are welcome.' She smiled back at the young woman before her.

'You've been amazing. I just have to find a way to deal with all this.'

'All this, meaning?'

'The parts of the past that are now in my present. These soldiers who took my parents from me. The same people who are looking for me now.'

'You want justice for your mother and father?'

'I do.'

'Sorry if I have been a coward, Seraphina. I loved Rebekah and Josef dearly. When they disappeared that night, I cried for weeks. I felt anger, despair, a whole array of emotions. I thought you had been lost too. When we found you, a lot of that came back. My instinct was to protect you. To keep you safe from harm. I thought that would be the best way to honour your parents. I was wrong.'

'Yadira, you aren't—'

'Please, let me finish. It is important I say this. You are right. Something must be done for your parents. For those other women too. It does not matter that it was so many years ago. It does not matter that we feel powerless. It does not matter even that we do not stand a chance. We must at least try. You truly are your mother's daughter. She would never tolerate injustice. Even back then, she wanted to go to the authorities. Josef stopped her. It made her furious.'

'You never told me that before.'

'I know. I am sorry. I was trying to convince you to let it go.'

'My mother wanted to find the soldier? The one who attacked Eliana?'

'Yes. Maybe if we had not stopped her, this all could have been avoided.'

'Maybe. You don't blame yourself, do you?'

She and Saul exchanged looks. Yadira was beside herself. Saul took his wife's hand in his.

'No,' said Saul. 'We do not blame ourselves. The fault lies with that soldier, or soldiers if there is more than one. Having said that, this has haunted us for years. Perhaps if we had your mother's strength, we could have stopped all of this a long time ago.'

'I can understand that.'

'Whatever you choose to do, we will support you as best we can.'

'Thank you, Saul. Both of you.'

'What will you do next?'

'I've been thinking about that. I do have one idea.'

'What is it?'

'Is it alright if I don't tell you just now? It's not a matter of trust, just that I am not quite sure how I will go about it.'

'Of course, Seraphina. Just let us know if there is anything we can do to help.'

'I will, thank you.'

'It is getting late, Seraphina,' said Yadira. 'Do you need to be getting back?'

'Probably. I wanted to talk to you more about my parents. To ask you about them, what they were like.'

'Sorry, I was not trying to rush you out. What would you like to know?'

'Actually, what I was going to say was that I have learned more about them tonight. Talking about the past brought up things I did not know about them yet.'

'Are you doing alright with all of this? I know it must still be hitting you quite hard.'

'I am. It's a lot to take in. Do you really think I am like my mother?'

'Very much so. She had an Egyptian grandfather, you know.'

'Wow.' Seraphina's eyes opened wide at that snippet.

'That is why your skin is a little darker.'

'Lucky thing too. It helps me pass as Egyptian, don't you think?'

'Without a doubt. I know you are Hebrew in your heart though.'

'Always.' Seraphina laughed. 'I had better be leaving.'

'Of course. Take good care of yourself and be safe. Will we see you again?'

'I hope so, and soon.'

'Whatever your idea is, I hope it works,' said Saul. 'We are always here if you need us.'

'Thank you both, for everything. Say hello to Joshua for me.'

'We will. Goodnight.'

'Goodnight. Come on, Maximus.'

Seraphina walked back through the city, thinking how fortunate she was which was an odd thought, given the circumstances. Despite all that was happening, she felt loved and cherished.

Afiz, Yadira, Saul, and even Maximus—all of them cared for her. Then there was Quintus. She knew he loved her too, and she longed to be in his arms again, and to feel that peace that he gave her when they were together. She eased back into the library, carrying Maximus with her.

Little did she know that she had been followed.

Cato had trailed her all evening.

She had been hard to keep up with, and her visit to the Hebrew village had surprised him. The spy watched as she vanished into the wall of the library. As the stone slid back into place, he smiled to himself. He had chosen this night by chance and had learned a lot about her.

The general would be pleased.

THIRTY ONE

He grew impatient. The men standing in front of him were too cautious. He did not like hiding like this, on peasant farms, far away from the palace where his father had raised him.

Caesar had made two big mistakes. The first had been releasing him, the second had been to allow his men to escape with their fleet, and Ptolemy thought it wise to capitalise on these mistakes, but Achillas and Pothinus seemed intent on waiting for the perfect moment.

Pothinus and Achillas were frustrated as well. They tired of explaining things to this boy. He was becoming more petulant by the day. They were both wise and patient men though. Plus, they knew that the boy was a valuable asset. He was the one with a claim to the throne. They would say and do what was necessary to keep him happy. Pothinus in particular was tired of hiding in the countryside. He was the real strength behind the young king, and he longed to return to the palace.

Pothinus' strength, however, was as a strategist. He knew that this attack could not afford to fail. He believed they could drive Caesar out of the city and force Cleopatra into exile. To achieve this, everything had to line up perfectly. His main worry was Caesar's movements.

Twice now, Caesar had arrived in the city and evaded the detection of Pothinus' scouts.

Part of their plan centred on Caesar's absence from the city. It alarmed Pothinus that he could come and go so easily without being seen, and he knew he couldn't admit such a weakness to Ptolemy. He had only confided in Achillas about it.

The scouts were men who could be trusted. Besides, they were too embarrassed about their own failures to tell anyone.

'Why do we continue to wait?' asked Ptolemy.

Pothinus and Achillas both paused, hoping the other would speak.

'Someone answer me!' shouted Ptolemy.

'Your majesty,' said Pothinus. 'There is nothing to worry about. We have been finalising our plans. The attack will happen any day now. We have been monitoring Caesar's movements. He is due to leave the city within the next week.'

'I am glad to hear it. I tire of hiding. I am the king of this land, and look at me, I am holed up on a farm like a peasant. Worse than a peasant. Peasants don't have to hide!'

'We understand, your majesty. We appreciate your patience,' said Achillas.

'Never mind my patience, Achillas. Are your men ready?'

'Yes, your majesty.'

'Pothinus, you are confident in our plan of attack?'

'I am, your majesty.'

'Good. Go and make your arrangements. Let me know the exact day you plan to attack.'

'Yes, your majesty,' said Achillas.

'Of course, your majesty,' said Pothinus.

'And gentlemen, do not come to me again saying this attack will be delayed. If you do, you will not like my response. Trust me on that.'

Pothinus and Achillas left the king's room. Pothinus was infuriated. He was a veteran of many battles. Yet here he was, being scolded by a boy who had not even reached his teens.

He shook his head and reminded himself of who that boy was.

He was the king.

Like Caesar, Pothinus was a man who worked towards long term goals. Once they took the city, Ptolemy would be back on the throne. Pothinus would live in the palace as his chief advisor. No more battles. No more hiding. For many years, he had fought for Egypt, but now he was weary, and ready for some calmer times in his life.

One more battle, he thought. *Just one more.*

Caesar was no pushover though. Pothinus knew that the man had his own goals. Only one man would prevail, and Pothinus believed he would be the victor.

THIRTY TWO

Seraphina waited. It had been a wonderful day. Afiz had taken her with him to the museum. She had spent the day with Gisgo and Khay, learning all sorts of things. She had spoken to Khay about astronomy and mathematics.

She had questioned Gisgo more about forgiveness and love.

'What makes you so curious about such topics?' Gisgo had lifted an eyebrow.

Seraphina said, 'My interest is purely theoretical.'

The look on Gisgo's face showed he did not believe her. He had smiled and let it go.

Maybe he knows I am in love, she thought.

She didn't care. She knew in the scheme of things, Gisgo had more important things to think about.

She had allowed her imagination to run wild. Walking the halls of the museum, she had spoken to many more scholars. Most had been reserved at first, but then spoke at length about their studies. She had impressed some of them with her knowledge, and many had asked her to come back and see them again.

There was no greater thrill for Seraphina than to be recognised by these scholars.

Well, perhaps the thrill of seeing Quintus came close, although it was a different feeling with Quintus. With him, Seraphina felt at peace. She could be herself without any sort of doubt or worry. She loved him for that. When she spent time in the museum and the library, with Gisgo, Khay and their ilk, she felt as though her dreams were coming true. Precious dreams, which she had envisioned and nurtured for a very long time.

Seraphina looked out over the water, considering how unbelievable the present trichotomy of her life had become. On one hand, the nightmare of what had happened to her parents had been brought to life, and the person who had done that was now looking for her, but at the same time, she was meeting some of the greatest minds in the world, having intellectual debates and discussions with them. Of all places, this was happening in the apex of knowledge that was the Great Library of Alexandria.

On top of that, she was falling in love with a beautiful young man.

Engulfed in her thoughts, she noticed Maximus suddenly turn, his ears alert and a low growl rumbling in his throat. Seraphina was startled and looked up. She relaxed, seeing Quintus walking towards them. She picked up Maximus, ruffling his ears.

'Silly Maximus, there's nothing to worry about. You remember Quintus, he is our friend.'

'Just your friend, am I?' Quintus raised his eyebrows then pulled Seraphina to him and gave her a soft kiss on her lips.

'You know what I meant,' said Seraphina. 'This is Maximus. Do you like dogs?'

'I do.' Quintus petted the adorable pup.

'I knew I liked you for a reason.' Seraphina treated Quintus to a broad, happy smile.

'I try. So, where are we going tonight?'

'Well, so far we have both shown each other somewhere new. I thought we'd keep our tradition going.'

'Our tradition. I like the sound of that.'

'I do too.' Seraphina moved closer to him as they spoke.

'So, where are we going?'

'I thought we could go to Lake Mareotis.'

'Have you been there before?' said Quintus.

'No. Have you?'

'No. So it will be new for both of us.'

'And Maximus.'

'Of course.'

'So, have you got any faster?' Before he could respond, Seraphina laid Maximus on the ground and bolted.

Quintus did not waste a second and sprinted after them. He barely kept them in sight. Before long, he watched Seraphina soar into the air. She had jumped off something, turning cartwheels and flips. She seemed to move as fluidly when jumping as she did when running. Somersaults, cartwheels, flips. Her gymnastic ability was second nature to her. He kept up a bit better than last time. Seraphina still bested him by a good margin. She waited for him at the edge of the lake with a smile on her face.

'Looks lovely,' said Quintus, catching his breath.

'Doesn't it? Look at those beautiful hills in the distance. It feels as though there are a million more stars in the sky tonight.'

'A perfect night. With the perfect girl.'

'You're sweet.'

'So, do you think next time you can tell me when we're starting a race?' He wiped a few beads of sweat from his forehead, still panting.

'I suppose that's fair.'

'Very gracious of you. When did you learn to run and move like that?'

'Lots of practice I guess. Years of it.'

'It is amazing. You are amazing.'

'Thank you. Now come here,' said Seraphina, pulling him close for another kiss.

'Why thank you.'

'You are welcome, good sir.'

'So, how long have you had Maximus?'

'Only a few months.'

'He looks very happy.'

'Yes, we've become very close in a short time. Sound familiar?' She ruffled the dogs head.

'It sure does.'

'When you hold me like this, it feels like the most natural thing in the world.'

'I feel the same way, Seraphina.'

They found a big rock to sit on, and sat side by side, with Maximus resting at Seraphina's feet.

Quintus sighed.

'Is everything alright?' Seraphina glanced over at Quintus.

'Yes. Well, no, not really.'

'What is it?'

'My father. He is so stubborn.'

'What did he do?'

'He is following through on his word. He said he has made arrangements for me to go to Rome. As soon as my classes finish. I am to enlist in the Roman army and train at a camp outside the city.'

'Oh, no. When do your classes finish?'

'About a month from now.'

Seraphina's head dropped. Quintus put an arm around her to comfort her. Her head rested on his chest, just beneath his shoulder.

'No,' she said.

'What do you mean, no?'

'I mean, no. You can't go. I have only just found you. I can't lose you so soon.'

'I don't have much of a choice, Seraphina. I haven't even thought about what he would do if I defied him. He is a man used to getting his way.'

'What would he do if you refused to go?'

'He would probably disown me.'

'You and I could go somewhere.'

'That's an interesting idea, but where?'

'I don't know. We'd be together though. We can even bring Maximus.'

Quintus paused for a moment. His rational side kicked in. This was crazy. They barely knew each other. Seraphina watched him. She could almost see the wheels turning.

'I know how I feel when I am with you. I know how much I care about you. That is all I need to know,' she said.

Quintus pondered her words. It was a crazy idea, but no crazier than enlisting in the army. That would be a life he hated.

'What are you thinking?' Seraphina edged closer to him.

'Lots of things. Being with you and leaving this place sounds a lot better than being stuck in the army, but …'

'But what?'

'He said I would have to be there for six months. Then we would talk again. Maybe after that I could end up in Rome. Studying in one of these colleges I dream of. Or under a famous scientist perhaps. You could come meet me.'

'Maybe, but I wouldn't see you for six months.'

As she said that, it hit him. He didn't want to be apart from Seraphina. Not at all. Six days, six months, any amount of time was too long. It didn't matter how many times he had met her. He didn't care how well he did or did not know her. There was a bond between them, and in his heart, he knew that whatever he did, wherever he went, he wanted to be with her.

'You don't want to be a soldier, do you?'

'No. Six months of military training would be hell. Even more so if it meant I could not see you.'

'Would your father really be that stubborn? To force you even if you hated the idea?'

'He would. He sees everything the army has given him and thinks it can do the same for me. I don't know what would happen if I disobeyed him.'

'Maybe it's worth talking to him one more time. You could tell him how you feel.'

'Maybe. It's worth a try.'

'He might change his mind.' Seraphina tried to sound hopeful.

'I won't hold my breath, but I will talk to him.'

'Great. There is actually something I need to talk to you about.'

'What is it? It sounds serious.'

'It is.'

'Is this about what you mentioned last time? About how you were orphaned and came to live in the library?'

'Yes, it is.'

'Well, remember what I said. You can tell me as much as you want to. I am all ears.'

Seraphina started to speak. She intimated what it was like for her growing up in the library. She watched as Quintus listened with raised eyebrows. He nodded as she spoke, and the soft smile on his face soothed her. Seraphina shifted gears, telling what she had learned about her parents. She saw Quintus raise his hand to his forehead and wipe away some more sweat from his brow. Then his hand moved to his cheeks, which he gripped. His eyes were wide, unblinking, and fixated on her. Seraphina's voice began to falter, and Quintus took her hand in his. He held it gently and stroked the top of it with his free hand.

She took a moment, and tears began to stream down her face. She saw Quintus move to hold her, and she put up her hand. Her tone deepened as she told him of the soldiers that were looking for her now. Quintus' eyes moved down, and shifted from side to side, then back up to Seraphina. Seraphina watched as his eyes repeated this pattern.

Finally, her face soaked, she lowered her hand, and she moved toward his embrace, almost collapsing on him.

He loved her for trusting him.

She loved him for listening and helping her get it all out.

'You haven't said anything,' she said.

'It's a lot to take in. Are you alright, my love?'

'Yes. I guess I'm worried that this might have changed things between us.'

'Of course not. If anything, I feel like we are closer. Thank you for trusting me enough to tell me.'

'I don't want to have secrets from you. It was time to tell you. After all, I love …' Seraphina caught herself.

'What were you about to say?'

Seraphina remained silent, but Quintus smiled at her.

'I love you?' asked Quintus.

Seraphina nodded. Quintus' smile widened.

'I love you too, Seraphina. I want to share everything with you.'

'I'm glad the feeling is mutual.'

'Of course it is. So, do you want to talk about it?'

'Yes. That's why I told you the whole story. I want to know what you think.'

'I am so sorry for what happened to your parents. Those soldiers! Terrible!'

'Exactly how I feel.'

'We should tell someone.'

'Who?'

'My father. He is very high up in the chain of command.'

'Do you think he would help?'

Quintus paused for a moment.

'Quintus?'

'I hate to say it, but probably not. How can I put this …'

'What is it, Quintus?'

'My father has poor views when it comes to the Hebrews. The Egyptians too. Basically, anyone who is not Roman.'

'Yadira told me of this problem.'

'Who is Yadira again?'

'My mother's old friend.'

'That's right. I'm sorry, there were a lot of details in what you told me.'

'It's alright, I didn't expect anything from you by telling you. I just wanted to tell you. It's a part of my life I have always wondered about. In the past few weeks, so much has happened. Old memories coming back, learning about who my parents were, and it just felt right that you know about it. So, you think we shouldn't tell your father?'

'Probably not. I don't think it would help. It would anger him to know I am spending time with you.'

'Because I am Hebrew?'

'Yes. Seraphina, please know that I do not have the same views as my father. I know what he is like though, and that is one of the reasons I want to be away from him.'

'I understand. I have lived in the city all my life, remember? I have seen the way Hebrews are treated by Romans. Even by Egyptians. Look at my parents.'

'I hope you know I am not like that. Not to any Hebrew, or any Egyptian. Not to anyone.'

'I know you're not. Sorry if it sounded like I was accusing you.'

'It's alright.'

'Will you forgive me?'

'Seraphina, really, it's fine. Of course I forgive you.'

'Forgiveness is something I have been thinking of a lot lately.'

'Why is that?'

'Forgiving myself. Forgiving others.'

'Yourself? For what?'

'For running out of the house that night. Everything might have been different.'

'You can't blame yourself for what happened, Seraphina.' Quintus took her hand again and held it tightly.

'I know, and it's not about that. Not anymore, at least. When I first remembered everything, I was devastated. I blamed myself. After I thought about it, I knew it was the soldiers who were responsible. There was something niggling away at me though. I feel that forgiving myself is important to be able to let go of any notion that I did something wrong. To help me move on.'

'I think I understand.'

'I have been reading a lot about forgiveness.'

'Reading about it?'

'Texts in the library. I also have been speaking to Gisgo. He is a philosopher currently staying at the library.'

'I have heard of him. We have studied him. He is here? In Alexandria?'

'Yes.'

'I love his texts.'

'I do too.'

'So, you spoke to him about forgiveness? In the context of philosophy?'

'Yes, only in theoretical terms. I did not tell him anything about my parents.'

'What did he say?' Quintus lifted his eyebrows, genuinely interested in what wisdom the philosopher he too had studied had to pass on.

'He said self-forgiveness is important. When we feel bad about something we have done, self-forgiveness can be useful to release the emotions. He also spoke of the importance of forgiving others.'

'You mean, forgiving the soldiers?'

'Yes.'

'Could you ever do that?'

'I honestly do not know. Everything is telling me that I must at least consider it.'

'Everything?'

'How I feel. What Gisgo had to say. The texts I have read about the effect of forgiveness. What it could be like to hold on to these emotions for a lifetime; I don't think I want to hold on to such terrible feelings for the rest of my life.'

'I understand, but still.'

'I am not there yet, believe me. So, if we cannot tell your father, is there anyone else we can tell? I want to do something about this.'

'Maybe there is someone.' Quintus' face lit up.

'Who?'

'An old friend of my father's.'

'That doesn't sound like the best idea.'

'He is nothing like my father. He has been like an uncle to me since I was a small boy. A kind and decent man. He and my father were in the army together, but years ago, he left the military although he stayed here, and lives close to the city. Maybe we could tell him.'

'What good would that do?'

'Benedict, that's his name, is respected by everyone who knows him, and he might still have some contacts in the army. To be honest, I don't know if it will do any good. I do trust him though, and he will listen to what we have to say.'

'We?'

'We would go together to tell him the story, wouldn't we?'

'Yes, I should come with you. Will it be safe?'

'Of course. Just another one of our adventures in the dead of the night.'

'Very funny. When shall we go to see him?'

'How about two nights from now? Benedict lives in the hills above those plains over there. We could meet here.'

'Alright.'

'Are you alright?'

'I am. Just a little nervous, that's all.'

'Benedict is someone we can trust.'

'If you say so, I believe it. Thank you.'

'You are welcome. Wait, for what are you thanking me?'

'For being in this with me. You have no idea how much it means to me.'

'I want to do whatever I can to support you through this.'

Seraphina smiled.

What more can someone offer, she thought.

To be with her in the midst of her problems. It was the sign of a selfless heart. She inched closer to him, and he wrapped his arm around her.

The young lovers spent the night talking about their dreams. They conjured wild possibilities for the future, and their ideas were only limited by their imaginations. For them, it was a beautiful evening, free of fear and unlimited by rationality or practicality. It was as if their bond could dispel anything that might go wrong. They laughed at some of their ideas and longed for what might be. They saw a bright future on the horizon and delighted in each other's company.

However, both Seraphina and Quintus were mindful of the present. There were complications in each of their lives. Yet on that night, those complications seemed like very minor bumps in the road.

A road that they would travel together for years to come.

A journey of adventure.

A life filled with love.

They held hands and looked out over the shimmering moonlit lake. As they sat there, the two adolescents saw a glimpse of a life neither had conceived of before, at least, not before they had met one another.

THIRTY THREE

Rufio sat in his living room and looked out the window of his house, sitting on a hill above most of the camp. Beyond the camp, he could see the vast sea. On the other side of that sea was Rome. Over the years, there had been many times when he had longed to return, but he had made the decision to stay in Alexandria. Part of that decision was rooted in ambition. Part of it was a desire to stay out of the politics that pervaded Rome. Both had turned out to be sound choices.

His plans were coming to fruition. He would send his son to Rome soon to be trained as a legionary which would leave Rufio with no personal responsibility to worry about.

He could focus on his new position.

He intended to exercise his new powers as far as he could by issuing a decree for Egyptians to be conscripted into the armed forces. The Egyptians were fierce warriors, but they lacked the training and discipline of his army. Despite that, they would provide valuable numbers on the battlefield, and there was a near endless supply.

Men could be sourced from cities and villages throughout Egypt. They would be sent into battle first. They would be lost in greater numbers, but that sacrifice would save Roman lives.

Those hardened by battle could train future conscripts.

It was a detailed plan, one Rufio had been working on for a while. He believed it could deliver him a large part of the African continent, if not all of it. Caesar would no doubt be grateful for his work. There would be rewards, and increased power.

With the Egyptian men gone, Rufio could usurp their businesses. The Hebrews would work in their place.

They would not be paid of course, and he dreamed of the riches he could amass, all of which would go to the Roman coffers, and expand his sphere of power and influence.

As Rufio fantasised about his scheme, there was an interruption to his solitude. Someone had knocked and entered his house. He looked up to see Cato, who had a nasty little smile on his face.

'Hello, Cato. You look like you have some news for me,' said Rufio.

'Hello, sir. How are you today?'

'I'm fine, Cato. What do you have to report?'

'Quite a lot, sir.'

'Well, get on with it.'

'I saw the girl leave the library late the other night.'

'What do you mean? How late?'

'It was a few hours before midnight.'

'Surely she does not work so late. No one is in the streets at that hour.'

'Exactly, sir. I suspect she lives in the library.'

'What?' shouted Rufio.

'Yes. I am positive of it, in fact.'

'She lives in the library,' murmured Rufio. 'Incredible.'

'It doesn't end there, sir.'

'Right. Where did she go?'

'To the Hebrew village of all places.'

'That *is* interesting. Did you see where she went in the village? Or who she visited?'

'A simple house. I have made a note of where it is. There was nothing unique about the place.' Cato shook his head as he spoke.

'Any clue as to why she was there?'

'Not really. She spent a lot of time in the house though.'

'You didn't hear the conversation?'

'No. I couldn't get close enough without being seen. There were a few people sitting outside their houses.'

'There was no other way to listen?'

'No, sir. I considered climbing on to the roof, but it was not viable. Besides, they would have heard me.'

'Fair enough. Did you learn anything else about who she went to see?'

'Yes, I have since returned to the village and seen who lives there.'

'Who are they?'

'An old Hebrew couple. Their names are Yadira and Saul. I learned nothing of interest about them.'

'It's hard to find out much from the Hebrews. They don't talk to strangers.'

'I was dressed as a Hebrew when I went there the following day.'

'Even so. If they did not recognise you, they wouldn't tell you much.'

'It was still worth asking.'

'Why do you say that?'

'Well, if they were friends with the couple who attacked you all those years ago …'

'We're unlikely to ever know that. You're right though, it would be very useful information.'

'I shall keep trying to learn more, sir.'

'Very well. Anything else?'

'Yes, sir. The first time I followed Seraphina, she was with the caretaker from the library. What's his name?'

'Afiz.'

'That's it. Afiz. Well, Seraphina and Afiz were walking through the marketplace. She does a very good job of looking Egyptian. She speaks perfect Coptic, you know.'

'Impressive. She spoke Hebrew when she went to the village that night?'

'Yes. Again, she was fluent.'

'I wonder how many languages this girl speaks.'

'At least three, sir.'

'Three? What is the third one?'

'I am getting to that.'

'Cato, I asked you a question.'

'The third language is Latin, sir.

'Latin? Now I am intrigued. Continue.'

'I overheard part of a conversation between Seraphina and Afiz. I didn't get much from it, except that she was planning to go to the Hebrew village soon.'

'This was before the night you followed her to the village?'

'Yes, sir.' Cato nodded.

'The day in the marketplace was the first time you followed her, correct?'

'That is correct, sir.'

'Why didn't you start with that?'

'My apologies, sir.'

'Never mind. Go on.'

'As I said, the conversation between Seraphina and Afiz did not yield much in terms of information. One thing was clear. Seraphina confides in this man. I wouldn't be surprised if he knows she lives in the library. In fact, I would almost guarantee it.'

'This Afiz, what kind of man is he?'

'I haven't observed him enough to know. He is a tall, stout man. He seems to do a great job of looking after the library.'

'He is Egyptian?'

'Yes, sir.'

'It could be useful to learn more about him.'

'Is that something I should focus on, sir?'

'Not just yet.'

'Very well, sir. The girl was wearing a necklace that day.'

'In the marketplace?' Rufio was looking confused at the relevance of this information.

'Yes. It was a very odd thing for her to be wearing.'

'A necklace? What was so odd about it?'

'It was a simple thing. A flat silver ring on a black string. It had Hebrew words carved into it.'

'What did it say?'

'The words translate to "our love" from what I read.'

'Our love? How touching. Any idea who would have given it to her?'

'Well, so far as I know, she only knows two Hebrews.'

'The old couple from the village?'

'That's right, sir.'

'There's nowhere else she could have got it from?'

'I don't know. It is only a guess at this point. Given the circumstances, at least, it's a well-informed guess.'

'I suppose, but I don't like relying on guesswork. I want to know if this is the girl I am looking for.'

'It's still early days, sir. I will find out more about her. Then we can be sure.'

'I like your confidence, Cato.'

Cato bowed his head slightly. 'I have no doubt, sir. I have been doing this for years. The information is always there. It just takes time.'

'I can appreciate that. I want to find out sooner rather than later. Now, what else have you learned?'

'Last night, I watched her leave the library again. She went to the edge of the city, where it meets the waterfront and the edge of the Hebrew village.'

'Another visit to our Hebrew friends?'

'No. She met someone else there.'

'Who?'

'A boy. He seemed to be Roman.'

'Seemed to be?'

'He was Roman.'

'Roman! What was his name?'

'I didn't hear a name.'

'How did you miss his name?'

'When the two first met and started speaking, some Hebrews came out of the house I was hiding next to. My attention was diverted, just for a few moments.'

'So, you didn't get his name? What did he look like?'

'Tall, dark straight hair, sturdy build.'

'Thank you very much, Cato. You have just described pretty much every Roman boy I have ever seen. How old was he?' Rufio was already irritated at the idea of a Roman and the Hebrew girl meeting.

'I would guess about seventeen or eighteen.'

'I assume this is how you know she speaks Latin?'

'Yes, sir. Her Latin was perfect. They spoke the entire time in Latin.'

'Old Imhotep must be running language classes in the library.'

'Excuse me, sir?'

'Nothing. What else?'

'After they spoke for a few moments, she put down her dog and raced away from the boy.'

'What do you mean, she raced away? She has a dog?'

'Yes, a small dog. Easily held in her hands. Anyway, she was speaking to the boy. Then, all of a sudden, she put the dog down and dashed off. The boy followed, and the three of them ended up at Lake Mareotis.'

'This is odd to say the least.'

'I thought so too. It took me a while to catch up with them too. Seraphina likes to sprint and jump her way through the streets. She is very fast. Then I had to wait for the boy to pursue them. So, it was his trail that I followed.'

'I see. You found them at the lake?'

'Yes, sir. By the time I got there, they were seated together. They sat there talking for a long time.'

'About what?'

'Lots of things. The two of them seemed close.'

'Care to provide some detail, Cato?'

'Of course, sir. Given that I followed them, I couldn't get too close without being seen. As you know, the lake area is quite open. The presence of the dog worried me too. So, I had to keep my-'

'Cato!' interrupted Rufio. 'I asked for details, not excuses. Did you or did you not hear what these two talked about?'

'Not much, sir. Some talk about running away together. She mentioned some problems she was having with her parents, and he was also talking about problems he was having with his parents. They then consoled each other.'

'How adorable. I am disappointed, Cato. I thought part of a spy's role would be to hear such conversations. To actually find out what is being said.'

'I apologise, sir. I did the best I could in the circumstances.'

'Never mind. I am coming with you next time.'

'Next time, sir?'

'The next time you go to trail her.'

'Are you sure, sir?'

'Yes. I want to know for certain if this is the girl I am looking for. It is clear I cannot rely on your observations.'

'Yes, sir. I will be sure to let you know when I am going next.'

'Do that. Now get out of here.'

'As you wish, sir.'

Rufio watched as the spy left. So much for being one of Caesar's best. Was it possible that this was the girl? She was suspicious, no doubt about that. Living in the library, sneaking out late at night to meet the old Hebrew couple, and a romantic tryst with a Roman boy.

It was all so odd.

He remembered the look of terror in her eyes that night. That look had given him pause. Remorse was not a familiar emotion to Rufio, but that night had changed him. The girl had lost her parents, and he had made Benedict a murderer, but if this was the girl, she had to be eliminated. There was no question about that. He just wanted to make sure it was her, because even at his most ruthless, Rufio would only harm a person if it served him in some way.

It almost made no sense to him, this last shred of humanity. He shook it off. His instincts told him that this was the girl. He would make sure, and then take care of it. Once he had done so, all that awaited him was a bright and prosperous future.

THIRTY FOUR

Seraphina watched. She had a look of deep concentration on her face. Khay was explaining his theories to a group of fascinated scholars; a group made up mostly of mathematicians, yet most of them had never seen or heard of the ideas being taught.

Meanwhile, Seraphina listened with great interest. She had read every available text written by Hipparchus since she had met Khay. She had learned all of Hipparchus' teachings.

Khay had been his protege many years ago, and now was an academic titan in his own right. Seraphina contributed to the discussion with great enthusiasm, and at times, it appeared as though she and Khay were having a private conversation.

The looks of surprise no longer impressed Seraphina. Of course, she still enjoyed the attention. The whisperings around the library about her intellect enthralled her. Afiz told her to stay humble. It was hard. Seraphina was by no means arrogant, but on the other hand, humility was not a concept she fully appreciated either. She was always respectful to others and believed in the importance of helping people in need, however, she saw humility as a dampener on greatness.

Afiz assured her she would learn, and she accepted that. If there was one thing anyone could say about Seraphina, it is that she was willing to learn new things.

She had also managed to get Afiz to make one concession. He admitted that part of what he meant by humility was for her not to draw too much attention to herself.

Afiz stood at the back of the room with Gisgo, watching the lesson wind up. They looked at her in the same way the scholars did. Neither of them understood what Khay was talking about, yet Seraphina seemed able to discuss the concepts with ease. Her intellect was impressive, and no one in the room would disagree with that. Once Khay completed his talk, Seraphina joined Afiz and Gisgo at the back of the room.

'Were you watching?' Seraphina's face was glowing with excitement.

'We were,' said Afiz. 'You have been reading up.'

'It is so fascinating. To think they discovered this branch of mathematics while studying astronomy. It's as if fate was at work.'

'How do you mean?' asked Gisgo.

'Well, the study of astronomy itself involves mathematics. To understand the planets, we need mathematics. Yet, in learning about astronomy, these new theories have been discovered.'

'That is an interesting way to look at it.'

Seraphina smiled, her mind abuzz. Nothing energised her like a good intellectual discussion.

'Seraphina! I am very impressed,' said Khay, coming to the back of the room.

'Thank you, Khay. The lesson was fascinating.'

'No one knew what I was talking about, except you, that is. You have been studying.'

'I have. No one else understood the lesson?'

'I don't think so. Some of them were asking me some odd questions just then.'

'Well, I thought it was brilliant.'

'Thank you. Now, are we having some lunch?' said Khay.

'Yes,' said Afiz. 'I have arranged some food, and we can eat in the garden. How does that sound?'

'Sounds good to me,' said Seraphina.

'I was actually asking Khay and Gisgo.'

'Oh, sorry.'

Gisgo and Khay laughed. 'That sounds wonderful to me, Afiz,' said Gisgo. 'Khay?'

'Perfect. I am starving. Let's go.'

The four strolled out of the study halls and into the garden. It was a beautiful, sunny day, and they found a spot in the shade to sit, the smell of the freshly cut grass permeating the air.

'What a beautiful day,' said Gisgo.

'I couldn't agree more,' said Khay. 'So, Gisgo, how are you enjoying your time in Alexandria?'

'It has exceeded expectations. The museum and library are unlike anything I have ever seen. Part of me wants to stay here permanently.'

'Why don't you?' asked Seraphina.

'It is a tempting thought, but my home is in Valentia.'

'We could find you a home here, I am sure,' said Seraphina.

'Stop pestering the man,' said Afiz.

'It is quite alright, Afiz,' said Gisgo. 'Seraphina's enthusiasm has been one of the highlights of my trip.'

'Maybe you could come and live here,' said Khay. 'You could learn some actual science instead of just writing about your thoughts.'

'I could, but then I would spend my days playing with wooden shapes and drawing imaginary lines around stars.'

The two laughed at one another.

'On a serious note,' said Khay, 'maybe I could come and visit you in Valentia some time.'

'You would be more than welcome, Khay. It is a little quieter than here, a lot quieter in fact, but it is a long voyage.'

'I think I would be up to it.'

'May I ask the two of you a question?' asked Seraphina.

'Of course, Seraphina,' said Gisgo.

'Yes, my dear, what is it?' said Khay.

'Where would you advise a young, aspiring academic to go to educate herself?'

'Seraphina …,' said Afiz.

'I am only asking hypothetically,' said Seraphina.

'My view is that you are in one of the finest centres of learning already. This place is unlike anything I have seen in Rome or Athens, or anywhere else for that matter,' said Gisgo.

Khay also offered a response. 'I am less travelled than Gisgo, but he is probably right. This library and museum is renowned around the world. My mentor, Hipparchus, thought very highly of it as well. Though, to be fair, that was many years ago.'

'There must be incredible colleges in Rome and Athens though, right? Also, what do you think of the idea of me studying under a mentor?'

'What kind of mentor?' said Gisgo.

'A mentor who is a well renowned scholar, who has expertise in a field that I want to study.'

'I think it is an interesting idea,' said Khay. 'I was only a boy when I met Hipparchus and began to learn from him. Our relationship as mentor and protege formed quite organically, so similarly, you might find someone who would take you under his wing. You have a brilliant mind, Seraphina, there is no doubt about that.'

'Thank you, Khay.'

'You will have some obstacles to overcome, however.'

'Such as?' Seraphina scrunched up her brows.

'May I be blunt with you, Seraphina?'

'Of course. Please.'

'You are a woman, and you are Egyptian. Both will be obstacles to you studying in a formal sense. Here in Alexandria, being Egyptian will obviously not disadvantage you. Being a woman will. You might have more of a chance finding a mentor, but even then, the most famous scholars can be closed-minded when it comes to certain things.'

'Most? You and Gisgo seem to be quite open-minded.'

'I cannot speak for Gisgo, but do you remember when you first met me? You have changed my mind, Seraphina, but when I first saw you, I wondered what on earth you were doing.'

'Oh.'

'Please do not misunderstand me. I am glad you changed my mind. You have an eagerness for learning that makes you a wonderful student. You grasp complex ideas faster than most, and you have a charming personality that helps you win people over.'

'Win people over? I don't want to win people over. I simply want to be treated the same as everyone else.'

'I can appreciate that,' said Gisgo. 'Some things are just the way they are. At least for now.'

'Gisgo, you spoke to me as an equal from the moment I met you.'

'Yes. I don't care if someone is a man or a woman, or where they are from.'

'Exactly. So how can you say, "things are just the way they are"?'

'You misunderstand me. That wasn't my intention in saying that. I take the world as it is, Seraphina, not as I would like it to be, which is why I added the part about it being that way only for now. I would much prefer to see a world where people have opportunity regardless of their origin or gender.'

'I understand. For us to have that world, there must be change, correct?'

'Yes, that is correct.'

'Which means someone has to be the first to try.'

'Also correct.'

'Why shouldn't that person be me?'

'Well said, Seraphina,' said Gisgo. 'Someone will have to be the first if things are to change. I think what Khay is trying to say is that it will be difficult for you.'

'I am up to the challenge.'

'Difficult and dangerous,' said Khay. 'I remember speaking to Hipparchus before he passed away. He told me how talented he thought I was and what a brilliant mind I had. I was not unlike you, in fact. He also told me that I should be realistic and stay here in Alexandria. Even though I had the skill, he told me I would never be accepted as a scholar outside of Egypt. I was outraged. As a young man, I was determined to prove him wrong, so I travelled to Athens. I went to one of the colleges at which my mentor had studied. I told them I was a protege of the great Hipparchus, and I was not permitted to set foot in the place. I travelled again in later years, once again to Athens, then once to Rhodes. The same thing happened.'

'That is terrible, Khay,' said Seraphina.

'It was. I decided not to go again. The second time I went to Athens, a guard stopped me outside the gate of the college. He questioned me about my business there. He threatened to attack me if I did not leave. I was a visiting scholar. I spoke perfect Greek. I was younger than I am now, but still an old man. I had no desire to be assaulted by a soldier.'

'Khay, I had no idea,' said Afiz.

'It isn't something I speak about. Seraphina, you can do anything you want. You are strong, capable, and intelligent. You've changed my mind in a short time. In doing so, you helped me realise that I was guilty of prejudice, just as those Greeks were to me all those years ago. I am the better for it. I tell you these stories now, not to scare you, but to prepare you. Some minds may not be easily changed, and you could experience hostility.'

'Even here, some of the scholars are not used to having a woman around. Have you noticed?' asked Gisgo.

'I have noticed odd looks. Some of the scholars are less eager to speak to me, and some do not at all. Yes, I guess I have noticed.'

'The mood is more passive here, most likely because you work for Afiz. Also, they consider you a harmless observer. I know, because some of them have spoken to me about it,' said Khay.

'What are you saying? That I should not come into the museum anymore? Or the library?'

'I am not saying that. What I am saying is that the situation could become different if you were a student here.'

'Why?'

'The answer again is simple prejudice.'

'Khay, what would you do if you were me? I love to study. Mathematics, engineering, philosophy, they all fascinate me. I love many of the other sciences as well. I know that I want to spend the next chapter of my life learning, so I can become a scholar one day.'

'That is a tough question, Seraphina. Knowing what I know,

maybe I would think of another ambition.'

'Never.'

'Seraphina, I think this conversation has gone far enough,' said Afiz.

'It is alright, Afiz,' said Gisgo. 'No one else is here. If Seraphina wants to ask me questions, it does not bother me. How about you, Khay?'

'I am fine with it too. So long as Seraphina understands that I will not simply say what she wants to hear.'

'I appreciate that, gentlemen,' said Afiz. 'This was supposed to be a hypothetical conversation. It no longer seems to be. I think it is best to stop.'

Seraphina's voice was raised and started to falter. 'I am not asking you these things, just so you can tell me what I want to hear. This is important to me.'

'Seraphina, please,' said Afiz.

'It is a coward who walks away from his or her dreams. Especially if it is just because of fear.'

'Seraphina, that was unnecessary,' said Khay.

'I am sorry, Khay. I apologise to you too, Gisgo. And to you, Afiz. I just don't think you can let things be as they are because you are afraid to do something.'

Seraphina began to weep.

'Seraphina, what is wrong? We're sorry if we upset you,' said Gisgo.

'I'm sorry,' she said.

Seraphina got up and walked away from the group. She wiped her tears away with her forearm. Her steps became faster, and she began to run. She heard Afiz call her name as she fled, crying her eyes out. She ran through the study hall, and out of the museum, through the library, into the lecture hall and up the stairs. She ran and ran until she was in her room, where she collapsed in a heap on the floor, hugging her knees to her chest.

The tears streamed down her face, and she wept and wept until she could weep no more. Finally, she was still. Maximus walked to her feet and sat. There he waited, watching his friend, and feeling her pain.

THIRTY FIVE

The general crouched, hiding behind the building. The spy was in front of him, watching the back alley. Rufio was a tall man, and his body was not built for such a position. He strained and moved, trying to find a stance that was comfortable. Cato was still and silent. The noises behind him were annoying. He dared not complain. Then, there was quiet. Cato looked behind him to see Rufio had stood up. He towered above the small spy. He looked up to the general.

'What? No one is going to see me,' said Rufio.

Cato looked back towards the library.

What an idiot, he thought.

He wondered why on earth he was here, with this tree of a man behind him, watching a library in the middle of the night.

Maybe Alexandria was not all it had cracked up to be.

Rufio had similar thoughts. Squatting and hiding in the dark, waiting for some girl to sneak out of a library. A girl who may be Egyptian, or Hebrew. In that moment, it seemed ridiculous to him. Yet they both knew why they were there. Cato was following orders. Rufio wanted to tie up loose ends.

The night was cool. The breeze from the Mediterranean blew

through the city. The light waves rocking into the harbour could be heard in the night's stillness.

The scent of the sea water was in the air. The calm heightened their senses. A door closed, and they snapped to attention. They looked at the alley. Nothing. They continued to wait. A few moments later, they heard an odd sound. Stone scraping. Then a thud. Both pairs of eyes fixed on the alley, where the sounds came from. The shadows obscured any vision of what was happening. The scraping sound again.

What the hell is going on, thought Rufio.

A moment later, Seraphina appeared. Cato was relieved. She didn't have the dog with her. Then Cato panicked. She was walking straight towards them. Rufio moved first. His eyes narrowed on Seraphina. Then, in one swift movement, he grabbed Cato and pulled him behind a horse cart that had been left on the street. Seraphina walked past them just as they ducked down.

Both men held their breath.

They listened to her footsteps as they faded into the distance. Cato poked his head out and saw her walking into the city. He had expected her to walk towards the waterfront.

Rufio grabbed him by the neck.

'Some spy you are!' he said through gritted teeth.

Cato was all about business. 'Come on, we'll lose her.'

The two followed Seraphina at a distance.

Rufio wondered where she was headed.

Cato suspected she was returning to the lake. That seemed to be the route she was taking.

After a little while, the girl started to run. Quickly. She took off sprinting down the street, and for a moment Rufio thought they had been spotted. Cato cut across one block and bolted in the same direction. Rufio followed. Several minutes later, Cato signalled to Rufio with his hand. The pair slowed down. Rufio made no sound, and Cato was impressed with the general's fitness. Seraphina stood for a moment at the edge of the lake and looked around. It was clear she was there to meet someone.

She sat on the same rock she had shared with the boy. Cato

watched for any signs of movement.

Rufio stared at the girl.

What was she doing here?

The spy saw him first. Quintus approached from the east, and spotted Seraphina.

Cato got Rufio's attention and pointed to the boy.

At first, the general could not believe his eyes.

Even with the distance between them, Rufio recognised his son, and his first reaction was to call out, but countless thoughts ran through his head, so he remained still.

Cato watched as the two embraced and kissed. He looked at Rufio and saw an odd look on the general's face. He turned his attention back to the young couple.

They had a brief conversation and walked away together.

Cato got his bearings, and realised they were heading towards the Eleusis Plain.

Nothing there but hills and countryside, he thought.

With Seraphina and the boy well out of earshot, Cato turned to Rufio. The same look was on his face.

'Is everything alright, sir? Should we keep following them?'

'That is my son.'

'That is Quintus?' asked Cato in disbelief.

'That is my son,' said Rufio again.

Cato paused. He watched the general, who was deep in thought. Rufio was looking at the ground, shaking his head. Suddenly, he looked up.

'Come on, Cato. We don't want to lose them.'

THIRTY SIX

Seraphina and Quintus held hands as they walked. As they left the lake behind them, the city gave way to beautiful countryside. The plains were spread out in front of them, dotted with ponds. Seraphina looked at each pond as they walked past, noticing the beautiful lotus flowers, and smelling their scent. In different circumstances, it might have been romantic.

The weight of their mission gave the night an eerie feel. Seraphina squeezed Quintus' hand and continued to walk.

'Are you alright, my dear?' asked Quintus.

'I think so,' said Seraphina.

'Are you sure you want to do this?'

'I am. Thank you for being here. Tell me more about Benedict.'

'He has been friends with my father for many years, they served in the army together. About ten years ago, he left the army, although I don't quite know why. My father continued to serve, and rose through the ranks, and Benedict and my father remained friends.'

'So, he is a Roman?'

'Yes.'

'He stayed here in Alexandria after leaving the army?'

'Yes, he always liked it here. When I was growing up, I saw him often. He was kind and patient towards me. Very unlike my father. I could never understand why the two of them were friends. I think I heard him say once that my father saved his life. Still, the two could not be greater opposites.'

'And you trust him?'

'I do.'

They arrived at the small farm. A rickety wooden gate swung with the breeze. Seraphina hesitated. She watched the gate go back and forth, like a pendulum. Quintus rubbed his thumb across the top of her hand. Seraphina looked up at him and smiled.

'Shall we go inside?' He smiled back.

Seraphina nodded.

Benedict heard the footsteps on his path and looked out of his window when he heard a voice he recognised, and opened the door.

'Quintus, is that you?'

'Yes. How are you, uncle?'

'I am well. Quite late, isn't it?' Benedict glanced at Seraphina.

'It is. Sorry if we are intruding.'

'Not at all. Who is this?'

'This is Seraphina. She is my … friend.'

'I see. Hello, Seraphina. My name is Benedict.'

'Nice to meet you.'

'Likewise. Come on in.'

The three entered the quaint cottage. As Benedict closed the door, Seraphina looked around. She had never seen such a home. It was simple, yet beautiful. Thick candles lit the room they stood in. The back of the house was shrouded in darkness.

'Have a seat. What brings you here, Quintus?'

'I haven't seen you in a while.'

'So, you thought you'd come and visit me in the middle of the night?'

Quintus hesitated for a moment. 'Ah, yes.'

The three sat in silence for a moment.

This was anything but normal, thought Benedict. *Where was Rufio,* he wondered. *Why were these two here?*

Quintus broke the silence. 'The house looks nice,' he said.

'I do love it here,' said Benedict. He allowed the change in subject, for now. 'So, Seraphina, how do you know this young rascal?'

'We met not long ago, near where I work.'

'I see, and where is that?'

'The Library of Alexandria.'

'The Great Library. That must be interesting for you. What do you do there?'

'I help the caretaker look after the library.'

'All those scrolls. I have been there once or twice. Just to look, of course. Do you like to read?'

'I love to read. In fact, that's what I do with most of my spare time.'

'Anything in particular?'

'If it's in a scroll and written by a scholar, I am interested. Lately I have been reading a lot of philosophy.'

'Greek? Roman?'

'Both, as well as Hindu and Persian.'

'How fascinating. So why has Quintus brought you here this evening?'

'There is something we need to talk to you about, sir.'

'I see. It sounds serious. Would you like something to drink?'

'Just some water, please.'

'Me too,' said Quintus.

Benedict got up and poured water from a jug sitting on the counter. Seraphina watched him. He was a tall man, lean and strong. He was older, but his movements were fluid and graceful. Seraphina could imagine him as a soldier. His neutral expression was one of kindness.

She noticed he'd had a smile on his face the entire time. That put Seraphina at ease, at least a little. She was still very nervous, and her left leg twitched up and down. Her fingers tapped the arm of the chair in rhythm with her leg twitching. Quintus rested his hand on top of hers.

'It's going to be fine,' he said.

Seraphina nodded and tried to still herself. Benedict returned and set the water on the table.

'Now, what is it that you have come to talk to me about in the dead of night?'

Seraphina just looked at Benedict. Quintus and Benedict both watched her in silence for a few moments.

'It's alright, Seraphina. You can trust him,' said Quintus.

'Seraphina, whatever it is, it will be alright. Just relax and try to tell me what is on your mind,' said Benedict.

'Very well. Here goes. A little over a decade ago, I lived in the Hebrew village.'

'You are Hebrew?'

'Yes, I am. I was having dinner with my parents. I was sulking and ran out of the back of our house. It wasn't to spite them. Then I got distracted and ran to play on the streets.'

Benedict wanted to interrupt and ask why she was telling him this. He decided to be patient and let this girl tell her story.

'I ran through the streets, and I got to the waterfront, near the library. Then I heard some noises, so I looked around, and followed them. There were shouts and screams. They got louder with each step. What I saw next was gruesome. A Roman soldier was on top of my father, bashing his head in with a helmet. My mother was on the ground, with another soldier on top of her. She screamed at me to run, and I did. As I ran away, I could hear them crying out for help. Then the cries stopped. I never saw my parents again.'

'These soldiers killed your parents? They were Roman?' said Benedict.

'Yes.'

'Do you know for certain that they killed your parents?'

'I didn't see it with my own eyes, but their screams stopped suddenly. They have never been seen again. They never returned to their home. I believe they were killed, yes. I am certain of it.'

Benedict held his head and looked at Quintus. He looked back to Seraphina.

'That is terrible, Seraphina. But why are you coming to me now to tell this story?'

'I told Quintus, and he thought if we came to you, maybe you could help.'

'I understand that, but what kind of help do you have in mind? This happened over ten years ago. Why are you only telling someone this story now?'

'I never returned to my home after that night. Until recently, I had no memory of what happened, or where I came from.'

'These memories have recently come back to you?'

'Yes, very recently. I have started to remember more and more about my parents. The memories of that night are now vivid.'

'I can only imagine. What do you expect me to do though? Quintus?'

'I don't know, uncle. Whoever did this to her parents committed a crime. Even if they were Roman soldiers, surely there must be some way to seek justice.'

As Quintus said the word "crime" a terrible feeling came over Benedict. It couldn't be! His memory wasn't what it once was, but it was coming back to him. His heart beat faster, and he gripped the arms of his chair. He squeezed so hard that his knuckles turned white.

'Is everything okay, Uncle?'

'Yes, Quintus. I am fine. Seraphina, tell me something.'

Seraphina.

His conversation with Rufio came back to him.

That was the name he had asked about.

No, please no.

'What is it?' asked Seraphina.

'What is the last thing you remember seeing before you ran?'

Seraphina thought hard for a moment. Her words were slow, recalling each detail as she spoke.

'One soldier, the bigger one, was standing over my father. My father was not moving. He may have been dead at that point. The other soldier had scratches on his face. He was on top of my mother, pinning her arms down with his hands. She twisted her neck to look at me, and then screamed. The other soldier walked towards my mother and picked up a dagger from the ground.'

Benedict slumped over, as if he had been punched in the guts. His hands still gripped the chair, otherwise he would have fallen to the ground. He pushed himself back up, and it felt like it took all his strength to do so. He looked at Quintus and Seraphina, then took his head in his hands, with his elbows rested on his legs. He looked as though someone had sucked the life out of him.

What did I do?

Quintus rushed to his side.

'Uncle Benedict, what is wrong?'

Benedict shook his head.

Rufio. That bastard.

'Uncle?'

Benedict nodded. Seraphina watched this man. She didn't know him, but something was not right. She waited for someone to say something. Benedict sat up and looked at Seraphina.

She was only a child.

She is still a child.

I took her parents.

That bastard.

A swirl of emotions engulfed him. Guilt. Anger. Regret.

'What is it?' asked Seraphina.

'I know what happened to your parents,' whispered Benedict.

'What did you say?' asked Quintus.

'I know what happened to your parents,' he said again.

Seraphina stopped breathing. Her eyes widened, and she glared at Benedict, who was staring straight back at her. His eyes looked empty, as if he was looking through her. His strength gave way to a frailty.

'Tell me,' said Seraphina.

'I am so sorry, Seraphina.'

Her voice was flat as she repeated herself. 'Tell me what happened.'

'I was on patrol that night with another soldier. We were keeping watch by the harbour, which was our usual duty in those days. Late in the night, my partner had not checked in. We checked in with each other each hour, in case we got separated for any reason. I went to look for him. I was searching near the library, and I heard something.

Voices and a scuffle. I followed the noises and came upon my partner. A Hebrew man was attacking him, and a woman behind him was hysterical, crying and screaming. I ordered the man to release my partner and he wouldn't. He said that my partner attacked his wife.

'The woman was distracted, like she was looking for something. My partner said they had both attacked him. I could see scratches on his face and arms. I repeated my order for the Hebrew man to release my partner. He refused. He looked strong, but afraid. I approached him to physically separate him from my partner, and he attacked me. We fought, and I tried to restrain him. As we fought, my partner attempted to arrest the woman. She screamed at him and resisted. I could see that she was pinned to the ground.

'Each time I tried to restrain him, he would push me off and attempt to help his wife. Then I would try again, and he would throw me off. The fight got worse, and I ended up on top of him. I hit him with my helmet several times, and thought he was unconscious. The woman had my partner's dagger. She lunged at me, screaming about how I had killed her husband. I defended myself and disarmed her. My partner got her pinned on the ground again, and I picked up the dagger from the ground. She seemed to give up resisting at that point. She just cried that we had killed her husband. That is when we saw you.

'She screamed at you to run. Then, something kicked in. Seeing you gave her a rush of energy. She got hold of my partner's sword and swung it at me, calling me a murderer. I retreated, trying to find a way to disarm her. She cut my arm and I fell to the ground. My partner saw she was distracted and struck her with his dagger. In the side of her torso. She went down. All this happened in a matter of seconds. I crawled towards the man, and he was not breathing. I realised he was dead. My partner was saying something to the woman, and a few moments later, she stopped breathing.'

Seraphina's whole body was shaking. Tears ran down her cheeks. She was face to face with the man who killed her father. Benedict's gaze stayed on the floor. He was unsure of what to do. It was still dawning on him that he had committed murder.

He didn't know.

He searched for a possibility, one that might exonerate him.

They were parents looking for their daughter, he thought.

Maybe Seraphina's mother had attacked Rufio. He knew that was his desperation speaking. He knew the truth. Rufio had lied to him. Now this girl was in pieces.

'Who was the other soldier, Benedict?' asked Quintus.

Benedict looked up at him. Quintus was dear to him. His head fell into his hands again. He had always regretted the actions of that night. With these revelations, the grief and guilt hit him a hundred-fold.

'It was your father. It was Rufio.'

Quintus fell back in his chair, heartbroken. Seraphina glared at him, and her eyes widened with even greater shock. Quintus turned and looked at Seraphina. He had no idea what to say. After a few moments, Quintus' head sunk into his hands. Seraphina looked at both of them, their heads in their hands as if it was their tragedy. She was finding it hard to breathe. She was furious. She hadn't said a word since Benedict finished the story. Quintus and Benedict were frozen, fathoming Rufio's betrayal.

Seraphina stood up. She had to get out of there.

'Wait!' said Quintus.

Seraphina spun around and looked him square in the eye.

'I didn't know,' said Benedict, as he stood from his chair.

'You didn't know?' shouted Seraphina. She charged at him, pushing him to the ground. 'You didn't know?' she repeated as she struck his head again and again. Benedict did not resist, and Seraphina hit him until she could move her arm no longer. Quintus took a step towards her, and his hand rested on her shoulder. For a moment, Seraphina felt comforted. Then she jumped to her feet.

'Don't touch me,' she said angrily.

Quintus stepped back, and Seraphina moved away from both men, retreating towards the front door of the cottage.

'You didn't know, Benedict? They were just Hebrews, weren't they? My father was protecting my mother. All you saw was Hebrews attacking a Roman soldier. Right? You didn't know. Did you know about the other Hebrew women? The others Rufio killed? The others who disappeared?'

'What others?' asked Benedict.

'It had been going on for weeks, maybe months. You served with the man, yet you didn't know he was attacking innocent Hebrew women. Well, one survived. That's the only reason I know.'

Quintus closed his eyes and remembered the story Seraphina had told him at the lake. Eliana. The other women. The anger began to rise in him at what his father had done. His fists clenched. He looked at Seraphina, who was in a rage. Then at Benedict, who looked thoroughly defeated. He was sitting on the floor, shaking his head in disbelief.

'Stop shaking your head!' shouted Seraphina. As she walked out of the cottage, she said to Quintus, 'well, I guess he won't be able to help us after all.'

Quintus followed her outside. 'Seraphina, please wait.'

'Why, Quintus? You heard him, didn't you? He and your father murdered my parents. What do you want me to wait for?'

'I don't know. I just don't want to lose you.'

'I think that is inevitable now.'

'But I love you, Seraphina.'

Seraphina softened for a moment. She looked into his eyes. Those warm eyes, so full of love and tenderness. 'Quintus, things will never be as they were. It's too much. I'm sorry.'

He watched as she walked away. There was nothing more he could say. He ambled back into the cottage, exhausted and bewildered. Benedict stood up and came close to him. He placed a hand on the boy's shoulder.

'Quintus, I honestly did not know. Please, tell me you believe me.'

His eyes pleaded with Quintus. In that moment, Quintus lost his final shred of hope that his father might be blameless in this. Looking at Benedict, he knew the truth. His father had lied.

'I believe you. He told you that Rebekah attacked him first?'

'Rebekah? Who is Rebekah?'

'That was her name. Seraphina's mother.'

'Quintus, we have to do something.'

'What can we do, Benedict? I'm not even sure Seraphina would want us to do anything now.'

'She wants justice for her parents, doesn't she?'

'Yes, but that was before all of this.'

Benedict looked Quintus right in the eye.

'My dear boy, if not for her parents' sake, then for the sake of every Hebrew in Alexandria, we have to do something. There is no telling what your father has planned. He cannot be allowed to remain in charge of Egypt.'

'What can we do?'

'I may have an idea.'

'What is it?'

Benedict explained to Quintus that he had a friend who was one of Caesar's personal guards. That he might be able to arrange to meet with Caesar and tell him the truth.

'What credibility will we have, Benedict? Caesar thinks enough of my father to make him general.'

'We have to try. The truth has to count for something. Do you want to see him in charge of every Hebrew and Egyptian throughout this land?'

'No, but isn't there a risk?'

'A risk of what?' Quintus felt a stab of fear.

'That my father will find out.'

'I should be able to speak to my friend without him knowing. He does not command Caesar's guards.'

Quintus shook his head. He was still reeling from the shock that his father was a murderer. Now Seraphina, whom he loved dearly, was lost to him.

'I don't know about this, uncle.'

'If we do nothing, many more will suffer. Just like Seraphina's parents, Rebekah and?'

'Josef. Her father's name was Josef.'

Benedict winced as he heard the name of the man he had killed. Maybe he could do something now, something to redeem himself. He knew it was a selfish motive, but he also knew the suffering that would follow if he did nothing.

'Very well. I will speak to my friend and see if he can arrange something. What are you going to do?'

'I don't know. She wants nothing to do with me.'

'Maybe things will get better in time.'

Quintus doubted that. Benedict talked some more and tried to comfort him. It didn't work. They agreed not to mention this to Rufio in any way whatsoever.

Rufio had heard the entire conversation. He and Cato had eavesdropped from a window at the back of the house. There was no way for them to be seen.

Cato was not easily shocked. Mainly, he listened and noticed the general's reactions. Rufio was surprisingly calm. He had prepared for this day for many years. He had always worried that Benedict might discover the truth. It had always been possible that the girl would resurface.

Rufio was devastated that Quintus had learned of his secret. He would forever have a tainted view of his father. It was the least of his worries for the moment. If Benedict could convince Caesar of the truth, the consequences were unthinkable. He would have to keep a close eye on his former comrade. It broke his heart that his son had agreed to keep the truth from him. In the circumstances, it made sense that Quintus was upset. In time, perhaps he would understand. For now, he had to deal with the situation at hand. He and Cato watched as Quintus walked from the cottage. When he was out of sight, they walked back to the city in silence. Near the barracks, Rufio climbed into his chariot.

'What are your orders, sir?' asked Cato.

'Follow Benedict. If he contacts anyone, I want to know immediately,' said Rufio.

'Are you sure you want to wait?'

'Benedict will have to arrange the meeting first. He won't just start broadcasting the story. He is much smarter than that.'

'Very well, sir. What about the girl?'

'Ensure she is followed. She can do little by herself, but I still want to know her movements. Tell me about anything significant.'

'What about your son?'

'You don't need to worry about him. I will deal with Quintus.'

Rufio whipped the reins of his horses and raced off into the night. After all, he wanted to make sure he arrived home before Quintus did.

THIRTY SEVEN

Afiz hadn't seen Seraphina all morning. He did a few chores, and went to look for her.

She must be sick or dying, he thought with a smile.

Both Gisgo and Khay were working in the library, and it was very unlike her not to be down there at the crack of dawn, peppering them with questions.

He knocked on the door.

No response.

He knocked again, then entered.

An odd sight awaited him. Seraphina lay on the bed, completely still. She usually rose before sunrise, and attacked the day with a vigour, but she was still in her pyjamas.

She hadn't reacted to Afiz's entrance, and Maximus sat in the corner of the room.

His gaze swayed back and forth between Seraphina and Afiz.

'Good morning, Seraphina,' said Afiz.

Seraphina sighed heavily but didn't return the greeting.

'I was wondering where you were. Gisgo and Khay are downstairs swapping lessons on philosophy and astronomy.' Afiz tried again.

Seraphina was unmoved. Afiz was worried, because the mere mention of those two usually had Seraphina in a frenzy to see them.

'Is everything alright?'

Seraphina began to cry. Her body shook as she wept, and she rolled to her side, away from Afiz. She stared at the wall, now blurry through her tears.

Afiz eased towards the bed and sat down, but he didn't speak. He just wanted Seraphina to know he was there for her. In that moment, it was all he could offer. His dear girl, his friend, was in pain again.

So much had come her way in recent weeks and, although it had been easy to forget it sometimes, she was only a child. Seraphina had a maturity and resolve beyond her years, but it didn't shield her from pain.

It could not shield her from fear, either.

Afiz thought about what must be going through her head; memories of her parents, meeting people from her past, Roman soldiers looking for her.

I should have seen this coming, he thought.

He rested a hand on her arm as she continued to whimper, as if to say *'It's fine. Let it out. I'm here.'*

Seraphina had been in turmoil the past couple of days. Yesterday, she had tried to act as if things were normal, but working in the library, she couldn't concentrate at all. She wanted more than anything to turn back time.

To go back to hiding in the library.

Having her late-night debates with Afiz, sprinting through the streets in the twilight with Maximus by her side, reading in her room, from the greatest collection of texts in the world.

It couldn't be as it was before. Everything was a reminder of what she had lost. In fact, she had lost more. Quintus, and the life of adventure and love they had imagined together. *How could they ever be together*, she thought.

His father. That lying murderer. Now, he's looking for me. It was only a matter of time. Maybe Yadira was right. She could flee to Israel and try to start over. What choice did she have?

Maybe she could take Maximus, she thought.

Everything else would be gone.

The library she grew up in. She would lose Afiz, the one who had always been there for her. She looked up at him, their eyes met, and she rose to hug him.

She buried her head in his chest and her tears soaked his tunic, but he held her, and they stayed that way for a few minutes, until Seraphina calmed down.

'Has something happened?' asked Afiz.

She nodded, her forehead still pressed against Afiz.

'Do you want to talk about it?'

She shook her head.

'Alright,' said Afiz.

Seraphina remembered the last time she kept something from Afiz. She let him go and knelt on the bed next to him.

'I should tell you,' she said, wiping her tears away.

'Only if you want to, Seraphina.'

She told him everything about her visit to Benedict. Afiz was speechless, and his gaze froze on Seraphina.

'What am I going to do, Afiz?' she asked.

He looked down to think. To try and process what he had just heard. 'I … I … have no idea. I'm … I have no words. I'm sorry, Seraphina.'

'I could take Yadira's advice.'

'Leave Alexandria? Go to Israel?'

'I don't see any other choice. Rufio is going to catch up with me eventually.'

Afiz nodded in agreement. He knew of Rufio and had heard many tales of his ambition and ruthlessness. 'You're probably right about that.'

'Do you know him? Do you know Rufio?'

'Not personally. I have heard of him though. You have good cause to be worried.'

'That's very reassuring, Afiz.'

'Sorry. Right now, the most important thing is to be honest.'

'You're right.'

Seraphina wiped her face dry and sat on the bed. She was alert now, thinking about what to do.

'Would you really leave Alexandria?' Afiz looked pained to just be saying the words.

'I don't want to, but it might be the safest option.'

'What did Quintus say?'

Seraphina described how she had attacked Benedict. Afiz could see the shame in her eyes. She told him where things were left with Quintus.

'He didn't have a chance to say much then?'

'He did say he loved me.'

'Do you love him, Seraphina?'

'I did, but now ...' Seraphina shrugged her shoulders. The resignation on her face was impossible to miss. Afiz felt for her. Her life had become so complicated.

'Will you see him again?'

'I'm not sure he would want to see me.'

'What do you mean? What was the last thing you said to him?'

Seraphina told him what she had said to Quintus. Her head dropped into her hands, the bottom of her palms pressed against her eyes.

'So, the idea of going to Benedict was that he might help you?'

'Yes.'

'Help you find the soldiers who killed your parents, and bring them to justice?'

'Yes. Sounds so silly now, doesn't it?'

'Maybe not. He used to be a soldier, right?'

'Yes.'

Seraphina described Benedict's demeanour after everything had been revealed, how he had not resisted when she had hit him, how he just lay there and took it.

'Maybe he'll want to help you.'

'Did you hear the story I told you? He was the one who killed my father.'

'Yes, but he said he didn't know, right? He didn't know that Rufio had lied to him?'

'That's what he said. Even if it were true, the man is not going to turn himself in.'

Afiz searched for a solution. It wasn't right that Seraphina would lose her life again because of all this. She already lost her parents, and spent her youth hiding away in this very room, so it was unthinkable for her to have to leave again, to leave everything she knew and held dear.

'You're probably right,' he said finally. 'So, what are we going to do?'

'I'll have to go and see Yadira. Start making plans to leave the city.'

'When?'

'As soon as possible.'

Afiz shook his head. 'Does it have to be so soon?'

'Once Rufio finds out I am here, he'll come for me, won't he?'

Afiz nodded.

'I'll go and see Yadira tonight.'

Afiz hugged Seraphina. He didn't want to let go. 'I am going to miss you.'

'I will miss you too. It's going to be strange, leaving this place.'

Seraphina looked around the room. It had been her refuge for so long. She had dreamed, slept, and learned for countless hours in this place. Afiz stared at the floor, his hands crumpling the sheet on which he sat. The thought of Seraphina leaving was one he had always considered. Not like this though. He felt like he was losing a part of himself, and it saddened him.

After looking around the room, Seraphina's eyes rested on Afiz. She took a deep breath and, like him, her gaze fell to the floor. In that moment, the silence was deafening. Time stood still, and the two sat side by side. Their eyes bored into the stone and they prayed for a miracle.

THIRTY EIGHT

Quintus loitered in the streets. It was late afternoon, and he hoped for the third day in a row that he might see Seraphina. He thought he had caught a glimpse of her two days prior. She had been working in the back of the library. It was too risky for him to speak to her there. So, he waited. Finally, his patience was rewarded. She and the caretaker came out of the library's rear entrance. He watched them, and it looked as though they were headed towards the marketplace.

They walked and chatted as if they didn't have a care in the world. He found it hard to take his eyes off her. She was so beautiful. Her good looks and striking smile had disarmed him from the moment they met. It was the heart and mind within that had truly captured him. His heart ached, and he hoped that not all was lost.

He followed them at a distance, starting behind them, then walking alongside them on a parallel street. There were only a few vendors left at this time of day, so he managed to keep them in his sights until he lost them. He doubled back to see if they had turned around. They were somewhere in the middle of that block.

Quintus thought of walking back to the street they were on, but he would be easily spotted. As he was thinking, someone tapped him on the shoulder. He flinched. Then he turned around.

'What are you doing?' asked Seraphina. Afiz was standing next to her. He did not look pleased.

Quintus was stunned. He just stood there with his mouth open.

'What are you doing?' Seraphina said again. 'Why are you following us?'

'This is Quintus?' asked Afiz.

'Yes, sir.' Quintus had finally found his words. 'Seraphina, I need to speak to you.'

'I thought I said all –.' She tried to be angry, but the sight of Quintus tempered her mood slightly.

Afiz interrupted. 'Let's get out of the street, there are a lot of people around.'

Afiz led them down the street, and turned into a small alley, gesturing for them to follow him. The alley narrowed and turned to the right, becoming a dead end. The walls had no windows, and they had complete privacy. Seraphina smiled at Afiz. Even she did not know about this place.

'Alright. Quintus, what is it you need to say?' said Afiz, keeping Seraphina protected just behind his shoulder.

'I just wanted to warn Seraphina,' said Quintus.

'Warn me? About what? Are you threatening me?' said Seraphina in a low growl.

Quintus put his hands up and took a step back. 'Of course not. I would never threaten you.'

'Then what do you want to warn me about?'

'My father. I know what he did to your family, and it stunned me, but—'

'Oh, it stunned you, did it? How do you think I felt?'

'Seraphina, perhaps you should let him finish.'

Quintus looked at Afiz, relieved for the support. He turned back to Seraphina, and hesitated.

'Well? Go ahead, finish what you were saying,' she said.

'He is a ruthless man, is what I was going to say. All my life, he has always been someone who gets what he wants. No matter how he does it. I came to warn you because I am worried about you. I am worried what might happen if he finds you and discovers who you are.'

Listening to Quintus' words, Seraphina's jaw softened. She had walked away from him that night, without even letting him speak. He had told her he loved her, and she had put an end to things between them. Even now, he had come to warn her, and she was on the attack. The boy was here putting her welfare before his own father. She felt ashamed. He had done nothing wrong.

'I'm sorry, Quintus.'

'It's alright, Seraphina.'

'No, it's not. I have been unfair.'

'In the circumstances, you're entitled to be upset.'

Afiz stood to one side and Seraphina took a step towards Quintus. She put her arms over his shoulders and hugged him, and he returned the embrace, breathing a huge sigh of relief.

'I thought I might lose you.'

'I'm sorry for what I said. None of this is your fault.'

'You have no idea how much I needed to hear that.'

Quintus was facing Afiz as he hugged Seraphina, and their eyes met for a moment. Feeling awkward, he released Seraphina.

'Don't stop on my account.' Afiz grinned.

Seraphina blushed and pushed Afiz. 'Stop it, Afiz,' she said as she smiled at Quintus. All three stood in silence for a few moments.

'So, you think Seraphina might be in danger?' said Afiz, more for the sake of saying something than anything else.

'Yes.'

'Excuse me while I play devil's advocate for a moment, but how would your father find out unless someone told him?' said Afiz to Quintus.

'Well,' said Quintus, 'he has a way of finding out things that he is not supposed to. Plus ...'

'What?' asked Seraphina.

Quintus explained how Benedict was planning to tell Caesar what he knew. Afiz and Seraphina were in disbelief. Either this Benedict was the craziest or the most honest man they had ever encountered.

'He's going to admit to Caesar that he committed a murder?' asked Afiz.

'I think the other night really shook him up. I know how upset you are at him, Seraphina, but believe me when I say that he is an honourable man. He would have believed my father though. Two nights ago, he learned he was a murderer.'

Seraphina actually felt sympathy for the man. She could not believe he was going to go to Caesar. He would be admitting a crime.

Quintus continued. 'He fears what might happen if my father remains in his new position. That he will abuse his power.'

'What new position?' asked Seraphina.

Quintus explained how Rufio had been recently promoted by Caesar. He went on to relay Benedict's concern for the Hebrews and Egyptians living in the city, and what might happen over time under Rufio's command.

'It might not matter to me,' said Seraphina. Quintus noticed Afiz's head drop as she spoke, and asked what she meant. Seraphina explained Yadira's idea to flee to Israel, and Quintus could see they were both saddened by the plan.

'Do you think Benedict will be able to meet Caesar and tell him?' asked Seraphina.

'I don't know. He said he knows one of Caesar's guards. Caesar's guards are not under my father's command. It is possible. Even then, Caesar would have to be convinced before he would do anything. Having said that, Benedict has an excellent reputation. Everyone who knows him has great respect for him.'

'Maybe there is a chance,' said Afiz.

'But not a good one,' said Seraphina.

The three stood in silence again. They searched for a solution, they despaired, and they angered at the injustice of the situation.

'May I come with you?' Quintus asked Seraphina.

'Come again,' she said.

'May I come with you?'

'To Israel?'

'Yes. To Israel. May I come with you?'

He had asked three times now. Seraphina thought of all that was happening, and the inevitable sadness of leaving Alexandria. She knew she loved Quintus. Almost since she met him, he had stood beside her through some of the toughest moments of her life.

She looked up at him and nodded. Quintus grabbed her and hugged her tightly.

'The two of you are getting ahead of yourselves,' said Afiz.

'Are we?' said Seraphina. 'If I have to leave, I will be alone. Quintus and I love one another. If he wants to come, I want him to.'

'I understand,' said Afiz. 'Let's see what Benedict does. It may be that no one needs to run away. Wouldn't that be better?'

'Yes,' said Seraphina, 'but I should still go to see Yadira, and soon.'

'Very well.'

'May I come with you?' Quintus grinned.

THIRTY NINE

Benedict's horse slowed to a canter. The Roman camp could be seen in the distance. As he approached the gate, he saw the legionaries spot him. An archer in the tower raised his bow. It was standard procedure for any visitor who was not dressed in uniform.

He slowed the horse to a trot and told a legionary he was a guest of General Rufio. The legionary signalled the archer to lower his bow. He welcomed Benedict, who dismounted his horse and handed the reins to the young soldier. The vast gates were opened, and Benedict saw the camp that had once been his home nearly ten years previously.

He walked alongside the legionary, recognising which buildings had changed and which had stayed the same. The camp looked so fearsome from the outside, but inside, it more resembled a village than a military garrison. He breathed in the fresh sea air. It carried with it the scent of the blue lotus flowers that grew in the ponds throughout the city, one of his favourite memories of his time here. They began to walk up a hill that pressed up against the far wall of the camp. He thought of the general who used to live on this hill. Now the general's quarters belonged to Rufio. The timing of the invitation had alarmed Benedict. Then again, Rufio had promised to invite him the last time they spoke.

I'm being paranoid, he thought.

They entered the house through the tall columns. The legionary went to announce Benedict's arrival while Benedict waited. The house was opulent by any standards. It was particularly extravagant for a soldier, even a general. As he looked around, Benedict resented his old friend. If he could even still be called a friend. He had betrayed his trust, and in the process a young child had been orphaned. The guilt had plagued him the past few days. No matter what, the blood of Seraphina's father would always be on his hands. His resentment turned into righteous anger.

Hopefully he could right this wrong.

Hopefully there would be justice for Seraphina's family after all these years. If he was to be punished as well, then so be it. Benedict was a man of integrity, and he would do what he believed was necessary.

'Benedict, you came,' said Rufio, entering the room.

The two greeted one another and made idle small talk. The general showed his old friend around the house. The house was massive and included every possible convenience and luxury. Benedict smiled as Rufio bragged. He cringed on the inside but remained polite. Once Rufio had given his tour, they stood at a window in the living room. They had a splendid view of the camp, the city, and the sea.

'You've done well for yourself, Rufio. Congratulations again,' said Benedict.

'Thank you.'

'Where's Quintus? I had hoped to see him.'

'He had some things to do in the city.'

Rufio looked into the distance and breathed in the fresh air. He talked to Benedict about the tensions in the city of late. Ptolemy had fled the city with his forces and ships, and there could be an attack any day now. The general was worried that innocent civilians might be killed if the young king attempted to take the throne. Benedict didn't trust a word that came out of Rufio's mouth. He did his best to look concerned, to play the role of a sympathetic friend.

'We think there may be spies in the city already,' said Rufio.

'Spies? Working for Ptolemy, you mean?' asked Benedict.

'Yes. They are uniting Cleopatra's enemies. When the fighting starts, these traitors will help the attackers in any way they can.'

Benedict nodded. He had no idea why Rufio was telling him this.

'Has anyone approached you?' said Rufio.

'No. I hardly visit the city, and no one comes to visit me.'

'No one has visited you recently?'

'Only you,' said Benedict with a smile.

Rufio smiled back. He asked about things at the farm and asked him if he was bored of the country life yet. It was a running joke between the two. Rufio had been teasing him about it for a decade, while Benedict had been telling him he loved it for just as long.

Benedict asked about Quintus, and how he was doing. Rufio played along, telling him that Quintus would be finishing his classes soon. They spoke about Quintus' future as a soldier. Benedict asked Rufio if Quintus was excited about it.

'I wouldn't say excited, but I think he will enjoy it once he is there.'

'There? Where?'

'He will be going to Rome to train as a legionary to begin with.'

'Oh, that's a shame. I will miss him.'

'I will too. I have a few things to do, Benedict. Thanks for stopping by.' Rufio began walking Benedict towards the front of the house. 'Come again and you can see Quintus before he leaves.'

'I'd like that.'

'You'll tell me if anyone comes to see you?'

'Right. Of course.'

As Rufio saw Benedict out, he reached for a dagger sheathed in his belt. He was behind Benedict, who never saw it coming. He plunged it into Benedict's back with great force.

'Actually, don't worry about it,' said Rufio, as Benedict screamed in agony.

Rufio pulled the knife out and stood in front of Benedict. He was still standing. Rufio stabbed him again, this time in the stomach. Deeply. Benedict howled in pain and fell on the steps at the front of the house. Two soldiers appeared on cue, and stood at the entrance, behind their master.

'You are a liar, and a traitor,' said Rufio, as he sat down beside Benedict.

'What? What are you talking about?' asked Benedict.

Rufio was calm and grinned at the response. 'I was there that night, when Quintus came to see you. With the girl.'

Benedict's eyes narrowed, and he said harshly, 'You bastard.'

Rufio laughed. 'First you lie to me, then you believe some bizarre tale a stranger tells you.'

He looked Rufio straight in the eyes. 'She wasn't lying, was she Rufio?'

Rufio looked off into the distance. 'I guess it doesn't matter now. You'll take it to your grave. No, she was not lying.'

'Why, Rufio?'

He turned to face Benedict. 'Why? They were only Hebrews, Benedict. I was young and impulsive.'

'All those women …' said Benedict, dropping his head.

Rufio shook his head at his friend's naivety. 'Yes, all those women. So what? Do you think Caesar would even have cared?'

'Then why not let me tell him?'

The general began to get angry. 'You are a fool, Benedict. This is just like you, to care about others and not your own kind. Both of us would be punished as murderers.'

'We deserve to be punished. We are murderers.'

Rufio stood up and gestured for his guards to come closer. 'Maybe, but that was a long time ago. I have other plans now, and I intend on seeing them through.'

'I know all about your plans.'

Rufio looked down at his old friend and asked, 'Did you know I stopped after that night?'

'That hardly matters. It is done now.'

'You're right, and now this is done too,' said Rufio as he knelt next to his old friend. He gripped the dagger in his hand and raised his arm. 'Any final words, traitor?'

'No. Actually, yes. Burn in hell, you rotten bastard.'

Rufio smiled. 'You are weak and a rat. You always were.'

Those were the last words Benedict ever heard. Rufio slammed the dagger into his chest. The blade ran clean through his heart. Rufio left the dagger there and admired his handiwork for a moment.

What a waste, he thought.

He could have been so much more. Once upon a time, he was an imposing soldier. Now look at him, nothing but a lowly farmer, and a traitor. Rufio walked back to his study. He told the guards to clean up the mess, and to make sure the body was never found.

FORTY

The Roman troops had changed their movements. They usually roamed the city by day, and once the sun had set, they would congregate in the harbour, not far from the library. They would drink, talk, and seemed more like a group of friends than soldiers on patrol.

The past few days were different, thought Seraphina.

They did not leave the harbour by day or night. They stood to attention, and there was no drinking. It also seemed as though their numbers had tripled. At least they were far away from the Hebrew village. As Seraphina watched them, she was reminded of her parents.

She cursed Rufio.

The past several days had been hard on Seraphina. The turmoil she felt of late had almost become normal. This was something different, though.

Since that night at Benedict's house, she felt weighed down. Perhaps this was the baggage the Hindu philosophers spoke of. She had spent time meditating and forgave herself every day. Her heart was telling her to do something else. Something she could not bring herself to do.

She shook off the thought and looked down at the clear streets.

No need to keep a lookout tonight, she thought.

Maximus watched her and knew she was going out. He was eager to go with her. Seraphina patted him on the head. 'Not tonight, Maximus.'

As she came out of the library's wall and into the night, a tinge of excitement crept into her. For a moment, she felt like her old self.

The empty streets beckoned.

The moon high in the sky lit the way.

She smiled and exploded into a sprint. She had just got into stride when something moved in front of her. Someone. They collided. Seraphina was dazed, but also alarmed. She got up to run away, then saw who it was.

Quintus sat on the ground, rubbing his forehead.

'Quintus!' said Seraphina. She was surprised, and her voice was far too loud. She looked around, and saw they were standing in the middle of an intersection. Anyone a hundred metres away in any direction could have seen them. She helped him to his feet. Once they were hidden, Seraphina asked what he was doing there.

'I came to see you, of course. Unlike some people, I don't roam the streets at night for fun. Do you know there are soldiers patrolling?'

'They're all in the harbour. I have done this before, you know?'

They smiled at each other, happy their old banter was back.

'I've missed this, you know,' he said.

Seraphina laughed at him. 'What? Colliding head on with each other in the street?'

Quintus took her in his arms. 'No. You making me smile, you silly goose.' He kissed her full on the lips.

'Goose, huh? You do know what the goose symbolises, don't you?'

Quintus shook his head. 'The Egyptian God, Geb,' she said. 'He allows crops to grow and is quite important. Some think of Geb as the force of ongoing creation on the planet.'

'Great, so I tried to mock you and ended up paying you a huge compliment? I need to read more.'

'That you do. You don't mind me educating you, do you, my love?'

'Of course not. So where are we going?'

'We?' Seraphina gave him a playful push. 'We are not going anywhere,' she said as a joke. 'I am going to see a friend.'

'Sounds cryptic. Should I be jealous?'

Seraphina smiled.

'We're going to see Yadira, now be quiet and follow me.'

She poked her head around the corner. She knew no one was around, but it was force of habit. The two ran together towards the Hebrew village. Seraphina slowed herself down, and Quintus ran alongside her. She smiled, enjoying the feeling of him being next to her.

I could get used to this, she thought.

Or maybe he could learn to run faster. Quintus noticed both her slower speed and her grinning face. He said nothing about either. He was happy to be with Seraphina again.

They belonged together, he thought.

His mind started to drift into the future, and it made him happy. There had been two days of severe heartache earlier that week, when he thought any future with her had been lost, and he hoped he never felt that way again.

'We're here,' said Seraphina.

It had just struck Seraphina that she was bringing a Roman to Yadira's house. She was not sure how that would go down. Fortunately, it was late enough that the street was empty.

Anyway, we're here now, she thought.

She shrugged her shoulders and motioned for Quintus to follow her. Quintus was oblivious, and wondered what Seraphina was thinking about. As she knocked on the door, Quintus took her hand. Yadira opened the door and gave them a quizzical look.

'Um, hello, Seraphina,' she said.

'Hello.'

They stood on the step to the house as Yadira examined Quintus.

'May we come in?' asked Seraphina. 'This is my friend, Quintus.'

'Of course, I am sorry. Please come in.'

As they walked into the house, Saul gave Quintus an equally odd look.

I was right, thought Seraphina. *This is weird.*

'Saul, this is Quintus.'

'It's good to meet you, sir,' said Quintus, approaching Saul, and offering his hand to shake. Saul hesitated, then shook it.

Quintus felt a little uncomfortable and regretted coming. Seraphina also felt awkward, and a bit stupid that she had not thought of this.

'Maybe I should go …' said Quintus.

'No, no, that's fine,' said Yadira. 'Come on, let's all sit down.'

Seraphina smiled at Yadira and apologised for bringing Quintus without warning. She introduced him properly, although she left out certain details for now. Yadira and Saul were fascinated. They had never met a Roman in a social setting. Their contact was limited to soldiers, who were often hostile. This young man, by contrast, seemed warm and courteous. The attraction between him and Seraphina was not lost on them either. As Seraphina spoke, the two could not stop smiling at each other. Yadira and Saul thought it was cute, and they asked Quintus some polite questions to make conversation.

'So, Seraphina, what brings you here tonight? Other than to introduce your boyfriend to us?' asked Yadira.

'Boyfriend?' said Seraphina, looking at Quintus.

Quintus smiled. 'Actually, Seraphina was on her way here when I ran into her. She wasn't even planning on bringing me with her.'

'I see,' said Yadira.

Seraphina told them what she had learned. She told them about her visit to Benedict. She told them about Rufio, and how he had lied to Benedict. Yadira and Saul listened, and everything began to fit together. The general's guards searching for Seraphina. How Seraphina had ended up at the library in the first place. Why the attacks had stopped. They listened with great interest at the idea that Benedict might confess to Caesar. Such a scenario was unimaginable in their minds. They wondered about Quintus' involvement, and Yadira watched him as Seraphina spoke. Seraphina bypassed the part about Quintus being Rufio's son.

Seraphina shared with them her fear of being found by Rufio. She was sceptical that Benedict would be able to do anything, if in fact he did help. She could not put her fate in his hands. She had decided that fleeing the city was her only choice.

Yadira was surprised. 'Wait. Now you do want to go to Israel?' she asked.

'Yes. I don't see any other way. If I stay here, this Rufio will eventually find me. Aside from myself, I could be putting Afiz in danger, as well as you and Saul.'

'Yes, but Seraphina. What you said last time—'

Seraphina interrupted. 'I know what I said last time, but things have changed. This Rufio is a powerful man. He commands all of Caesar's forces throughout Egypt.'

'Are you afraid?'

Seraphina admitted she was. The four of them discussed the situation. Every angle was analysed. All possibilities were considered. Yadira wondered how Rufio might even find out about Seraphina's existence. Saul agreed with his wife, and it made Seraphina wonder. Even if they were right, her relationship with Quintus came with its risks. Yadira asked if they would flee together, and they answered together in the affirmative.

'Won't your family miss you?' Yadira asked Quintus.

'Yadira,' said Seraphina. 'There is something I have to tell you.'

'What is it?'

Seraphina told her who Quintus' family was. Yadira was in shock, but she and Saul allowed her to finish. Seraphina told them all about Quintus, and how much he had stood up for her. By the time she finished, they looked at him with admiration. Quintus explained his own issues with his father. He told of the hurt and devastation of realising who his father truly was. He wanted to be with Seraphina and leaving his father behind would not be difficult in the circumstances.

'You are a good young man,' said Yadira.

'Thank you,' said Quintus.

Yadira went back to her notion that Rufio might never find out. As they continued to discuss things, it became evident they were going in circles. No one could guess if Rufio would ever learn about Seraphina and her true identity. If Quintus and Seraphina stayed together, it increased the chances that he would discover her. Having said that, it was clear to everyone in the room that Quintus and Seraphina wanted to stay together. To call this a quagmire was a huge understatement. There was one thing Yadira felt compelled to say.

'Seraphina, do you remember the last time you were here?'

'Of course, Yadira.'

'Do you remember what you convinced me of?'

Seraphina sighed. 'I do.'

Seraphina listened to Yadira and considered her words very carefully. Yadira spoke of Rebekah, and the kind of person she was. She told Seraphina how much she was like her mother.

'Even if you go, you will always wonder about this. I am worried it will haunt you,' said Yadira.

Seraphina hung her head in resignation. For a moment, she despaired, then she thought of her mother. She thought about how Yadira had spoken of her gritty and spirited personality, of how her own memories of her mother were of a strong woman, then she looked up and into the faces of the three people in the room. As she looked at each of them, she saw unconditional love and support. Yadira had first suggested she flee. Now she was proposing an idea that verged on the insane.

'What could I even do?' she asked, to no one in particular.

'We. What could we do,' said Quintus, as he took her hand.

Seraphina smiled at him, and a tear ran down her cheek.

Yadira and Saul beamed at the young man.

If all Romans were like this, Yadira thought, *it would be a different world.*

'Very well. What could we do?' asked Seraphina.

'We could go and talk to Benedict. See if he is serious about going to Caesar,' said Quintus.

Seraphina bit her bottom lip. 'I would be so embarrassed. I hit him last time. A lot.'

'You hit him?' asked Yadira. She was amused by the idea.

Seraphina kept biting her lip and shook her head at herself. 'Yes. I lost my temper. Badly.'

Quintus moved closer to Seraphina and rubbed her shoulder to comfort her. 'I spoke to him afterwards, Seraphina. He understood you were upset,' he said.

'What if he doesn't want to help? Or if his plan doesn't work?' Seraphina leaned forward.

'Then we will figure it out from there,' said Quintus.

'Is there anything we can do?' asked Saul.

'Find out what we would need to do to leave the city,' said Seraphina, standing. 'Just in case.'

She hugged Yadira and Saul, perhaps for the last time. The Hebrews hugged Quintus as well. It was the first time either of them had hugged a Roman. After they said their goodbyes, Quintus and Seraphina walked out into the dark night, holding hands, and remaining silent, daunted by the prospect of what they were about to do.

FORTY ONE

Gisgo paced around the lecture hall, pondering thoughts as usual. He looked up at the rows of seats.

What a grand room, he thought.

He imagined all the people who had learned in this room, then he thought about all the people who were yet to learn in this room.

There was nothing quite like education, to his mind. It came in all forms, not just from the reading and writing of texts, and the old philosopher had learned many lessons in his time.

Despite his age, he was still open to learning new things.

His logic was that if he stopped being willing to learn, it meant he had reached the peak of his knowledge, which went against the very fibre of his being. He loved learning and had decided a long time ago that he would continue to learn until his dying day.

The quiet of the room was interrupted by a small click. He turned around. Seraphina was carefully closing a small door. It was right at the back of the lecture hall. She turned around and froze. She had not expected to see Gisgo.

'Hello, Seraphina. I haven't seen you in a while.'

Seraphina remembered the last time they had seen each other.

She had run from the museum, upset and in tears.

They chatted about what each of them had been up to. Seraphina edited her side of the conversation heavily. She did not think it wise to tell Gisgo of the events in her life. It wasn't that she didn't trust him, her instincts just told her it would be a bad idea. Besides, he would be in utter disbelief. Some days, even she was in disbelief.

'You were quite upset the last time I saw you. Is everything alright now?'

Seraphina nodded. 'Yes, thank you for asking.'

'No problem. So, what is on the other side of that door?'

'Oh, just a storeroom. Nothing interesting.'

They talked about Gisgo's visit and how much he had enjoyed it. He and Khay seemed to have become very good friends. Seraphina listened, feeling a little miffed. Because of all the drama in her world, she had missed out on spending time with these great minds.

Yet another reason to be angry with Rufio, she joked to herself.

At least she hadn't lost her sense of humour. Gisgo was only halfway through his trip, so maybe not all was lost.

'I'm going to do some reading in the library. Would you like to walk with me?'

'Absolutely.' She nodded happily.

The two walked out of the lecture hall, chatting about this and that.

'Will you be writing anything while you are here?'

'Possibly.'

'Perhaps a scroll you will leave in the library?' She smiled and raised her eyebrows.

'Actually, I've already started working on something.'

'I can't wait to read it.' Seraphina skipped for a step, and then halted. She stared at the ground, her smile giving way to a slight grimace.

'What do you think happens if someone does a wrong upon you, and you never forgive the person?'

'Remember how I asked you before if everything is alright now?'

'Yes, I remember.'

'It's not, is it?'

Seraphina did not make a move. She made eye contact for a second, then looked away. Her forehead pressed against her palm, as she leaned forward. Her fingers tapped the top of her skull. Gisgo watched and waited. Seraphina's fingers stopped tapping. She looked out from behind her hand. Gisgo was still there, with a concerned look on his face. She looked back down. There was plenty she wanted to say, but she wasn't sure she should say any of it.

Gisgo decided to speak. 'Look, Seraphina. This is none of my business, but you have talked to me about this before. You have asked me about it today. I know you are inquisitive, but this doesn't strike me as idle curiosity.'

Seraphina spoke in general terms. 'There is someone who has done something terrible. Something that hurt me and impacted my life. I'm not sure if I want to forgive this person, but it is eating away at me. There is something I am very curious about.' She was still staring at the table, her head planted in her hand.

'What is that?'

'How does the idea of forgiveness work when it comes to justice?'

'How do you mean?'

'Well, say someone commits a crime. The crime affects someone in a very significant way. If that person feels compelled to forgive, does that mean she should not seek justice?'

Gisgo said, 'The two are not mutually exclusive. Take the example of a thief. If a man were to rob a family, the family might be inclined to forgive him. Even if the family did forgive the thief, they may still wish to seek justice. That could be some time in the dungeon to repent for his crime, or some form of restitution for what he stole.'

'Interesting,' said Seraphina. Her chin was now on her hand, as she reflected on Gisgo's words.

'Do you know of a crime that has been committed?' asked Gisgo.

'No.'

Gisgo's eyes were filled with doubt, but he let it go.

He stood up, walking towards the shelves to find some texts, but as he left the table, Seraphina moved as if to say something. He turned his head back, his eyes inviting her to speak. She looked down to the table, her chin resting in her palms.

'Look, Seraphina. If something has happened, if a crime has been committed, you should tell someone. The problem with criminals is often that they repeat their behaviour when there are no consequences. If someone has done something to upset you, then of course you may forgive them. In fact, I always think it is better to forgive. Then you can move on. The act of forgiveness can often be more important –'

'For the forgiver than the forgiven. I remember,' said Seraphina.

'Yes. But if a serious crime has been committed, it would still be wise to do something about it. At the very least, to tell someone in a position of authority.'

Seraphina nodded without looking up. Gisgo went to scour the shelves.

'Thank you, Gisgo.'

FORTY TWO

The lake was perfectly still.

Seraphina played with Maximus, who enjoyed the attention. He ran around her lap, snapping at her fingers as she tickled him.

He is such a funny little dog, thought Seraphina.

She waited for her Quintus.

With the city behind her, there was nothing but empty space in front of her. Green plains stretched as far as the eye could see, but beyond that, there was harsh desert.

At least, that's what she had been told.

The trip to Israel would have them crossing the desert, if it came to that. She held Maximus up and wondered how he would fare in such wilderness. He squirmed in her hands, trying to wrap his mouth around her thumb. She giggled.

He'd probably have a great time, she thought.

She lifted him high up in the air and stood. Turning around, she said, 'You'll always be with me, won't you Maximus?' As she turned, she saw Quintus approaching.

You will too, she thought.

She hoped.

She put Maximus down in anticipation of a big hug. As he got closer, she saw his face. It was pale. He looked almost faint.

'What is wrong, Quintus?'

He just shook his head and continued walking towards her. He planted his face just below her shoulder and was completely still, and out of instinct, she wrapped her arms around him. She had no idea what was wrong. At that moment, she knew all there was to do was hold him. She walked with him, and they sat together on their rock.

He looked off into the distance, unable to speak. She watched him, and he held her hand. Seraphina held his hand with both of hers and squeezed to let him know she was there. She looked up and saw he was crying, tears in freefall down his gentle face.

Finally, he muttered, 'Benedict is gone. My uncle is gone.'

'What do you mean, he's gone?' whispered Seraphina.

'He's gone. He's dead.'

'Dead? What happened?'

Quintus explained how he had found out from his father. He had come home in the afternoon. His father was in the living room. He seemed to be waiting for him. There was some bad news, he told Quintus. Then he asked him when was the last time he had seen Benedict. Quintus lied of course, and his father gave him an odd look.

'Are you sure?' Rufio had asked him.

'Of course, father. What is the bad news?'

His father said, 'Benedict's cottage had been burned to the ground. There is no sign of Benedict. It must have been bandits.'

'Bandits,' mumbled Seraphina, who by now was also in shock.

'There were no bandits,' said Quintus.

Seraphina asked what he meant. Quintus went on to explain his father's demeanour when he told him. Blank face, neutral tone. As if he was talking about some everyday event.

'He killed him, Seraphina. Or had him killed. It's the same thing.'

'I am so sorry, Quintus.'

The two sat, hand in hand, with nothing left to say for now. Quintus' grief was almost palpable, and Seraphina felt powerless.

Now he has lost someone as well, she thought.

Gisgo was right. If something wasn't done, this would never end. This man would go on ruining lives to get what he wanted. After a while, Quintus sat up straight. He let go of Seraphina's head and wiped his face with his palms.

'I'm sorry I cried so much,' he said.

'Please, Quintus. You do not need to apologise.'

'I know. It just doesn't feel right.'

'Makes you feel like less of a man?' She couldn't help but tease.

Quintus laughed. It made him feel better. 'Something like that, I guess.'

'You are the most wonderful man I have ever known. Tears or no tears. You got that?'

Quintus nodded. 'We had better start making arrangements, don't you think?'

Seraphina knew what he was suggesting, and she took his hand back in hers. 'We can't, Quintus.'

Quintus was confused.

'If we go now, this will stay with us forever,' said Seraphina.

Quintus listened to her words, but he thought only of protecting her. He looked at her. The strength in those eyes. He had lost someone dear to him, and he was ready to run away. This girl was ready to stay and face whatever came their way. In that moment, Quintus' love and respect for Seraphina deepened beyond measure. He smiled and embraced her. They would stick together, they decided. No matter what.

'So, what's the plan?' asked Quintus.

'I have no idea,' said Seraphina.

The two of them spoke long into the night. Quintus shared his fondest memories of Benedict, and he laid the memory of his uncle to rest. Seraphina had remembered more about her parents. She told Quintus every single detail, and he listened, enjoying the way her face lit up when she spoke about them. She showed him the necklace at least four times as she told her stories. He smiled and looked at it.

Our love, he thought.

Seraphina's father had given it to his wife when they were married.

He watched Seraphina talk, and could feel his heart beat. He wanted to give this girl everything he could, everything she desired. If it was up to him, all her dreams would come true. Like Seraphina, his mind would often drift into the future. Well, that wasn't true. It only happened when it came to thoughts of the two of them.

They talked about what they were going to do. They both knew that Caesar stayed in the palace when he came to the city. Seraphina knew his ship. They would have to be careful, because the area around the palace was crawling with soldiers.

They had both heard gossip.

The feud between Cleopatra and her younger brother was about to reach breaking point. Caesar was enmeshed in the situation through his alliance with the new queen, so the palace would be surrounded.

They thought of how to approach the situation. The only person who had authority over Rufio was Caesar, so the idea of trying to tell anyone else was discarded. Lots of plans were formed, then ditched.

'I can't think of anything. He is a hard man to get to, after all. Many kings and warlords have tried before us,' said Quintus.

Seraphina nodded her head, glaring at the pebbles at her feet. As if they might somehow give her the answer. Then suddenly, her head shot up and her eyes widened.

'I have an idea.'

She told Quintus her plan. She said what he would need to do, and how she would get past any soldiers and guards. Quintus poked a few holes in it, but it was the best idea either of them had come up with.

'Of course, there are some risks,' said Seraphina.

What they were thinking of doing was crazy.

FORTY THREE

Rufio was looking at a giant piece of parchment. It was a sketch of the harbour. He looked at the headlands that jutted out into the waters, and pictured soldiers posted there. His scouts had still not found the missing Egyptian ships. The general did not believe they would stage an attack through the harbour. It was too daring. His military advisers thought otherwise.

Caesar had ordered him to plan a defence of the bay. *Our ships must not be cut off from the sea.* Those had been Caesar's exact words. He had selected a crew of men who knew the harbour well. They would have to sail into the waters. It had to be scoured for every point of advantage and weakness. Rufio believed in meticulous planning. If Ptolemy dared to enter their harbour, he would regret it.

He saw his son in the living room. He called him in.

'Quintus, how are you today?'

'I'm well, father,' came the brief reply.

'Look, I know you must be struggling. I am sorry we didn't speak much the other day about Benedict. I was in shock. I still am.' He motioned for his son to sit down.

The boy seethed at his father's deception. He gave no outward indication of his feelings and sat. Rufio talked to him about how these things sometimes happen. It was unfortunate, but Benedict would not want him to be unhappy.

I know what Benedict would want me to do, thought Quintus.

He just sat and nodded, as if he were absorbing the words of a wise man. His father told him that things would be better soon. He would finish his schooling, and before he knew it, he would be in Rome. Rufio told him about the training camp he was going to. Quintus feigned enthusiasm, and this pleased his father.

'I haven't completely come around to the idea, but I am looking forward to the new experience, Father.'

'Once you are there, you will enjoy it. I am certain of that.'

They talked about the rest of Quintus' classes, which were due to finish in a couple of weeks. Quintus seemed worried about the war gossip around the city. Rufio assured him it was nothing of concern. As they spoke, Rufio became curious. Quintus seemed in good spirits. He had opened his mind to the thought of being a soldier, however slightly. Maybe he had just accepted how things were going to be.

Rufio had spoken to Cato, who reported nothing unusual in the girl's movements. She had not seen Quintus since the night at Benedict's house. At least, not according to Cato. However, Rufio did not have the full story.

When Rufio had ordered Cato to spy on Benedict, it had meant he could not monitor Seraphina. Another operative had been assigned to watch her. Unknown to Cato, this spy was not nearly as reliable as he believed.

Cato's information was bad, and Rufio was misinformed. Had he known the truth, Quintus would have been confined to the camp days ago, so, as it turned out, Seraphina and Quintus caught a huge break, and Rufio's suspicions remained just that, merely suspicions.

My son has come to his senses, thought Rufio.

There was no future for him with that girl, regardless of the circumstances, and he was confident that Quintus had realised this.

As they chatted, Quintus noticed all the papers on his father's table. He asked about them. Rufio, pleased by Quintus' curiosity, showed him the sketches of the harbour. It showed the positions of ships and soldiers throughout the city and its waters. Quintus showed a lot of interest and made mental notes. He memorised the area around the palace as best he could.

'I'm going to be gone most of the day, son.'

'Oh? Where will you be?'

'I have to go out into the harbour. We will spend most of the day there. All in a day's work of keeping our city safe.'

Quintus said goodbye and watched his father leave the camp. He raced away on his chariot. Quintus took a deep breath.

It's now or never, he thought.

He walked out of the camp like it was any other day. He looked back for a moment and realised he might never see it again. The thought made him smile. He headed towards the city and did not look back.

FORTY FOUR

Afiz and Seraphina worked the morning away. They went through the library, putting things back in place.

Some of these scholars are slobs, thought Seraphina.

Nevertheless, she helped Afiz tidy the library from top to bottom. Now that she was no longer in hiding from Imhotep, such tasks could be done in daylight. It made a miserable chore a much easier one, because they could work with two hands, and without the need to carry a lamp.

Once they were finished, they went to Seraphina's room. They had not spoken in a few days, and she wanted to give him an update. Seraphina sat on the bed and Maximus jumped into her arms. Afiz moped around the room. He looked at every crack and crevice as if he might never be there again.

Not long ago, they would talk in this room nearly every morning. Now, each passing day brought them closer to never seeing each other again.

'So, how did it go with Yadira?' asked Afiz.

Seraphina thought of telling him about Benedict first, but she decided to answer his question instead. They talked about her going to see Yadira. Afiz was amused that Quintus had come along. It had gone quite well, Seraphina assured him. She told Afiz how she had asked Saul to find out how they could leave the city if they needed to.

'So, you're definitely going?' asked Afiz.

'Well …' muttered Seraphina.

'Well, what?'

Seraphina explained. She talked about her parents. Then she mentioned her conversations with Yadira and Gisgo. She knew it would haunt her forever if she ran away. Rufio could not be allowed to get away with his crimes.

'I can't leave, Afiz. Not like this.'

'Seraphina, this is madness. I understand how you feel, but Rufio is not a lowly soldier anymore. He is a powerful general. What happened was over ten years ago. I'm not saying that you shouldn't feel hurt. Of course you should. In time, you may feel differently.'

'Well, there is something else.'

At the moment, there was a knock on the door.

Seraphina and Afiz froze and stared at each other.

Even Maximus' eyes shifted across the room in suspicion.

They were the only three who were ever in this room.

Another knock.

Seraphina's neck clenched, and she looked at the door. Afiz motioned for her to hide under the bed.

Once she had, Afiz shrugged his shoulders to loosen up and faced the door.

One last knock.

Afiz creaked the door open.

'Quintus?' he whispered. He yanked the boy into the room, checking the corridor before closing the door. Seraphina materialised from under the bed and asked him how he got inside the library.

'Um, you showed me, Seraphina,' he said. 'Remember, the other night when we came up with our plan? You told me how to come and find you when it was time.'

'Time for what? What plan?' asked Afiz. He folded his arms and glared at Seraphina.

'Oh, I completely forgot.' Seraphina clasped her head in frustration.
'You forgot?' asked Quintus.
'Forgot about what?' asked Afiz.
There are too many people talking at once, thought Seraphina.

She told Quintus she had forgotten about telling him how to get into the library. She hadn't forgotten about their plan.

'What plan?' asked Afiz again. He was about to implode with worry. The two of them calmed him and explained their plan. He was not impressed.

'What?' yelled Afiz, as he sprang to his feet. 'When I came in here this morning, I thought you were running away to Israel with him.' He pointed at Quintus. 'Now you're telling me you plan to infiltrate Caesar's palace? To tell him about a crime committed by his most senior officer?' Afiz was exasperated and marched around the room as he spoke.

'Afiz, please calm down,' said Seraphina.

'Very well. I'm calm, but you need to listen to me, Seraphina. Even if you do somehow get to speak to Caesar, what happened was a long time ago. That is how he is going to think of it.'

'I have to try, Afiz. Besides, there's more to the story.'

Afiz's breathing became heavier again. He could not take many more of these surprises. Seraphina and Quintus told him about Benedict's death. About how Rufio had spoken to Quintus afterwards. He was a good man, said Quintus, and now he is gone.

'I am so sorry, Quintus,' said Afiz.

Quintus nodded and thanked him. Seraphina took Quintus' hand and looked to Afiz. 'Now do you see why we have to do something? This man will continue like this, hurting people to get what he wants.'

'I just don't know if it's going to work.'

'Trust me, Afiz.'

'You're crazy, Seraphina. Fine, I trust you. Wait, you said something about a plan? That Quintus was coming to get you when it was time for your plan?'

Seraphina grinned at him. 'That's right.'

Quintus noticed Afiz's stare and was more tentative. 'Ah, yes.

I came to get you because my father will not be anywhere near the palace today.'

'How do you know that?' asked Afiz.

Quintus explained what his father had told him. Afiz argued that it could be a ruse. Even if it was, Quintus said, there was no time to delay. Caesar was due to leave that afternoon.

'If we don't catch him now, we may not get another chance,' said Quintus.

'So, what exactly is this plan?' asked Afiz.

'Well, we've been talking about that,' said Quintus. 'I've spent a lot of time at the palace, especially recently.'

'What do you mean?' asked Afiz.

'My father often had to go there as part of his duties when I was growing up. I went with him.'

'And recently?' said Afiz.

'As part of this plan, I thought I should check out a few things. This is the exact uniform the servant girls wear in the palace.' He reached into a small bag he had with him.

Afiz's raised his eyebrows and looked at Seraphina, who was smiling at him.

Quintus continued. 'I've also worked out where the servants' entrance is and have a pretty good idea of the layout of the palace.'

'You think Seraphina will be able to walk in wearing that uniform and all will be fine?' asked Afiz.

'No,' said Quintus. 'Of course, there is a risk, but knowing how the servant girls look, how they wear their hair, and how they come and go from the palace will give us some advantage at least. From there, it's up to Seraphina.'

'Sounds like you two have thought of everything,' said Afiz. He gripped Seraphina's shoulders and looked into her eyes. 'Are you sure about this, Seraphina?'

She looked at Afiz, smiled and nodded. 'Yes.' Afiz did not release his grip, and a tear ran down his cheek. It splashed on the ground.

'We have to go, Afiz. You have to let me go.'

Afiz nodded, but his hands continued to clutch her. He hugged her tight. 'Make sure you come back, alright?'

'I will, Afiz.'

'Promise.'

'I promise.'

Seraphina patted Maximus on the head and left with Quintus. Afiz was left alone in the room with the small dog. He went to the window. He looked down and saw the two of them walk away. He looked up and said a prayer for them.

Please bring her back safe to me.

Seraphina watched Quintus. Once again, he was by her side. He had risked a lot in recent days. They went over the plan again. Quintus did not like that it involved Seraphina going into the palace alone. It could not be helped though. His presence would be suspicious. At least one soldier was bound to recognise him. That certainly would not help things. He had a grimace on his face as he walked. The poor boy had been through an emotional whirlwind of his own. Seraphina could relate to that.

'Are you alright, Quintus?' she asked.

Quintus nodded. 'It's just my father,' he said.

'What about him?'

'I'm so furious at him. I'm glad that I'll never see him again.'

Seraphina nodded. Quintus watched her, and she looked so peaceful. He asked how she felt.

'The past few weeks have been unlike anything I ever imagined. Remembering the truth about my parents was tough. Hearing Benedict tell me the full story was even more difficult. It has taken me time, but I have forgiven myself for running out the door that night.'

'I'm glad to hear that. It wasn't your fault.'

'I have forgiven your father too.'

Quintus stopped dead in his tracks. He could not fathom what Seraphina had just said to him. He forgot his surroundings for a moment, and asked Seraphina how she could do that. It was a short walk from the library to the palace, and there were soldiers everywhere, so they moved to a less open spot.

Seraphina took Quintus' hands in hers and looked into his eyes with earnest. She described the emotional rollercoaster she had been on. The heartbreak, the sadness, the anger, the regret.

'I felt nothing but rage against your father. I still do when I think about it. What that feeling did to me though, that was the biggest surprise. It changed me. From the happy girl I was to a creature burdened by hate. It made me think of the future. Did I want to have that with me for the rest of my life? I decided I did not. I am forgiving him, so I can let go and move on. I don't know if he is sorry, and maybe I never will. The attacks stopped after that night. My guess is that something changed in him. Whether it was remorse or something more practical, I don't know. What I do know is that I don't want to spend the rest of my life thinking about Rufio. So, I have forgiven him.'

Quintus was astounded. He had never imagined forgiving his father for the things he had done. To Seraphina's parents, let alone to Benedict. Then there were all those other women he had attacked. He thought about what they were doing and understood. Seraphina wanted to let it go. She wanted to remember her parents with love in her heart. Not hatred for their murderer. She wanted Caesar to know the truth about his general.

It wasn't driven by hate.

It was simple.

It was justice.

He smiled at his girl, who was unlike anyone he had ever known. They shared a hug and continued towards the palace.

FORTY FIVE

Caesar was tired of Alexandria.

He loved Cleopatra, without a doubt. The young queen made outrageous demands though. The city was on high alert, and soldiers surrounded the harbour. Not to mention every one of its buildings. The amount of men protecting the palace was ridiculous, even to Caesar. Yet she demanded that battalions be dispatched to capture her brother. Time and again, Caesar had explained that the protection of the city was their best strategy, but she refused to listen.

The most frustrating and expensive case of sibling rivalry ever, he thought.

Still, he remained patient. He had not got this far through acting on impulse. Keeping the queen happy was essential to his plans. He was leaving the city today. He was happy about that, but then again, plenty of problems awaited him in Rome.

'I have told you. The city will be much safer once Ptolemy is captured,' said Cleopatra.

'My men have everything under control. The city is safe,' said Caesar. 'Now please, leave me be. I must get ready to go to the docks.'

'The docks? Where are you going?'

'To Rome. I told you this.'

'Rome?' shouted Cleopatra.

This set off another tirade. This time, Caesar listened without responding. He got together a few things and tuned out the young queen's voice. She spoke louder and louder, trying to get Caesar's attention. By the time he looked back up, she was screaming at him.

'Enough!' Caesar's voice boomed through the room.

He asked her to get out.

The tone of his voice jarred her, and she left without a word. A few moments later, he heard the door creak open. Caesar spun around, prepared to rebuke Cleopatra if she had returned. It was not her. Seraphina entered the room, dressed as a servant. She stood in the doorway, carrying a bundle of sheets. Caesar looked at her, wondering why she was just standing there. Seraphina had not expected to find Caesar alone.

'May I come in, sir? I'm here to clean your quarters.'

'Please, can you come back later?' said Caesar, turning his attention back to other matters.

'Certainly. When should I return?'

Caesar shot her an angry look.

What kind of servant was this, he thought.

'In a few hours,' he said through gritted teeth.

Seraphina retreated from the room. As she walked down the hall, a Roman soldier hurried past her. He did not so much as look at her.

At least the disguise was working, she thought.

She looked back at the soldier, and saw he was almost running. She decided to follow him and see what he was doing.

Caesar was now fuming at yet another interruption. He looked up this time to see a soldier, panting.

'What is it now?' yelled Caesar at the soldier.

'A problem with your ship, sir.'

Caesar shook his head and asked what the issue was. The soldier started to explain something about the sail, but Caesar cut him off.

'Never mind,' said Caesar. 'Just fix it.' The soldier was about to run out of the room.

'Hold on,' said Caesar. 'How long will it take?'

'It shouldn't be more than a few hours, sir.'

Caesar dismissed the soldier and lay down on his lounge. If he had to wait here a few hours longer, he would at least do so in peace.

FORTY SIX

Peace was far from Ptolemy's mind. He screamed at Pothinus, who had found yet another reason to delay their plans.

'Your majesty, Caesar is leaving the city at any moment. As soon as his ship is out of sight, we will attack.'

'He was supposed to leave already. Is that right?'

'Yes, your majesty.'

Ptolemy sat up in his chair. He may have been young, but he was still the king. 'Let me make this very clear to you, Pothinus. Our forces are ready. Our ships are hidden within striking distance of the city. This attack is happening today. I do not care whether Caesar is in Alexandria, in Rome, or in the middle of the sea. We will follow through on our plans. If that does not happen, come tomorrow, you will no longer be in command of anything. Do you understand?'

'I do, your majesty.'

Ptolemy smiled, and relaxed back into his seat. 'Good. The plan is to attack as the sun goes down, correct?'

'It is, your majesty.'

Ptolemy pointed a finger at Pothinus. 'The moment that sun starts to set, sound the attack.'

Pothinus bowed and left the room.

FORTY SEVEN

Caesar woke from his nap. It was late in the afternoon, and he had heard nothing about his ship.

It is best to wait, he thought.

He picked at some grapes, popping them into his mouth one by one. He thought of his days as a child. Sometimes he wondered if he had made the right choices. Much of his journey had not been a result of choice though. His father's death had been a pivotal moment in his life, and he became head of his family at a young age. Responsibility was thrust on him, and it became a habit. Now, he was responsible for an entire republic. That came with its benefits. Still, he wondered what a simpler life might have been like.

A knock on the door disrupted his thoughts. The same servant girl was back. He gestured at her to get on with her business. Seraphina moved towards the bed, thinking of what to do next. She started changing the sheets and watched Caesar. He ignored her, and sat on his lounge popping grapes into his mouth.

The plan has worked, thought Seraphina.

She was in the palace, and Caesar was right there. There was no obvious way to start a conversation. She decided to go with the direct approach.

Setting the sheets down, she walked towards the lounge.

'Caesar, may I ask you something?'

Caesar sat up. He had a disoriented look on his face. 'What is it?'

'I have something to tell you. It's important.'

Caesar did not understand.

'What would a servant girl have to tell me that was important?'

Seraphina told him it was about something a soldier of his had done. A serious crime committed many years ago. Caesar held up his hand to interrupt her.

'Do you actually work in the palace?' he asked.

'Well, no, but—'

'Guards!' shouted Caesar. 'Guards!'

Seraphina panicked and started telling him the story. She mentioned Rufio's name, which caught Caesar's attention straight away. Then she started babbling about her parents. That Rufio had killed them. Then something about other Hebrew women. It made little sense to Caesar, who had stopped listening. He shouted again for his guards, who finally came.

Seraphina had just finished telling him about Benedict. As the guards pointed their spears at her, she finished her story with 'he was a Roman soldier too, and Rufio murdered him.' Caesar ordered the guards to take her away and to keep her away from the palace.

What the hell is going on, he thought. *Why was an Egyptian servant girl in his living quarters? Why was she telling him about Hebrews who had been killed? More than anything, why was she accusing Rufio of such terrible crimes?*

He shook his head.

None of it made sense, he thought.

He was about to ask the guards to bring her back, when yet another person ran into his room.

It had been a busy day.

'What is it now? Is my ship ready at least?' said Caesar.

'No, it's not that, sir. The city is under attack!'

FORTY EIGHT

The Egyptians were well organised. They swarmed the city as planned. The Roman soldiers were not prepared. Most of the city was lost due to the concentration of their forces in the harbour. By approaching from the rear of the city, Pothinus had taken them by complete surprise. The people hid in their homes as soldiers clashed in the streets. The first phase of the attack had been a huge success for Ptolemy's forces. Pothinus gathered his men, and headed for the bay.

The fate of the Roman camp was much worse. Achillas had been clever. One of his men, disguised as a Roman soldier, rode towards the camp. Once the gate had been fully opened, Achillas had sounded the charge. Hundreds of men, including heavy cavalry, attacked the camp. The fighting was fierce, but brief. The Romans had not anticipated such an attack. Most did not even have time to arm themselves.

Caesar ran to the front of the palace. He could see the enemy forces advancing. One group from the east, and the other from the city. They had perfectly flanked his forces. Outraged, he screamed at a nearby soldier.

'Where is Rufio? Where is the general?'

The soldier was terrified. He simply pointed into the harbour.

Caesar's eyes followed, and what he saw panicked him. A lone Roman sailboat was in the harbour. It carried the general's standard. An entire fleet was nearing the entrance to the bay.

'Signal them!' shouted Caesar.

Rufio's crew were looking at some rocks. One of the sailors said any attacking boats could be forced on to the rocks with ease. As he heard the words "attacking boats" Rufio spotted them.

He snapped his head back to the shore, and saw the soldiers signalling his boat.

A bit late, he thought.

He snapped his fingers, and the sailboat raced to the docks.

Seraphina was still being led away when Caesar dashed past her in the corridor. The soldiers had not restrained her. They had their spears pointed at her back, and ordered her to keep walking.

She could not tell if they might harm her.

Maybe they would just kick her out of the palace. They were walking down a narrow corridor where a small door was ahead. As they approached it, Seraphina heard a huge commotion, but she opened the door, as commanded. It was a wild scene.

Soldiers were fighting.

Carnage everywhere.

The amount of blood alone astounded Seraphina.

Her captors were stunned, and that was all the chance she needed. She bolted away from the fighting and the palace, and the guards did not even chase her.

Their orders were to keep her away from the palace.

Mission accomplished.

They stayed inside, away from the mayhem, and closed the door.

They had to hold the docks. Caesar stayed in the harbour, barking commands at senior officers. He could see Rufio's boat returning to shore. The Egyptian fleet was in pursuit, but they would not catch him. The size and speed of the smaller sailboat outran the enemy attackers, and meanwhile, the Roman soldiers fought hard to keep the harbour. The Egyptian forces had caught them by surprise, and now began to overpower them.

Rufio jumped off the boat as soon as it docked. He ran towards Caesar.

'You call this a defence?' Caesar yelled at him. Rufio could think of nothing to say. Caesar shouted at him to get his men in order. As Rufio went to leave, Caesar pulled him back by the collar. Caesar rushed his words.

'This may not be the time or place, but I heard something very odd today, Rufio. Some story about murdered Hebrew women. A long time ago. An Egyptian girl managed to find her way into the palace to tell me this story. Does it ring any bells?'

Rufio shook his head. Caesar didn't believe him. It didn't matter for now.

Caesar, facing the water, saw something of much greater concern. The Egyptian ships were moving into position. His fleet was being cut off. Those ships were now useless to him. He had an idea and grabbed Rufio again.

'Set those ships on fire, now!' Caesar pointed to the Roman ships.

'Sir?' Rufio was in shock that Seraphina had somehow spoken to Caesar, and now he was confused at the orders being barked at him.

'Our ships. Set fire to them. Now!' Caesar glared at him as he walked away. His face was filled with rage. Rufio wasted no time. He ordered his men to set fire to the ships.

All of them.

The soldiers lit torches and ran to the edges of the harbour. The ships were ablaze in only a few minutes. The move caught the Egyptians by surprise. They had been sailing into the harbour at full speed, as Achillas had ordered.

The high speed of the Egyptian ships would cause heavy damage to the Roman fleet.

Achillas watched in horror from the shore.

A wall of fire now awaited his men, and their ships were moving too fast to stop. They crashed into the flames, which filled the sky. The smell of burning wood spread throughout the harbour. A thick, black cloud of smoke engulfed the fighting.

It was pure chaos.

Achillas and Pothinus watched as their men abandoned their ships. They were the lucky ones. Those at the front of the ships had not survived. They were burned alive, and their screams pierced the sky.

Caesar stood on the steps of the palace and smiled. The Egyptians had no naval support for their forces. He looked out over the harbour.

It had become a vicious battlefield.

Fire, blood, and destruction.

The Egyptians might win this fight, he thought.

It did not matter. If they did, he would return with his warships and decimate them. For now, it was time for him to leave. His ship was ready. There was no one to stop him. Every other boat in the harbour was on fire. As he sailed away, he saw the flames rush from the boats to the docks.

As his ship left the bay, the library caught on fire.

FORTY NINE

The soldiers did not follow her. The streets were empty. After a few minutes, Seraphina slowed down, walking past a few homes, seeing families huddled inside.

She could still hear the fighting, and wondered if Quintus was safe, as she had no idea where he might be. When the fighting broke out, he may have gone back to the library. He may have gone into the palace to look for her.

Guessing would do no good.

She looked up. There was nothing but empty street between her and the library. She ran towards it. Maybe Quintus was there. As she got closer, she smelled something burning. Her home was on fire! The roof of the library was engulfed in flames.

For a moment, she panicked.

Afiz. Quintus. Maximus. She collected herself and thought of the small dog trapped in her room, so she went in to get him.

There was pandemonium in the library. Imhotep and Afiz scrambled to save scrolls. Those who were studying in the library were helping them, starting with those scrolls on the highest shelves, because the roof was on fire.

The scholars looked nervous.

They had collected a lot of the scrolls from the shelves but had no idea what to do next. Imhotep had a look of panic in his eyes and was no help at all, so Afiz took two men with him and returned with a stack of crates. He told the scholars to put as many scrolls as they could inside. Imhotep just stood there, looking up at the burning roof.

'Imhotep,' said Afiz, taking him by the shoulders. 'Are you alright?'

Imhotep nodded slowly, not taking his eyes off the roof.

'Imhotep!' shouted Afiz. Imhotep looked at Afiz. 'Once those crates are full, get them out through the back.' Afiz pointed, unsure if his words were registering. 'Away from the fighting.'

Imhotep nodded. Afiz searched his eyes for some indication he understood. 'Alright?' Imhotep nodded again. Afiz ran off to check the library. He had to make sure that everyone got out before the roof collapsed.

FIFTY

It was the one and only time he would be dressed as a soldier. Quintus had knocked out a legionary, and now wore his uniform. He found his way inside the palace which was huge.

Where could she be? he thought.

There was no one in sight. As Quintus searched, it became obvious that the palace had been deserted. He ditched the sword and spear and ran through the palace.

Front to back.

Top to bottom.

There was no sign of Seraphina. He feared the worst.

There is no point staying here, he thought.

He circled the building and found an exit away from the fighting. Once he was out safely, he sprinted to the library.

FIFTY ONE

Not far away, Rufio was screaming orders to his men. The battle was not lost yet, but they had suffered heavy losses. The general was expecting reinforcements from Columbarium. The news had not yet arrived that the camp had been obliterated. Everywhere he looked, the Egyptians outnumbered them. He ordered a retreat to the docks. Regardless of anything else, Rufio was a dedicated soldier. He stood with his men and ordered them to form a phalanx.

This might be our last stand, he thought.

Caesar had left them, and now they faced defeat at the hands of soldiers commanded by a child. Rufio refused to believe this was his fate. He left a commander in charge and headed for the palace. There was a legion of guards stationed inside. They were needed in battle.

Rufio took two men with him. The three of them searched the palace. Completely empty, they reported. He told one to run to the nearby barracks and bring back whoever they could. The other was ordered to ride to Columbarium and find out what was happening. As they left, he saw Cato running into the palace.

'I've been looking for you, sir.'

'I sent for you hours ago, Cato.'

'I'm sorry sir, I got caught up in the fighting. Some of your men saved me. I got here as fast as I could.'

'Never mind that. Where is the girl?'

Cato had no idea, so he gave his best guess. 'At the library, sir.'

Good, thought Rufio.

It was time to finish this.

FIFTY TWO

Afiz checked throughout the library. He found Gisgo and told him to go to the museum. It was safer there.

Gisgo did not hesitate, but he asked if Seraphina was alright.

Afiz assured him she was, even though he had no idea if she was or not. More than anything, he wanted to run to the palace to find her. This thought ran through his mind as he checked the final rooms in the library.

Maximus, he thought.

If anything happened to him, Seraphina would never forgive him. He moved his stocky frame as fast as he could up the stairs. The door was ajar. No Maximus, and no Seraphina.

What is going on, he thought.

Seraphina had left the dog here when she went with Quintus. He heard the door creak behind him and turned around to see Quintus. The two looked at each other in confusion.

'She's not here?' asked Quintus.

'Come on, let's get out of here,' said Afiz.

The two ran out of the room down into the library.

'I thought she was with you?' said Afiz, panting.

'No,' said Quintus.

'What happened?'

Quintus spoke frantically. He told Afiz how Seraphina had gone into the palace. She had not come out for hours. Then the fighting started. He had looked for her, but by the time he got in, the palace was completely deserted. He told Afiz about what had happened in the harbour, and how it had set the library on fire.

Afiz absorbed all of this.

'Maximus is gone. No one else would have gone up there but you, me, or Seraphina,' said Afiz. 'I think.'

'Maximus was there when we left, right?'

Afiz nodded. 'Even if someone else went up there, why would they take Maximus?'

'Who knows? Afiz, we should get out of here. We have to find Seraphina before the fire gets worse.'

Afiz thought out loud for a second. 'If we are looking for her ...'

Quintus finished the thought. 'Then maybe she is down here looking for us.'

The two of them ran into the main atrium.

FIFTY THREE

Now that she had Maximus, the next thing was to find Afiz. She came out of the back alley. The fire was getting worse and had spread to the sides of the building. Undaunted, she walked in through the front entrance. She saw Imhotep and a few others.

They were trying to salvage as many scrolls as they could.

Others ran to the back of the library, carrying crates full of Seraphina's beloved texts.

The scene was chaotic.

Seraphina thought of Quintus and hoped no harm had come to him. She asked Imhotep if he had seen Afiz.

'He was here a little while ago,' said Imhotep. He was much more animated now and shouted out directions to the men around him. 'He went that way.' The curator pointed to the back of the library.

Great, thought Seraphina. *I'm just running around in circles now.*

She looked down at Maximus and rushed into the depths of the library. She had to find Afiz.

Imhotep saw the fire spread to the walls. It began to burn through the shelves on the upper floors. He despaired, as he saw his library in ruins. He cursed the Romans, and Ptolemy, and Cleopatra. Their politics and power games had resulted in this destruction. Those idiotic barbarians fought outside, killing each other. Meanwhile, he and the few who were left fought to save knowledge. Learnings and wisdom passed down through the ages, so that future generations might have its benefit.

He cursed all of them.

Imhotep watched the flames spread to the front of the library, then he told the remaining men to get out through the back.

'Tell the girl too,' he said.

He was about to follow them and remembered he had left something in his office. It was a family heirloom, and his father had given it to him. He went back to get it. He could not believe what he saw next. Rufio, in full armour. He looked up at the burning building and entered.

The general was some distance away, but Imhotep could see the look in his eyes. It was one of pure rage. The curator slithered out of sight and fled the library.

FIFTY FOUR

There were men everywhere. Afiz and Quintus were headed in the wrong direction. Scholars carrying crates full of scrolls were fleeing the library, while they were trying to go in. The men held them back, saying it was too dangerous. There was no one left inside, they said. Afiz and Quintus relented, and two more men came out. Afiz asked if they had seen the girl.

'What girl?' asked one.

'The girl who works in the library,' said the other.

'Where is she?' said yet another.

'We thought you found her.'

'No, we came out here. We didn't see her.'

'How about you?'

Afiz put his hands up to stop them, asking if anyone had seen her. They all shook their heads. Quintus and Afiz pushed past them and went to look for her.

Seraphina could not see anyone. The smoke was getting thicker, as she looked through all the rooms in the back of the library. She called out Afiz's name and began to cough. She could not see anything or hear anyone. Walking back into the main hall, the entire building was on fire. A lot of the shelves had been emptied, but so much was going to be lost. She kept calling out Afiz's name.

Through the smoke, she saw someone near the front of the library. She walked towards the entrance. The figure was walking towards her. Maximus coughed from the smoke. She stopped. It was a Roman soldier.

He was an older man and was dressed in full armour. He looked vaguely familiar. A sword hung from his belt and he wielded the thick handle of a spear. His eyes fixated on her, and his teeth were gritted.

'Who are …' began Seraphina. She took a step back, realising who it was.

'It's been a long time, Seraphina,' said Rufio.

She shuddered when he said her name and took another step back. 'Rufio?' she asked. It was more of a statement than a question.

A big smile appeared on his face and he nodded, advancing towards her. 'That's me,' he said. 'You don't recognise me? From all those years ago?'

Seraphina's teeth clenched, and her eyes began to water. The fire surrounded them both now.

She continued to retreat, and he continued to advance. She looked down at the tip of his spear.

The metal was razor sharp.

Seraphina gulped.

'You're not going to cry, are you?' said Rufio. 'Tell me, how did you manage to speak to Caesar?'

Seraphina stopped backpedalling. 'It doesn't matter now, does it? What matters is that I told him.'

Rufio also halted. He was now only a few metres from his target. 'You think you made a difference? He didn't believe you. Who would believe a lowly, worthless Hebrew like you?'

Seraphina smiled at him. Rufio was impressed with her grit. 'If he didn't believe me, then why are you here?'

Rufio smiled back, showing all of his teeth. 'I'm here to do what I should have taken care of a long time ago.'

'Father, stop,' said another voice. Quintus came out of the smoke and walked towards Seraphina.

'Stop now!' yelled Rufio at his son. He pointed the spear at Seraphina. One lunge and he could strike her. Quintus stopped, and raised his hands to calm his father.

'Father, you don't need to do this,' said Quintus, staying completely still.

'Silence!' screamed Rufio. 'This does not concern you, Quintus. Now stay back.'

Like Quintus, Seraphina had raised her hands once Rufio started screaming. She saw a figure approaching behind Rufio. It was a large man, moving very slowly. Afiz inched closer and closer, careful to make as little sound as possible. Quintus spotted him and started to bargain with his father.

'Father, we can leave. I'll come home with you and go to Rome. Whatever you want. Please, just don't harm her.'

Quintus' words made Rufio hesitate for a second, and that was all Afiz needed. He raised the wooden beam and knocked the general to the ground. They all looked down. There was blood on his head, and they could not tell if he was unconscious or dead.

'Come on, let's go,' said Afiz. Seraphina smiled, and went to leave. She saw Quintus and stopped. He was looking down at his father. He didn't want to leave him, even after everything that had happened. It was written all over his face.

'Quintus,' she said. 'Come on.' She took his hand.

Afiz yelled at them to hurry up. The walls were beginning to collapse. Quintus hesitated, then whispered his father a last goodbye. As he turned, he saw the entrance of the library collapse. The flames illuminated what was left of the library, and the three searched for a way out. Afiz could see some light through a wall that had cracked. He climbed a small pile of rubble to see if he could force his way through. Using a rock, he started to smash away parts of the wall, which had been weakened by the fire. The rubble beneath his feet gave way. Quintus and Seraphina held him up. Afiz kept striking the wall, like a man possessed. Bit by bit, pieces of the wall fell outside.

Afiz looked down at his friends in relief and smiled. As he reached down to pull Seraphina up, his expression turned into one of alarm. Maximus barked, and Quintus saw his father just in time. He pushed Seraphina out of the way, and Rufio's dagger plunged into his son's rib cage. His son screamed in agony, and Rufio recoiled in horror.

He looked at his son in anguish, then his eyes met Seraphina's. There was a loud crack above them, and the roof finally gave in. A huge chunk of the stone ceiling above fell. Seraphina looked up in horror. With Afiz's help, she dragged Quintus out of the way. Rufio scrambled towards them but tripped on some rubble. The last thing he saw was the rock falling from above.

He let out a piercing scream as it landed, crushing the life from him.

FIFTY FIVE

One month later. Ptolemy's forces had scored an unlikely victory that day. Pothinus' planning and execution of the attack had been flawless.

Cleopatra was forced to flee Egypt.

The young king sat on the throne, but his luck was not to last.

Caesar remained in Rome, which was consumed by civil war which he would eventually win and return to Alexandria. Just as he had planned, the final victory belonged to him and Cleopatra.

Ptolemy, Pothinus and Achillas all met their end when Caesar's armies returned.

The library was completely destroyed.

Imhotep and Afiz saved many of its scrolls, but a lot was lost. Imhotep had gone into hiding that day. After a few weeks, and being convinced of Rufio's death, he came out of hiding. He told his side of the story, and of Rufio's threats, and apologised to Seraphina.

Naturally, she forgave him. Imhotep and Afiz worked together to determine what had been lost. In time, maybe the scrolls could be replaced. They persuaded the king to build a new library. Construction took its time though, as the city had more pressing priorities. Even though the library had burned to the ground, Rufio was the only casualty of the tragedy.

In the weeks after the destruction of her home, Seraphina spent a lot of her time in the Hebrew village. She and Yadira spoke for hours about Rebekah and Josef. She could come and go as she pleased, by day or night. This freedom took some time to adjust to. Some nights, she and Yadira would sit at her favourite spot. They would talk and laugh the night away, reminiscing.

Saul, a carpenter like Josef, taught Seraphina his trade which, unsurprisingly, Seraphina picked up with ease. Her time with Yadira and Saul was precious in those days. The memories of her parents were bright, with the horrors of the past now left behind, and Seraphina was grateful for that.

Gisgo left after his month in Alexandria. Seraphina begged him not to go, but the pull of home was too strong. The city was in tatters, and the library's destruction reduced its appeal to the old philosopher.

Seraphina thanked him for everything.

She told him the whole story.

Gisgo was amazed and very proud of Seraphina. He had come to regard her as something of a protégé, and he told her as much. She walked with him to the very end of the dock where the two said goodbye in the same place they had first met.

Maximus adjusted very well to his new life of freedom. With the library gone, there was nowhere to leave him, and also no reason to hide him.

He went everywhere with Seraphina.

She would often watch him, his freedom reminding her that theirs was a life that could now be free of hiding. It felt wonderful. Still, the two would share an occasional run through the city in the middle of the night.

Quintus survived his father's attack.

It had been touch and go that day. Seraphina had knelt before him and cried like never before while Afiz had rushed to find a doctor.

Seraphina begged every god she could think of to spare him and finally her prayers were answered. Someone came just in time. It took a lot of rest, but he slowly regained his strength. The trauma of his father's actions and his death would take much longer to heal.

Seraphina did not leave his bedside the entire time.

Quintus was comforted by her presence, but those were still challenging days for him. That day's battle had taken both of their homes, and to some extent had scarred their souls.

Afiz's home had never been so full. For a man who loved his solitude, he adapted well. In fact, Afiz had never been happier. Seraphina was now free to live her life. She had found a wonderful young man to love. Together with Maximus, his house became something of a family home. As overjoyed as he was, he had a feeling it would not last.

The three of them sat around an old table, built many years ago. Seraphina pressed her hands on the wood that her father had shaped with his own hands. Yadira had offered it to her, and Seraphina had decided to take it to Afiz's house. That was home for now.

Afiz had made his mother's spiced chicken. As he laid the food down on the table, he watched Seraphina and Quintus. There was a look of mischief on their faces. The two rarely stopped smiling at one another, and Quintus' sporadic sadness was fading by the day.

Young love, he thought.

He sat, and Seraphina offered some words of gratitude for the food. Afiz started to eat and looked up at Seraphina. She would typically wolf this food down, but her attention was only on Quintus. She looked at him, nodding her head towards Afiz. He did the same.

'What is it, you two?' asked Afiz.

Seraphina turned her attention to Afiz. She shook her head and said it was nothing. They continued to eat. It became obvious to Afiz that they wanted to talk, so he asked again.

'Well, Afiz, we've been thinking about the future,' said Seraphina.

Afiz had a sense of what was coming. His instincts were right. Seraphina and Quintus were both passionate about education. With the library and museum now destroyed, they thought of where else they might go. Rome, Athens, and many other places were considered. Afiz told them the library would be rebuilt, but knew their adventures lay elsewhere. The little orphan he had first taken in was now a woman. She was safe and happy, and that was all he had ever wanted for her. He knew it was time to let her go, for good.

He half-heartedly asked if they had a plan. He knew they would figure it out.

One afternoon, while Seraphina was meditating, she heard a knock at the door, but she tried to ignore it, thinking that someone else might answer.

The knocking persisted.

She opened her eyes and saw the crate of scrolls in front of her. She had managed to 'borrow' them after what happened at the library, figuring they were as safe with her as they were with anyone else.

Another knock at the door.

She got up in frustration, looking around as she walked through the house. No one else was home. She opened the door to a familiar face.

It was Khay.

'Hello, Khay. What a surprise,' said Seraphina.

'It's good to see you,' said Khay.

Seraphina invited him in and the two of them sat down. As Maximus sniffed around Khay's feet, Afiz returned home. His eyes turned to Khay and he raised his eyebrows.

'What brings you here, Khay?' said Afiz.

'Matters of some importance,' said Khay.

'It sounds serious,' said Seraphina.

'It could very well be,' said Khay. 'An old friend has come to see me. There have been rumours about the general, Rufio. Do you know who Rufio is?'

Afiz and Seraphina looked at one another.

'Seraphina, it is very important that you trust me,' said Khay.

'Yes, I know who he is.' Seraphina sighed.

'Well, the rumours are that he left the battle when it was at its fiercest. Do you know why he would do that?'

'Khay, would you excuse us for a moment?' Afiz nodded at his friend.

'Afiz, this is a very serious matter.'

'I understand. Just a moment, please.'

Afiz nodded for Seraphina to follow him. Seraphina trudged after Afiz.

Afiz turned to face Seraphina. Her head was hanging down. A blank stare on her face as she examined the courtyard floor.

'Seraphina …' said Afiz.

No reply.

He rested his hand on her shoulder. 'Seraphina, we need to think here.'

'Can we trust him, Afiz?'

'I think so,' said Afiz.

'Then let's tell him what he wants to know. I don't want to hold on to it any longer.'

'But what if—' Afiz started to speak.

'It will be as it is meant to. I believe that now. No more secrets. No more running. It's time for me.'

'Time for what?'

'Time for me to stand and face whatever is going to happen next,' she said.

'I'm proud of you, Seraphina.'

Seraphina smiled and stood tall. She took a deep breath and looked up to the sky.

Bright blue. Perfect.

She felt her heart beating and looked at the old ring dangling from her necklace.

Our love, she thought.

Her mother and father could be at peace now, and the thought gave her strength.

Khay's heel was tapping the floor. He saw Afiz and Seraphina come back into the room. The heel became still.

'I don't know for sure, but I believe Rufio left the battle to come and find me,' said Seraphina.

Khay's eyes were wide with shock. He looked at Afiz, then back at Seraphina.

'Wh … why would he be looking for you?' Khay looked more than a little confused. 'Wait, come to find you where?'

'The library. He was looking for me because he wanted to kill me.'

Khay put his hands up and exhaled deeply. He wasn't sure how much he wanted to know.

'Who is your friend, Khay?' asked Afiz.

Khay's hands were on his knees. Looking down at the floor, he shook his head.

'Khay?' asked Seraphina.

'Yes?' said Khay.

'Who is your friend?'

'Oh, an old acquaintance, and someone I trust.'

'You weren't expecting to hear what I just said, were you?' asked Seraphina.

'No, I was not.'

'So, what do we do now?' asked Afiz.

'There's more to the story, isn't there?' asked Khay.

'A lot more,' said Seraphina.

Khay looked at the young woman. Her face wore a peaceful smile. She wanted to tell.

'Tell me everything.'

Seraphina proceeded to tell Khay the tale. She left nothing out, but protected Yadira's and Saul's identities. Khay was riveted and leaned forward in his seat. Halfway through, the door opened. Quintus walked in to see the three in deep conversation.

He was confused. Introductions were made, and Quintus was assured of Khay's integrity. He was uneasy, but he trusted Seraphina. He sat as Seraphina finished telling of their foray into the palace and her meeting with Caesar.

'One question,' said Khay. 'How did you escape the palace?'

'The guards were taking me away. The palace was surrounded by fierce fighting. Once we were outside, the guards were stunned by what they saw. I ran and never looked back.'

'Amazing,' said Khay. He fell back into his chair. 'Just amazing. You have all been through so much.'

'So, what now?' asked Seraphina.

'Let me go and talk to my friend.'

'Who is this friend?' asked Quintus.

'I can't tell you his name, but he can be trusted. I'm not going to tell him everything you've told me. In fact, he doesn't even know I'm here. However, he does want to get to the bottom of Rufio's death. My plan is to find out what he knows and take it from there.'

'Alright,' said Seraphina.

'Alright?' said Khay.

'Yes. Whatever happens from here, we will face together,' she said.

Khay smiled. The love between the two youths was palpable.

'So, what are your plans from here? Seraphina? Quintus?' asked Khay.

'Hey, what about me?' Afiz laughed.

Khay shook his head as Seraphina and Quintus spoke of their ideas. Their energy was as fanciful as it was contagious. Hours passed as the four of them discussed the future.

The past was now resolved.

At least they hoped it was.

FIFTY SIX

They sat and waited. Seraphina held Quintus' hand and looked out over the water. It all looked so familiar, yet so much had changed.

'Seraphina, is it?' came a voice from behind them.

She turned to see a portly man standing behind them. She nodded, and he gestured for them to follow him.

The building was more for function than form. The atrium was wide yet dull with its grey stone. Eight plain rooms sat on the sides, four on the left, four on the right. Their guide continued walking. He was headed for the far left-hand corner.

He ushered them into the room and asked them to have a seat. He vanished as suddenly as he had appeared.

'This is a weird place,' said Seraphina.

'Looks more like a Roman administration building than anything Egyptian,' said Quintus.

'You've seen places like this before?'

'Vague memories, from when I was a baby.'

Seraphina nodded. She wasn't sure what to expect from this meeting. Khay had not told them much.

'Are you alright?' said Quintus.

'Yes,' she said. 'Just want to get this over and done with.'

'We don't even know what this is.'

'No,' she said, laughing. 'I suppose we don't. Khay was quite mysterious, wasn't he?'

'Yes. I'm not sure what to expect,' said Quintus.

Khay and another man came in to the room. They sat down on the other side of the table, facing Seraphina and Quintus. Khay's friend was an odd-looking man. Tall and bald. He was dressed in a similar fashion to Caesar, and Seraphina assumed he was Roman.

'Hello, Seraphina. Please allow me to present my friend, the senator Cicero,' said Khay.

'Senator!' said Seraphina.

'Cicero?' whispered Quintus.

Cicero smiled at the pair. He already knew a great deal about the two. He watched as their eyes shifted between Khay, him, and each other. He placed his hands on the table and told them not to worry.

They talked about what had happened in the library. He had heard the rumours regarding Rufio and wanted to talk to her first hand. Seraphina told him what he wanted to know, and none of it seemed to surprise him.

'I never liked Rufio, you understand,' said Cicero. Turning to Quintus, he then added 'though I do understand he was your father. I am sorry for your loss and mean no disrespect.'

'Thank you,' said Quintus.

'I am only beginning to learn the extent of Rufio's crimes. I am so sorry for what happened to your parents, Seraphina.'

'I appreciate that, sir. You need not apologise.'

'He was a Roman soldier, however much of a rogue he was. He was here on the authority of the Senate, and that's why I'm apologising. We must take responsibility for what he did.'

Seraphina nodded and offered a weak smile.

'Is there anything I can do for you?' asked Cicero. 'I understand you have been through a lot.'

'No,' said Seraphina. 'It is done now, and I am happy to be moving on with my life.'

Cicero nodded. He explained what he did more fully. In addition to being a senator, he was a lawyer and an author. He lived in Rome and moved in academic and official circles.

Seraphina smiled and listened. She thought the senator a little boastful. She noticed a curious smile on Khay's face. Her attention returned to Cicero.

He spoke some more about life in Rome. Then he asked Seraphina what her plans were.

'We have discussed many things,' said Seraphina.

'I understand you are something of an academic yourself?' asked Cicero.

'Well, I spent most of my life living in a library.' She laughed at her own joke.

Cicero smiled and turned to Quintus. 'I'm also told you have done very well in your schooling here.'

Quintus nodded.

Cicero painted a vivid picture of life as an intellectual. His descriptions of Rome, its colleges and libraries and museums, all had Seraphina salivating. Quintus smiled as he listened to what he had imagined. What he had begged his father to allow him to do. Khay and Cicero reminisced, and the mood lightened. The four continued to talk for some time.

Cicero asked about Seraphina's life in Alexandria. Leaving out a few details, she told of her past. Seraphina talked about how she had met Quintus. Romance wasn't mentioned. Cicero, like Khay, could read between the lines. He smiled as Seraphina told her story. Inside, he was saddened that they were now both orphans.

As she finished, the senator leaned forward.

'How would the two of you like to come with me to Rome?'

ACKNOWLEDGEMENTS

I am so grateful for my mother, Samadara. She has instilled the desire to learn in me since before I can remember, and has always encouraged me to be the very best person I can be. I love you, Mum.

I also wish to acknowledge my writing coach, Azul Terronez and my editors, Graham Toseland and Tracey Govender. I will value your insights, generosity and dedication to my project for many years to come.

Thank you for purchasing your copy of Reading Seraphina!

Please leave a review on Amazon or Goodreads.

Thank you!

ABOUT THE AUTHOR

Stanley is a former lawyer turned writer. He has travelled to over 80 countries, and loves his continuous adventure across the globe. When he's not writing, you can catch him eating beef rendang, practising yoga, or hanging out in an airport.

Printed in Great Britain
by Amazon

15991798R00181